Praise for *Twenty-Seven Minutes*

"*Twenty-Seven Minutes* is th[illegible]e-vated prose, characters with [illegible] a pitch-perfect mood that is wo[illegible]of a small town's obsessive hold [illegible]ur people in its grip try to move on, is both poignant and pacy, an unforgettable portrait of grief and the darkest ties that bind. A must-read debut that marks Ashley Tate as a brilliant new voice in literary suspense."

—Ashley Audrain, *New York Times*
bestselling author of *The Push*

"A twisting, beautiful, deeply affecting mystery from a commanding new talent. *Twenty-Seven Minutes* is by turns evocative and unpredictable, truly gripping and deeply satisfying. I loved it."

—Chris Whitaker, *New York Times* bestselling
author of *We Begin at the End*

"I raced through this suspenseful debut. I loved the smart dialogue, the sense of foreboding, and the stunning setting. But, most of all, I was hooked by the characters, the twists, and the 'Who on earth could have done this?' puzzle. Definitely a writer to watch."

—Jane Corry, internationally bestselling author of
Coming to Find You and *My Husband's Wife*

"*Twenty-Seven Minutes* by Ashley Tate is a ride and a half. Tate nails the small-town vibe and the messiness of human emotions, making this an all-consuming read. If you're up for a story about regret, memories, and the ripple effect of one decision, this book is for you."

—Caroline Mitchell, author of the DI Amy Winter series

"I was completely transfixed by *Twenty-Seven Minutes*, a taut, raw, powerful suspense that centers around a decade-old tragedy that's traumatized a community. Every character carries both a darkness and moments of goodness inside them as they grapple with their own memories and secrets of the night that took one of their own. Ashley Tate has written a masterful collision course of pain, sorrow, and grief that sliced open my veins and tore out my heart."

—Samantha M. Bailey, *USA Today* bestselling author of *Woman on the Edge* and *Watch Out for Her*

"*Twenty-Seven Minutes* is a beautifully written story of family secrets, dangerous obsessions, and the unsolved mysteries that can haunt a small town for years. With her well-rounded characters, breakneck pacing, and emotional depth, Ashley Tate is a new thriller writer to watch."

—Robyn Harding, international bestselling author

"A great read! *Twenty-Seven Minutes* vividly brings to life the long-term impact of grief and loss alongside an intriguing mystery. Well-paced with a satisfying ending and unexpected twist, I found it unputdownable."

—Patricia Wolf, author of *Outback*

"In *Twenty-Seven Minutes*, Audrey Tate creates a tense and deeply affecting story of desperation, dysfunction, and tragedy that stays with the reader long after the final twist. Skillfully plotted and darkly atmospheric, I thoroughly enjoyed this gripping debut."

—Rosemary Hennigan, author of *The Favorites*

TWENTY-SEVEN MINUTES

TWENTY-SEVEN MINUTES

ASHLEY TATE

Cover design by Jonathan Bush
Cover images © David Wall/Getty Images, Spoon/
Getty Images, Pongstorn Pixs/Shutterstock
Internal design by Laura Boren/Sourcebooks

Published by Poisoned Pen Press, an imprint of Sourcebooks
P.O. Box 4410, Naperville, Illinois 60567-4410
(630) 961-3900
sourcebooks.com

Library of Congress Cataloging-in-Publication Data

Names: Tate, Ashley, author.
Title: Twenty-seven minutes : a novel / Ashley Tate.
Description: Naperville, Illinois : Poisoned Pen Press, [2024]
Identifiers: LCCN 2023024236 (print) | LCCN 2023024237
(ebook) | (trade paperback) | (ebook)
Subjects: LCGFT: Thrillers (Fiction) | Novels.
Classification: LCC PR9199.4.T35648 T84 2024 (print) | LCC PR9199.4.T35648
(ebook) | DDC 813/.6--dc23/eng/20230602
LC record available at https://lccn.loc.gov/2023024236
LC ebook record available at https://lccn.loc.gov/2023024237

Printed and bound in the United States of America.
KP 10 9 8 7 6 5 4 3 2 1

To Agatha and Archer, everything is for you

No one ever told me that grief felt so like fear.
I am not afraid, but the sensation is like being afraid.

—C. S. LEWIS

PROLOGUE

She was too young to die.

She was too young and too beautiful and too good to die. And yet none of that mattered, because in that moment she was lying awkwardly on her back, starting to convulse, gaping at the dark night sky, dying. The pouring rain mixed with the blood from her body, gathering beside her on the bridge in hurried torrents.

Her ribs were broken, snapped like dry tinder; her lungs punctured and emptied of air. Her legs and right arm and the right side of her face, crushed beyond recognition. They'd have to use her dental records officially, although unofficially everyone would know it was her because it was a small town, and in a small town everyone knew everyone else.

But they didn't know everything.

She was interesting and kind; she demanded truth and trust and loyalty. She would have hated knowing that over time she would become everyone's shadow. Forever a lingering presence, never there but always there; slipping into moments without warning—at the dinner table, on a walk by the bridge, when the leaves started to turn.

The rain continued to pour but the pain that had been white-hot and angry was starting to fade; she knew this was a bad sign. She willed the pain back desperately because it was better than the fear that had taken root in its place, that flooded her perfect young body, that replaced the blood in her veins, pumping outwardly to her four remaining functioning organs—now three.

Now two.

She willed her last thoughts to be profound—a crystallized understanding of the world she was leaving behind or the tragedy of her life ending this way or what she might have accomplished. She wanted her last thoughts to be worthy of this moment but she was too cold and too terrified to think straight.

Should she think of her mother? Of her brother, Grant? What this would do to them, to him? This was ending her life; how would it alter theirs?

Nothing profound came. To her horror her thoughts turned to how she might look lying there; she wondered if her jacket was still intact, wondered if it was still pretty. Thoughts she couldn't bear to have, but who was she to argue with death? Could you still tell it was real leather and expensive? Had she expected too much of him? Had she been wrong about him? The jacket had cost her four months of mindless babysitting jobs but had made her feel grownup. And feeling grownup had meant that she was closer to leaving this small town, that she was closer to having more.

We'll leave together, they'd whispered, clutching hands, dreaming the same dream. But they were only children really, not yet sculpted into the imperfect people they'd become. *We'll be okay.*

The distillation of her life into her many awards and accomplishments—*so impressive for someone so young*, they'd all say with tears in their eyes—would be front-page news in the small local paper for an entire week. And then a half-page, and then, after a month, sinking to a footnote for the sake of her family. For her mother and Grant. To help them *get through this*, to help them *move on*, to help them *heal*. Although of course they'd never do any one of those things.

If an ambulance had been called right away she would have survived, with some scarring and residual aching in her shoulder and right thigh, and the near-death experience would have infected her with even more drive—feverish, obsessive now. First, a scholarship to a good college in a faraway city; then, a warm, successful husband, and three children who would grow up taking for granted the one thing she'd always craved: choice.

But the ambulance was called too late—twenty-seven minutes too late. Something that would weigh on him forever.

She lay unseeing up at the harsh night sky, half of her jaw exposed with its stark white beautiful bone, and as her oxygen ran out and her heart stopped beating—and five miles away her mother bolted straight up in bed—and as she closed her eyes, or maybe they were already closed, she wondered who would be the first to tell the truth of what had happened that night.

She was so special she glowed.

This is what they'll think when they think of her. When they think of young Phoebe Dean. Because over time all of her flaws will become slightly blurred, slightly vague, and without her around to age or mature or correct them, the complicated girl will fade away until all that is left is the girl that they just remember. The special one. The perfect one. The one who died in a tragic accident as it rained, on a bridge, over the river; even if the truth is a little more nuanced.

But the truth, it will come out. Nothing can keep the truth buried; it will always unfurl itself, lay itself bare. It is unstoppable—like the tide, or a storm, or a ghost.

It will hunt you down.

TEN YEARS LATER

JUNE

Three Days before the Phoebe Dean Memorial

June shoved the soggy tissue in her pocket and stared at the fresh dirt at her feet. The oval hill of soil was larger than she'd expected it to be. She looked around, worry blooming in the pit of her stomach. Should she ask someone about this? A groundskeeper? That unhelpful woman on the phone who'd slotted her in at dawn? Would this mound of loose dirt wash away the next time it rained, fully exposing her mother's cheap wooden casket, allowing her to climb out and roam free?

"Well, June, I think this is just lovely." Her elderly neighbor, Evelyn Lloyd, patted her briskly on the arm. June tried to smile, but the jerk of her mouth let more tears spill out. "Oh, there, there," Evelyn clucked. "She's at rest now. No more suffering. Your poor mother is finally at peace."

June opened her mouth to speak but a watery cough silenced

her. Evelyn took a small step backward, as if June's grief might be contagious and seize the old woman. Evelyn clucked again sympathetically, but her eyes were glassy. Evelyn was bored.

June wasn't a fool; she knew Evelyn had only come out of obligation because she lived down the road. Just like she'd bring the obligatory banana muffins every Thursday afternoon, rain or shine.

That old bag should mind her damn business, June's mother would caw from the couch if she were sober enough to notice they'd had a visitor. *She's just coming so she can gossip about us. Now they care about us? Now they're checking in? Vultures, all of them, June. Never forget what they did to your brother and us, promise me.*

"Thank you for coming, Mrs. Lloyd," June mumbled to Evelyn. "My mom would have appreciated it—that someone came."

"Oh dear—everyone must have just got the details mixed up, or are still in shock after Rosie Wilson's accident. Ninety-three years old and blind as a damn bat! She had no sense to be driving at night, no sense at all." Evelyn sighed. "But I'm sure they'll wish they'd come, the whole town. Every last one of them." She brought her coat up around her loose turkey neck. "I'll leave you alone then, to say goodbye. It's a fresh start for you, June, no more demons."

Demons? June nodded curtly, hoping Evelyn would notice the change in her demeanor and think twice about passing judgment on her family when she knew. She knew all of it. Evelyn lived far down the road, but she'd still have been able to hear the shouting and the dishes being thrown against the walls when

June's father and brother were fighting. But then her brother had taken off, and her father a year later, and the silence had probably been just as noticeable; more so.

Evelyn shuffled off on her cane, and June stared at the dark hump again. She knew there were no guarantees that her mother's body was actually down there, but she could feel a slight tug coming from below all the same.

"I'll miss you," June said, tears drying on her throat like cold fingers. "I'll come back soon to visit."

June found the overgrown narrow path back to the main part of the cemetery, where the plots were large and meticulously cared for, with real flowers and lit candles in glass lanterns and sprinklers on timers so the grass was always green. The small cemetery had been deserted when she arrived, but now there was an older woman kneeling at a marble headstone gripping fresh-cut roses. June startled, not having expected to see anyone she knew. She slid her sunglasses on so she wouldn't be recognized or have to make small talk, especially not with that woman, especially not today.

As she neared the front gates, she spotted a crew digging a fresh grave—three tired-looking men leaning on their shovels, smoking, talking quietly. June walked by quickly, not wanting to know who would be filling that new hole or whether the body could expect a large funeral with real tears and kindness and support, but none of the men noticed her or even looked her way. June was invisible to them, something she had long grown accustomed to.

GRANT

Grant was still heavy with sleep, slumped in his chair at the breakfast table. He yawned and then noticed the newspaper tucked neatly under his mug. He caught a sliver of headline: TOWN MEETING CALLED TO VOTE ON BRIDGE REMOVAL.

He stood up quickly, to distance himself from what he'd just read. He rubbed his eyes and stared unblinking at the letters until they bled together and his mother dropped a plate in front of him. It clattered and he flinched, praying nothing would spill, praying that his breakfast would remain securely on the plate and not slop onto the table, giving her another reason to resent him. Wide awake now and on edge, he sat back down carefully, his eyes shooting again to the front page: WEST WILMER BRIDGE CLAIMS SECOND LIFE.

The kitchen was too warm all of a sudden. Had his mother read the paper? She never folded it like that for him. She never did anything for him except feed him—anything else would be more than she could bear. Had she put it there for him to see? Grant's eyes darted nervously around the kitchen, landing on the gardening shears by the sink, crusted earthy green. Maybe she'd been to the cemetery that morning, something she did occasionally around this time of year.

With the memorial in just a few days, the memorial he'd do anything to have her cancel, things were already bad. And now this. Attention back on the fucking bridge. He clutched his fork in one hand, his knife in the other; a foolish way to fight off what he feared could barrel down on him. He considered climbing the stairs back to his room, to hide under the covers, to start the morning over again. Instead he turned slowly in his seat. Over his mother's hunched shoulders, out of the large window in their kitchen, the wind was rattling the wooden frame, and overnight the leaves had started to turn.

"Damn old woman fell asleep at the wheel." His mother spoke with her back to him. "Not wearing her glasses either. She shouldn't have been driving over that dangerous thing in the dark."

Grant cleared his throat and unclenched his jaw. He avoided looking at his mother, the local town paper, the sharp shears. He stared harder out the window. The leaves outside were a premonitory yellow. Fall. It was usually the worst season of the year for him. For them. His mother and him. When that night could still blow in and settle like frost, delicate and cryptic. Resentment, blame. But rarely mentioned aloud.

And now another accident on the bridge, another life taken, drawing everyone's attention back there, to the deep river, to the rickety danger hanging above it. What did a bridge removal involve? How deep were the posts in the water? The town claimed to love his sister still; would they dare disturb the place she took her last breath?

He couldn't have this. He couldn't have the spotlight turned back on and everyone feeling like they had permission to talk about it, to split open the wound that for him had barely healed in the first place.

"It should be taken down—that old thing." His mother spoke quietly while flipping an egg in a pan on the stove. "Should have taken it down years ago, after…"

She trailed off but Grant could swear he'd just heard soft footsteps on the stairs, and he was now paralyzed in his chair. He gripped the utensils in both fists even tighter. He exhaled loudly, a forced hiss, felt his bad leg bob under the table on its own, his eyes burning from staring out the window so as to avoid the shadowed hallway and that strange, fleeting thought that he'd heard her coming down the stairs, had even smelled her before she walked through the doorway. Rose water. Toothpaste.

"Oh," his mother said and then stopped. Grant waited. "I've been looking through some of her things for Sunday."

She stopped again and he waited again, barely breathing; there was nothing to say and so he didn't speak. Silence shrouded the warm kitchen, morning shadows skittered and danced.

"I'm looking for those bracelets she loved. And her necklace."

Grant stopped chewing. He rubbed his leg to stop the bobbing. He tried to remember if he'd taken his pain meds that morning but couldn't.

"Grant—have you seen them?"

"No. What necklace?"

"The gold one with the locket. I want to have it cleaned."

"No," he repeated. "I haven't seen it."

"I'll look again, then. Probably just missed them. Or maybe they've crawled off to join your father's watch."

Grant touched his bare wrist; let his hand slip away, clammy. "Maybe."

"Eat up, can't be late again. That Dean charm'll wear off one of these days." She jerked around to smile briefly, a vestigial maternal afterthought, but her eyes were pointed and cold. He returned the smile mechanically until she went back to the stove and he could relax his face. *Why bother trying at all?* he wanted to ask her. Maybe things would be better if they were just honest with each other—that she hated him, that he deserved it. But he never said it, because the subject of his sister and her accident was taboo, which suited him fine; better.

Grant scooped baked beans onto his fork even though he'd lost his appetite. His harried pulse vibrated below the surface of his skin; he could see his nerves gliding through his bloodstream, like ripples. Like rushing black water, like the river. He closed his eyes as he shoveled the forkful down. When he finished he stood slowly, pushed his chair back gently—no sudden movements to draw attention to himself—and gingerly placed the plate in the sink while his mother's rounded back was still to him. This is what he saw most of and had for nearly ten years: the back of her. He still lived at home but could go weeks without seeing her face; sometimes he could forget what she looked like.

His mother moved from the stove to stand in front of the large paper calendar on the wall. It was new, and the first thing that she had hung in their kitchen in years. Everything else had been taken down long ago. All of the colorful art they'd created in junior school, all of the family photos. Their happy unknowing faces too hard to witness first thing each morning.

Grant heard a creak above him and looked up. He shook his head, feeling foolish. Phoebe couldn't be upstairs. He heard the creak again and covered his mouth to stifle the sound his body wanted to make—a scream or a wail, something tortured. He saw the river again, the rain that pounded relentlessly onto it, the water so angry it churned and frothed white, violent.

But that was ten years ago. What he'd lost that night was gone forever. And she wasn't upstairs. She wasn't upstairs and she wasn't about to come flying into the kitchen with her toothbrush in her mouth, foam in the corners, smiling because she knew he'd cover for her. She'd have snuck out again to study all night in the old barn at the edge of the field; she had SATs coming up and was so determined she was practically manic. The barn calmed her, she'd say, like when they were young. Just another couple of months, she'd say, grinning at him about their plan, the one they'd had since they were kids. The one she'd made him promise he'd keep. That they would leave together when his scholarship was clinched. That he would focus, that he wouldn't let her down. Phoebe would graduate early; they'd rent a cheap apartment with the money he'd been saving up, who cared if it had rats or roaches, they'd have everything; they'd be together and they'd be free. *Just us, we'll be okay*. All of the years spent smothered in their small house in their small town, by their stagnant widowed mother, could be left behind and eventually forgotten.

The creak came again. Why was his chest so tight? Why was it so bloody hot in the kitchen this morning? What had she known before she died? Would she have forgiven him in time? He'd caught her in the days leading up to that night trying to pick the lock of his bedroom, and the fear of what she might have found made it hard for him to breathe.

What are you keeping from me? she'd asked, backing away from him, eyes wide, to her own bedroom. *I will not let you ruin this for us. You promised me.*

Grant blinked the sweat from his eyes, refocused on his mother standing at the wall, at the small hole in the elbow of her sweater, because he hadn't heard a creak, he hadn't heard anything. Phoebe was not about to walk into the kitchen with a playful wink and those big dark eyes shining. Because he hadn't heard her moving around, set to burst through the kitchen doorway to start the day with her bright light, to try to keep him on track—because Phoebe was dead.

TEN YEARS AGO

8:45 a.m.

Grant Dean sensed her standing there before he was even awake—his lurking judgmental shadow lately.

"What is it?" His throat was so dry it felt raw. He cracked an eye open but there was no water on his messy bedside table—that would have taken foresight, which he lacked—just a lamp that hadn't worked in weeks and empty beer bottles that he could now smell. He grabbed his watch, slid it on, the familiar weight causing a lump in his throat that he swallowed away. It was just a watch. It was just a watch that had belonged to a father he had no memory of, that was worth more money than he'd make in a year. He screwed his eyes shut, and huffed loudly to the ceiling of his bedroom so he wouldn't yell at his little sister, who was a real self-righteous pain in the ass to come in here and treat him like a child.

What did she really know about the things he had going on? She wasn't the only one who was under immense pressure, was she.

From behind his closed eyes he sensed Phoebe frown. The feeling of her disappointment caused him to bolt straight up in bed. "I said, what is it, Phoebe? Why are you in my room? It's too early for your lectures."

"But it's not. Early." Phoebe strode to the window, drew the curtain loudly; he shielded his eyes from the burning morning sun. "You're going to be late for school—again. Coach'll bench you, you know he will. And you have that big math test, the important one, the one you said you were going to study for last night. You promised me you'd take it seriously. These things matter, so I know I didn't hear you come stumbling home at two a.m. I know I must have dreamt that because you wouldn't lie to me."

Grant felt the slow stir of movement beside him, drew the covers to his chin to try to muffle it. Phoebe's head shot back to his face and then her eyes slid down to the bed. She looked away quickly, but he caught her biting her lip.

"Okay, okay, I'm sorry." He raised his hands in mock surrender. "I'm getting up right now, I'm hurrying, I promise I studied for that test, I'm ready. Thank you for waking me so I won't be late for school."

Phoebe rolled her eyes and balled her small hands into tight fists, and he wondered if she'd dare throw the blankets off to make a point. He braced himself for it:

You have practice, Grant.

No distractions, Grant.

I will not let you lose everything, Grant.

You promised me.

If she only knew, he thought, his pulse thumping the longer he watched the worry on her pretty face. A tongue was out now, licking his hip bone, and he tried his very best to smile at his little sister.

"It really is late," Phoebe repeated, but she didn't come any closer, so he tried to relax. "It's almost nine, I'll drive you. I made you oatmeal but it's probably cold—I can warm it up."

"Don't you dare touch my truck. You're a terrible driver." He tried to sound light but there was hot breath under the blankets, a finger running down the inside of his thigh. He flicked it away under the covers, locked eyes with his sister, grinned at her, so she wouldn't see the movement.

Phoebe nodded, satisfied, throwing her long black hair into a ponytail. "Smells in here." She opened the window and looked around the room again. His mind raced, trying to remember getting home last night, fumbling up the stairs, whispering and ripping off clothes, and he prayed there was nothing left out in the open that Phoebe could see, regretted that he'd been too wasted to lock his bedroom door. This whole scene could have been avoided if only he'd been smarter.

"See you downstairs. You'll be happy to know that Mom's already left for work."

"Okay."

Grant waited until he heard Phoebe on her way down to the kitchen and then flung his legs over the side of the bed. "Just stay in here until we're gone. We'll talk later." He stood, speaking *over his shoulder to the pile of sheets and a secret Phoebe could never find out about: "Whatever you do, don't let her see you. You know she'd lose her mind."*

BECCA

Becca used her pretty gold-handled scissors to cut the front page neatly along the crease. She smoothed the paper carefully on the kitchen counter beside the sink. She'd splurged on the scissors for exactly this reason, but now they were a bit dusty because it had been a very long time since their bridge was written about. She had kept all the articles about the accident back then; there had been twelve. And now they were voting on taking it down? Gone forever? The timing—it was heartless, wasn't it? Or was it poetic maybe? She wasn't sure. But certainly, old-as-dirt Mrs. Rosie Wilson shouldn't have been driving at night without her glasses on. Who could have let her do such a reckless thing?

Of course, Becca would keep the page, a small inflection of pain so she'd never forget. *Survivor's guilt*, her therapist would call it—something she struggled with still. Grief never went away, it just lurked and sometimes hibernated. So she'd definitely keep the page in her box, along with her many other treasures and a notarized copy of the affidavit she'd signed nearly ten years ago to the day, her hand trembling, bandaged, three fingers broken, swearing officially that Grant's truck had hit a deer and spun out of control in the dark and the teeming rain, that poor Phoebe in the passenger seat without her seatbelt on had taken the brunt of the impact when they slid headfirst into the guardrail. That in every way it was the single worst night of her life; that she'd lost so much more than anyone could possibly know.

Becca looked out of the window above her sink. The leaves were turning and she felt the prick of tears in the corners of her eyes. The guilt rushed in without warning sometimes, but other times she could sense it was coming, about to claw at her. Yes—Becca nodded to herself in her empty kitchen—the timing of this accident was indeed heartless. Unfair. She had a right mind to drive herself to the Best Rest Retirement Home to yell at Darryl Wilson for letting his ninety-three-year-old senile wife get in her car and drive over their bridge, mere days before the memorial for Phoebe Dean; had no one any decency left when it came to what had happened there?

The bridge was already a thorn in people's sides. It was old and rickety and ugly, and many thought it should have been taken down years ago. Becca expected this vote next week would turn everyone in town into irritating little bees, flitting around, buzzing loudly about something that really had nothing to do with them.

Becca tried to turn her attention back to what she'd been doing before she caught sight of the paper just now. She stared down at her phone on the counter and the unanswered calls stared back. She shook out her arm, listened to the soft chime of silver, a lovely gift from Grant that usually made her feel better, but not today. She chewed on her cheek, to stop herself from counting how many times over the last couple of weeks she'd called him, only to get his voicemail—until his voicemail had filled up and she couldn't even leave a message.

But Grant was probably still asleep. Or on his way to work and couldn't pick up. It was actually better that he hadn't picked up; she didn't want him driving recklessly and getting in an accident. Another accident. The rumors still floated around—that he'd waited to call the ambulance on purpose, that he'd been driving blackout drunk—but she'd been there and knew that neither of those things was true, and she had the affidavit in her box to prove it. They'd never even been officially questioned, which they would have been if anyone had suspected anything more than it being just a terrible, awful accident! And look, another terrible awful accident had just occurred in the same exact spot. If anything, old Rosie Wilson's crash should help people see how innocent Grant really was.

Becca sighed. They'd connect when Grant was ready, she just had to be patient. He'd come around—he always did. He was a great man; if only everyone could see what she saw, or knew what she knew. How far he was willing to go for those he loved; how good and caring and dependable he really was.

Tears came again and this time they stung. She rubbed one away angrily. Why couldn't she even think about how wonderful Grant was without feeling wracked with guilt? Without it bringing up awful memories of that night? No one knew the burden she carried every day; what she'd had to give up, and what she had to continue to keep to herself.

Becca sighed and swiped to an app, but the digital graph just worsened her already terrible mood. The flashing red line looked like a frown, horribly disappointed in her for the twenty minutes of REM sleep she'd managed last night. She slammed her phone down on the counter. She wanted to delete the app altogether, but it was new and her mother had paid for the whole year's subscription *in advance*, as she told her every chance she got, and Becca suspected her mother had found a way to track Becca's problematic sleep patterns herself.

She'd already ignored three calls from her mother because she had to hurry or she'd be late for work, and with Rusty's new clocking-in system, which she knew he'd implemented because of her, now she had to work a full—full! Like her seniority didn't matter for anything!—eight hours before she could clock off from her job at Kramer's, the grocery store in town. She had her AA meeting tonight, and walking into those late was worse than getting reprimanded at work. She'd found a group a couple of weeks ago, when things began to feel dire. It was big, so she could sit in the rusting foldout chair with her scalding coffee and be more or less invisible, which was the whole point because she wasn't an alcoholic, she just went to learn about them so she would know how worried to be about Grant.

Becca was thoughtful like that—what she did for him on her own time, during the periods that he wasn't willing to talk. Sometimes they lasted weeks and sometimes months; once it was a whole year. She called them his *dark spots*, and she accepted them and she was patient, even if it was hard. But she loved him and they didn't need to talk all the time; their bond was unbreakable after what they'd been through together. And they'd been through so much more than anyone knew. *Unbreakable*, Grant would say. *Solid as a rock. But we have to keep it to ourselves.*

Becca picked up the phone to call Grant, maybe just one more time, but then threw it down; he'd call her when he was free. He'd need her, he would.

She stretched out her neck and breathed deeply, like she'd been taught. She touched her beating heart; she was dreadfully worried about him, he was drinking too much lately, spending every night the last couple of weeks in Reggie Nash's garage, which made Reggie Nash nothing but an enabler. When Reg's wife, Heather, got fed up, they'd slink off to Flo's, the local bar, where she'd heard Grant had been yelled at last week by someone who'd had one too many and dared to think they could bring *that night* up with him. That they could flip a switch and it was suddenly okay to talk so openly about what had happened. This person, this nosy prick, had been so drunk on cheap whiskey that he'd accused Grant of monstrous things. Of *lies*. Said Grant was jealous of his sister and wanted to hold her back. That he was probably glad she was dead. That drinking and driving was a scourge on society, and that had Grant not been on the football team, the sheriff would have charged him for the accident. That he was lucky he wasn't rotting in jail.

If the rumors still hadn't faded away, would they ever? And now another deadly car accident on the same bridge.

Becca saw the headlights cutting through sheets of rain,

felt Phoebe's head in her lap, heard the sickly sound of her wet breathing. She gripped the edge of the sink until her fingers stung. These memories were like waves that rose up from time to time, knocking her flat and leaving her winded. She scratched at the raised scars on her chest. The kitchen walls tightened.

Becca forced a smile at her reflection in the window. She thought of Grant, his big brown eyes, how they lit up his whole face. She knew she had her work cut out for her this time; Grant was clearly so depressed that he was having trouble returning her calls.

It certainly couldn't help that his wicked mother was hosting a memorial at their home. Not that Becca was terribly surprised. Ellen Dean didn't seem to care for her son—never had. Ellen may have pulled the wool over the townspeople's eyes, playing the part of long-suffering widow and mother, but Becca knew the truth. That Grant had never stood a chance, that living in the shadow of his perfect little sister was hard enough when she was alive, and impossible now that she was dead.

But still, they were family, and so over the last few weeks a small part of Becca had hoped Mrs. Dean would come to her senses and cancel it. It was downright cruel to shove Grant's face in it after ten years—as if he hadn't suffered enough! It had been a car *accident*. Rumors or not, insidious gossip or not, there'd never been any charges laid because Becca had seen the deer despite the rain; it had stood frozen there in the headlights of the truck, too big to avoid hitting it. That's what they said, for god's sake: deer caught in the headlights, it was like a metaphor or whatever. No, she didn't need a lawyer back then, of course she'd swear to those events to keep Grant out of jail; she'd do anything for him. She'd loved him then and she loved him still. Nothing could ever change that.

"A memorial? But—why?" Becca asked, appalled, when Mrs. Kilsworth mentioned it at the grocery store. "Are you sure about that? In their house?"

"It is the decennial, so it's lovely to remember Phoebe finally. Officially. Of course, we all understood that Ellen couldn't bear to hold something when it first happened, when that darling girl was ripped away from us..." Mrs. Kilsworth, their ancient English teacher, sighed long and hard, and Becca found herself souring despite it being very early in the morning. "It's still such a loss—for the whole town! She would've put West Wilmer on the map, no doubt. She was my best student. No one has even come close, but then she was just robbed—" Mrs. Kilsworth dabbed at her baggy eyes with a handkerchief, gripped by a grief she had no claim to. Becca was disgusted by the woman's fat crocodile tears and imagined unhinging her mouth to tell her what Phoebe was really like, see how special Mrs. Kilsworth thought Phoebe was then, but of course she didn't. She'd kept a lot to herself for the last ten years, and she wasn't about to let it slip now.

"It's a nice gesture, although it will be hard to attend, very emotional, as these things always are." Mrs. Kilsworth's reedy voice shook, which made Becca's skin hot. "That darling Phoebe always had a smile for everyone, and all those awards! I chaperoned the spelling bees you know. To see her at work was like

magic in a way. Just such a good, smart girl. I heard her mother kept an entire room in their house for her awards. So..." The old woman glanced at Becca indifferently. "Will you be going then, dear? To the Dean house on Sunday?"

"What?" The question caught Becca off guard. Was this old woman going senile and forgot she'd been there that night? "Of course I'm going. Of course I'll be there. It will be difficult for me, but how could I miss it? Grant will want me there for support."

Mrs. Kilsworth frowned and Becca threw her hand up to stop whatever it was the old woman was about to say, whatever complaints she'd dredge up, whatever rumors she'd hiss out of her hideous mouth. Becca straightened up at the cash register and smiled bigger, but it took effort. Did this woman know how hard her life was? That living with the burden of that terrible night sometimes felt like she was drowning?

"Mrs. Kilsworth." Becca cleared her throat. "I shouldn't have to remind you that I was in the truck that night! My goodness!" She leaned across the register and tugged on her scarf so the old woman could see the scars that ran crisscross from her neck to her chest. "These are from the impact. The seatbelt nearly took my head clean off. You know, sometimes when I wake up I forget that it even happened, and then I have to relive it all over again. It's like a never-ending nightmare." Becca wiped one eye and then the other with the back of her sleeve. She watched the wet marks slowly bleed out from the cuff until the urge to scream at the old woman had passed. "Shoot, look at me! But it's been hard, with people bringing it up again, like it's nothing more

than idle gossip." Becca smiled wider. "No offense, I know you mean well and that she was in your English class—and so was I!—but that whole stages-of-grief thing? It's not true. There are no stages and so it never really goes away. Complicated grief is a very real disease."

"Yes." Mrs. Kilsworth pursed her thin lips. "Well—thank goodness you were wearing your seatbelt when poor Phoebe, only sixteen years old with all of that potential—"

"I was knocked unconscious." Becca glared at the woman. "Fully blacked out. Horrible concussion. The truck nearly flew into the river, so it's a miracle that I'm alive, standing here listening to you gossip about Phoebe Dean."

"How are you holding up then, dear?" Mrs. Kilsworth gave her a tired look and Becca bristled. She knew Mrs. Kilsworth didn't care to hear how she was holding up. Even after ten years, the only person they cared about was Phoebe. Always Phoebe.

"Some days are still hard, even after this long, Mrs. Kilsworth," Becca answered curtly. "I try to keep busy, so I don't slide backward. I was in the hospital for eighteen days you know, and then I had years of therapy to try to heal from the trauma—"

"I simply cannot imagine what her poor mother is going through right now," Mrs. Kilsworth interrupted her. "Leading up to her own daughter's memorial—"

Becca sighed loudly, frustrated. What about her grief? Her suffering? "Well, I can tell you from experience that sometimes it feels like it just happened yesterday, and what I wouldn't give to go back to that awful night and take back what happened, so that Grant and I could still—" Becca clicked her jaw shut, flashed a tight smile. "Just listen to me rambling on, the memorial is bringing it all back up, it's been hard."

Mrs. Kilsworth raised a bushy white eyebrow before collecting her small bag of groceries. "I'll see you in a few weeks then I suppose, Rebecca. You take care of yourself."

Becca looked down at the kitchen counter as her phone rang for the fourth time that morning. But it wasn't Grant. And so she closed her eyes, bracing herself to answer.

JUNE

June wiped the sweat from her forehead and rubbed her sore eyes. She stopped on the side of the road to catch her breath. The walk from the cemetery had gone by in a blur of jumbled thoughts and moving legs, and it took her a long minute to orient herself. She looked back over her shoulder but there was nothing but open fields and long empty highway behind her; no markers to ground her. She looked ahead, squinting into the bright sun until she was sure she could make out the edge of the McCrays' old property, which meant she'd been walking for nearly two hours and was almost home. June was exhausted, but she took a deep breath and kept going.

As she neared her turn, passing by the McCrays' weather-beaten farmhouse with brittle brown ivy creeping up the siding and three cars on cinder blocks guarding the front, June saw a table set off to the side of the highway, with two pink balloons and two young girls behind it.

June wondered if this was a mirage. She rubbed her eyes again. Was she imagining the lawn chairs and pretty balloons and swinging, carefree legs? Because she couldn't quite believe that people had lives continuing to spin on normally when hers had just been shattered. Again.

June continued on her way. The girls waved, and up close she recognized them as her neighbors who lived a mile away—AJ and Linda Hill's nine-year-old twins. AJ had known her older brother, Wyatt. June hesitated on the dirt road. Wyatt. She tried her best not to think about him, but he was creeping in lately; she'd thought of him just this morning.

June forced herself to keep walking but she was shaken, the ground below her feeling increasingly uneven and rutted, and she wished desperately to avoid these girls and their lovely pink balloons and whatever it was they were doing on the side of the deserted road so early in the day.

"Morning, Miss June," the slightly taller one said with an eager smile. "We're sorry to hear about your mom passing on. Our parents told us about it. We're to draw you a card and leave it on your front porch to cheer you up."

"And did you know about Mrs. Wilson?" the shorter twin asked. "She was very old but it's still sad she died."

"Because every passing is a loss, Pastor Paul says," the other twin added. "Are you doing okay without your mom now, Miss June? Must be lonesome on your own even though your house is so small."

"Thank you, I'm fine," June said, facing up to the expanse of stark morning sky, unable to stomach their hollow words and that they had each other and two living parents with jobs and two cars and a newly paved driveway. "But I do have to get home—good luck out here with this."

The twins smiled a practiced smile. "Actually, Miss June, we're out here this morning raising money for the Phoebe Dean memorial this weekend—for Mrs. Dean? We're doing it on behalf of our church youth group, so anything you have will help, even a dollar or two for soda. It's to remember—"

"*Commemorate*, Livvy—"

"To commemorate the tragic accident that happened on the bridge—"

"The *first* tragic accident on the bridge, Livvy—"

"Yes, I know," June interrupted. "It's been in the paper all week." She thought again of her brother without wanting to, but he had always loved running on that bridge, despite it being so high and narrow and frowned upon. *Dangerous*, her mother would fret. *Fucking stupid*, her father would scream.

"I had a brother once, you know," June said to the sky. "*Have*. I *have* a brother. Your dad knew him—they ran track together in high school. But then he left, ran away, the same night as that car accident you're raising money for, so it's been a decade for him too I guess." June smiled at them quickly. These girls weren't even born when Phoebe Dean died, and yet here they were, out on the side of the road in her memory, when there was certainly no attention being paid to June's mother, or her brother for that matter.

June was used to being unseen, but this morning she was so done in that it overwhelmed her more than she already was.

She sighed loudly, unable to keep it in. The twins' smiles inched wider on their young faces but their eyes narrowed; one started chewing on her thumbnail. June knew she was making them uncomfortable as she watched the girls exchange a quick sidelong glance.

"Why'd your brother run away?" one finally asked.

"Wyatt." June ignored the question. "His name is Wyatt."

The twins pursed their small pink mouths in unison and then nodded at her gravely, dismissing her. "Sorry for your loss. Have a nice day, Miss June."

June set her shoulders firmly in the direction of her house, a lump burning her throat as she neared her driveway and turned down it at a jog.

She took the four crumbling steps to stand at her front door, noticing for the first time that the knob was about to break off. She bent to pick up the local paper, could feel the sun hot on her back. VOTE ON BRIDGE REMOVAL—she shoved the paper under her arm. Tearing down the bridge was something that the town could fight over, but she had other things to worry about, like cleaning and keeping the electricity from being shut off.

"I'm fine." June spoke to the peeling knocker that resembled a disfigured face. "Fine." She reached for the handle and saw that her palm was chapped and bright red from rubbing it along her thigh; a nervous habit she'd had in childhood. She thought the habit had long died. She opened and closed her fist, which made her palm ache. June cleared the tickle in her throat; she wasn't fine, she was very far from fine.

She pushed on the door, swinging it open to reveal the

cramped living room. After nearly a week, the smell of alcohol was faint now, finally overpowered by bleach and that fake pine scent of neon liquid cleaner.

Cleaning kept her body moving so she couldn't sink to the floor and drown on the linoleum or the threadbare rug in the hallway. It made the days push on. On her hands and knees, scrubbing, sweating into her eyes until they stung—it was the only thing that emptied her mind.

June still hesitated in the open doorway. Was she ready for this? Her mother was really gone, buried in the ground now, seven miles away. Shouldn't she feel a small weight lifted? Wasn't that what people felt?

She'd put her life on hold for years to care for her mother, who hadn't wanted to be cared for and had made that clear every chance she got—in looks of resentment, in refusing to eat for days, in tears and screaming that the child she wanted to come back never did.

Why, June? her mother would ask, and June would shake her head because there was no proper answer to give. *Why hasn't he come home?*

And June would reply: *I'm sure he will. Soon.*

But where Wyatt had been for the last ten years, after running away the night of a terrible fight with their father, June didn't know. The help they needed from the sheriff to look for Wyatt, to find wherever he'd slunk off to and then drag him home, as they had done several times before, hadn't been available because of that car accident. Their town was too small for more than one problem, she supposed, and they'd chosen her. Phoebe Dean.

She'd drained all of the resources and air and sympathy, and all that June's family was left with was an empty chair at their table and a steady stream of questions that would never be answered.

June took a deep breath, crossing the threshold and then closing the door behind her. She wouldn't think of the memorial on Sunday, of how everyone was thinking about Phoebe Dean again, caring about her again. June looked around; the threadbare pillows were still on the couch, the fraying curtains were still drawn and tied, and she could see the sun streaming into the kitchen in fat panels on the polished tile floor. She didn't remember cleaning the floor, but she was quite pleased that it had been done. She nodded to herself, and then bit her lip because it was trembling. She thought of the twins on the side of the road and the river and the bridge, and fresh tears came to her eyes. The familiar feeling of nausea rose, and the fear of the endless day ahead reached for her as she opened the closet for her cleaning supplies. The bathroom needed to be done.

But you can't clean forever. A noiseless whisper from the house, a threat, tickling the soft hairs on the back of her neck.

"I know," June snapped aloud to the empty living room, the walls breathing around her. She had felt lately that the house was closing in like a cocoon—a chrysalis perhaps—with milky filaments something she could almost see.

WYATT

The light hid behind clouds and Wyatt had to walk with his eyes down at his feet so he didn't trip and fall onto the darkening highway. He had to be careful; his eyesight was poor, and with no one around for miles, people drove recklessly on such deserted stretches of road.

By the time he reached the familiar turn, where the broken fence ended, his feet were numb. He saw that the grass and weeds had grown wild and untamed; the property looked a right mess. Wyatt snickered to himself, pleased by this embarrassment, knowing how much it would anger their father, who had cared so much about the exterior property but cared nothing at all for what was within it.

He stepped without looking over the large grooves in the driveway, where the car would sink and then spring up, making him and June squeal in delight when they were children. That he still knew where all the potholes were seemed like a good sign—that it wasn't too late. He should have come back earlier. She'd already been through a lot. Too much maybe.

Wyatt's big toe caught on something, and he tripped. A new groove in the road, he realized. He wondered if June would be able to forgive him.

You're not worth it anyway.

Wyatt ground his teeth until they ached, driving his father's voice away. He needed his head clear so he could think, so he could come up with an explanation for why he'd been gone so long.

June would be full of questions that had no good answers—about where he'd been, and why he was back now but not before, when he could have reset the course of everyone's lives. He had left, and then their father, who couldn't take the guilt of pushing him to leave, and being a weak man, had left too. He, Wyatt Chester Delroy, had been the catalyst for it all, he knew that. Or he *thought* he knew that. Sometimes he was unsure of what he could know or understand; he was unsure of who he really was as he stood in the middle of his crumbling childhood driveway. Ten years was a lifetime to be gone from a place.

Wyatt lit a cigarette. The pack was damp and it took a few tries, but when it finally caught, the smoke calmed him. He sat on their old tire swing, planting his feet firmly on the dry, fractured ground. Through the cracked window, he watched June at the kitchen table, staring at some empty middle space, lost.

June's hair was long and thin and she had aged. Her sweatshirt slipped down one shoulder; Wyatt could see her sharp collarbone. The sweatshirt had belonged to him but was now faded and misshapen. Wyatt remembered they fought over it long ago, until their mother threw it in the trash. *The Solomon shirt*, she'd yelled, *doesn't belong to either of you now*. That June must have snuck out later that same night to dig around in the trash and then washed it in secret formed a lump in his throat that he briskly swallowed away.

Wyatt moved the swing back until he hit the tree, the solidity of the trunk grounding him. The tree and its damp earthen smell reminded him of when he was a child and would dig in the dirt, for delicate sinuous roots, for worms, for the feel of cool silk sifting through his fingers.

Wyatt spat forcefully on the ground and stood. He was an adult now, grown, no longer interested in dirt and spiders and wriggling worms, those silly childish things. He'd come home because it was time. He knew the town still cared about that goddamn accident, that goddamn family, but he also knew their blind spots and their preoccupations—the scary bridge! A second accident! The fucking adorable memorial!—meant he could slip back in and go unnoticed for as long as he needed, until all the pieces were in place.

From his spot under the tree, Wyatt could tell the kitchen had changed only subtly since he was last in it. The door to the old yellow refrigerator was bare, no fading Christmas cards or handwritten messages or to-do lists, those totems of mundane life that most homes displayed—but not this one. This one was not a normal home; this one was stagnant with grief and ghosts.

He leaned forward. The ancient white stove was rusting in one corner and missing a burner. Three of the cupboards were without knobs, one door hung off its hinge completely; pity hardened in his gut.

Wyatt flicked his wrist sharply, once, twice, and squinted against the brightness of the kitchen light as he walked closer. On the linoleum table where June sat were mounds of crumpled tissues and a white mug that he had bought at a school fair with a pocketful of change: *World's Best Dad.*

Wyatt let out a bitter laugh at the cruel irony of the chipped ceramic. The first thing he'd do would be throwing that fucking mug against the wall. What their father had done was unforgivable, didn't June realize? Was she still so naive? Did she still expect so goddamn little from people? Wyatt felt a ripple of anger, that hot vestige of his past, and pushed it away with another flick of his wrist. They didn't need their parents; they'd have each other, like when they were young and would tap on their shared bedroom wall in Morse code, and smile together behind books about birds and dinosaurs at the library while their father snored in a chair.

Wyatt watched June until he started shivering in the cool air. Her eyes weren't bright like he remembered, but bloodshot and vacant; he wondered if she was lost in her grief, searching for their mother.

Wyatt heard an animal keening and looked behind him, alert. There were coyotes here, wolves. But he saw nothing, just dead fields and solid country emptiness. No furtive movements, no hungry eyes stalking him.

He turned back to the window and realized the sound was June. He watched his little sister break down and felt something splinter inside of him. Her sobs leaked through the cracks in the window and under the front door and over to him. He dropped his cigarette, stubbed it out with his boot, and reached out to see if he could catch the sound. He wanted to taste it. Wyatt quickly made a tight fist instead, embarrassed. It was a silly gesture.

He watched as June took two fistfuls of tissues and pushed them to her eyes, but then jerked up suddenly as though spooked. He held his breath and stared into his little sister's hardened face.

She glanced to the stove—perhaps at the old black kettle, he wondered—her face expressionless. Could she sense that he was there? That he'd finally come back?

Wyatt had kept the truth to himself for ten years, gnawing at him, writhing around inside of him, but now it was time to set it free, unburden himself of it before it was too late.

Before he ran out of time.

He began coughing until it winded him and unease took hold in his gut, winged insects battering in a jar, that June might not recognize him or allow him inside. That she might be too afraid. He sat back down on the tire swing; he would wait until night fell. June would be less reluctant to turn him away in the dark.

GRANT

The kitchen wall was bare but for the new paper calendar and a spackling of tiny black holes where nails had once been. Grant was going to be late for work but it didn't matter. His mother didn't really care about his job, and he couldn't leave until this macabre new ritual was completed. His mother had bought the calendar a month ago, the same day she'd decided to hold the memorial—to make up for never holding a funeral, to remember Phoebe finally. She'd told him curtly of her plan to host it at their home, and he'd been unable to think of anything to say and so, like usual, had said nothing.

Grant watched her uncap the fat marker and ceremoniously cross out the day prior, the tip squeaking, its high-pitched sound a daily reminder that they were getting closer to it, to the tenth anniversary of Phoebe's death, and that he was a terrible son.

"There." She recapped the marker. "Oh." She turned to him now, running her arthritic hands along her apron. "Grant." She frowned slightly at his name and he gripped the squared top of his chair. "I'm making a roast, ordered a special cut from Kramer's. It'll be ready tomorrow morning for pickup. For your sister's memorial on Sunday."

She rarely referred to Phoebe at all and so *your sister* landed like a slap, bitter and unforgiving. Grant swallowed, the taste of egg and coffee lodged in his throat. He'd hoped that she'd change her mind about this idea to have people here in his house, crying and drinking and judging and asking questions, but with it three days away now, he knew it was inevitable; knew it was closing in.

"Sure, I'll pick it up." Grant eyed another line from the newspaper: VOTE TO BE HELD NEXT WEEK. He heard a door slam upstairs and cringed.

"You still haven't fixed that." His mother spoke to the wall again. "It's going to come straight off the hinges soon—it's been twenty-seven days, Grant."

"What?" Grant froze, glad that his mother's back was to him. "What did you say?"

"The bathroom door upstairs, it's been three or four weeks now, can you fix it, please? And the porch light is still out. And the railing outside. Your father would roll over in his grave."

"Right..." Grant stared at the back of his mother's head, at her loose ponytail and thinning gray hair. That was two mentions now of his father. This morning was a ripe nightmare he wished he could wake from. He felt his phone through his jeans. The vibration felt desperate and so he knew it was her. He jammed his hand into his pocket, fumbled, but was too late, the call stopped.

The screen stared at him, dangerously silent. Until the texts came through:

Did you see the paper?

We should talk.

You're not ignoring me, are you? Xo

Grant frowned as he scrolled back through the dozens of unanswered texts and calls from her over the past few weeks; she was becoming restless.

"Did you hear..." his mother said, and he held his breath and wondered if she would bring it up for once, that the place where his sister died was being talked about again, that there was so much misery in their house that sometimes it was hard to breathe, "...that Birdie Delroy passed?"

"Oh." Grant emptied, let his breath go. "No."

"Cancer," his mother went on. "But all that stress wouldn't have helped any, and the drinking. Who could blame her, though, with her boy running off like he did." She kissed her teeth. "Now that girl's been left alone in that house. Have you seen the place? It's falling apart. What was the girl's name? It was strange—typical of Birdie though, to choose something so odd. Summer?"

He cleared his throat. "June."

"June. That's right—June Delroy. But if that boy of Birdie's was going to turn out anything like his father, maybe it's best he's gone. Hank Delroy was bad news, even when we were in high school ourselves. Not everyone is cut out to be a father."

The Delroys were the absolute last family Grant wanted to be reminded of, and so he said: "You're right." A definitive plea to end the conversation, although he agreed, it was for the best that Wyatt Delroy was gone.

"That boy Wyatt was a real bad seed. I saw him in the back of the sheriff's car plenty. There was something off with him."

Grant refused to consider fathers and bad seeds and especially Wyatt Delroy, and prayed not for the first time that morning to wake up from this nightmare. He stood, sweating, waiting for his mother to drop it, *please, god, please.*

"But the girl—June—now she's all alone. You should go to Birdie's funeral, ask June if she needs anything done around the house." She kissed her teeth again. "It's the neighborly thing to do."

"Yeah," he said, but he knew he wouldn't go. "Okay."

"Well, go on then," she said, her smile barely a twitch this time. "Please don't be late for work."

"I won't, I'm leaving now."

His mother filled the frying pan to soak, and left the kitchen but paused in the hall. "By the way," she said, as if a casual afterthought—but he knew from her pinched tone that it wasn't. "I found her journal. It was out in the barn after all. Mustn't have looked hard enough before, but it's in her room now, where it belongs."

"Oh," he said, uncomfortably. He'd looked out there years ago—was this true or was his mother toying with him?

"I can't bear to read it, not yet, but in case you wanted to."

"Why would I want to do that?" he said far too loudly, but he was drained of patience.

His mother stood stock-still a few feet away. Her back was

to him, but he knew she was wrestling with whether to engage with his tone or ignore him altogether.

Grant released his hands from clutching the top of his chair, and hot blood flooded back to his fingertips.

"I'll leave some dinner in the fridge," his mother said finally before walking away. The door to her bedroom closed and he was dismissed by the soft hum of her television set. Grant watched a large black crow land in the oak tree outside and shit on the yellowing grass below it. He grabbed the newspaper from the table and shoved it deep in the trash under the sink.

Grant shifted his weight; his leg was really bad now, he had to practically limp to the front door, balancing on the knob to tug on his coat. He didn't bother checking the clock on the wall, he knew he was late. But that was just one of the many problems piling up, and the day had only just begun.

BECCA

Mom?" Becca answered her phone. "It's too early for you to be calling me nonstop already—what's wrong?"

"We pay for your phone, honey, just answer the first time and save us all the trouble, especially when you know how much your father and I have been worrying—"

"Yes." She grabbed the juice from the fridge and drank straight from the carton. "Yes—I know how much you've been worrying because you keep telling me. But listen, I can't talk, I cannot be late. Rusty has this whole new clocking—"

"Have you read the paper?"

Becca sighed loudly at the floor. "Yes?"

"That poor woman—sixteen grandkids! And now they want to take the whole bridge down, but you know who's leading that charge? AJ Hill! That horrible man and his mother-in-law, Nancy Kilsworth! She was always so hard on you in high school, wasn't she? Well, they're leading the charge, and we should vote against it." Her mother snorted. "That AJ was always a righteous pain, accusing you of those awful things when you were just a child really—"

"Mom—"

"I'm rambling, sorry." Her mother paused just briefly before continuing. "And also Birdie Delroy! Did you hear? A few days ago—cancer in the end, liver I think, so now I can't stop thinking about poor June. You should check in on her, bring her something to eat. The last time I saw her in town she was very thin."

"I haven't spoken to June in years."

"I'm sure she'd be happy to see you. I should call her myself, find out when the funeral is." Her mother sighed dramatically and Becca considered hanging up; she didn't have the time or the energy for this. "Rebecca, I ran into Eileen Tucker yesterday and she was asking if we're going to the Deans' this weekend, and of course we're not stepping foot in that house, but then she asked if you were going and you're not, are you? Your father and I don't think that would be a good idea—"

"Yes, I'm going!" Becca spat into the receiver. "Why does it seem like people have forgotten that I was even there that night? When I lost *everything*."

"Oh, honey—"

"It would be weird if I wasn't there." Becca snatched her keys from the basket on the counter. "You haven't forgotten that I was there that night, have you? That I was in the truck? You saw me in the hospital, right? For eighteen whole days?"

"Rebecca—"

"You wouldn't be minimizing what I've been through, would you, Mom? You wouldn't be trying to erase my trauma?"

"I'm not, honey, but you're getting worked up and I would hate to think what Dr. Murphy would say about all the feelings—all the very hard feelings—this might stir up for you if you were to go on Sunday and see that man. Maybe we should just call Dr. Murphy—"

"But I thought you wanted me to *feel everything*," Becca snapped. "I thought that's why you forced me to therapy in the first place! So I'd remember everything, so I could *feel* everything, otherwise I wouldn't be able to process it—that's what Dr. Murphy said. God!" She left the house and stormed to her car, her phone clutched to her ear. "Didn't Dr. Murphy say that I had suffered a *very serious traumatic event* but that I was finding my own ways to cope? I know it's been a few years since I last saw him, but surely you remember all that! That there is not *one* way to grieve but that everyone grieves in their own damn way?"

"Please, Rebecca, you don't have to yell—"

"Please stop checking in on me, because I can handle this weekend, just like I've handled the last ten damn years!"

There was a long pause and then her mother very quietly said: "I would hate to think that you're fixating again."

"I am not fixating! Sunday will be good for my grieving process—complicated grief, remember? It's a real disease? And Grant needs me, imagine how hard this is for him—"

Shit. Becca clenched her teeth to shut her big mouth, but it was too late. She heard the soft click of her mother's jaw tightening. Her mother had upset her and now she'd let something slip that she shouldn't have. Her parents didn't know the full story of her and Grant back then, but the very little that they did know, they hated. Hated that Grant had been driving the truck, hated that Becca had been there at all, hated that she still had gaps in her memory, even though it was totally normal!

"She's lucky, Mrs. Hoyt," the resident doctor explained. "Very lucky to remember anything at all. Rebecca suffered a serious concussion, so having gaps surrounding the impact is normal. We often see retrograde amnesia in cases like these. Now she needs to rest."

"But what if she never remembers?" her mother asked, stricken, looking over at Becca lying in the hospital bed. "We're just not sure why she was in his truck, or at that wild party, in the first place. She hasn't always had the best judgment when it comes to boys—"

The doctor frowned impatiently. "A young girl is dead, Mrs. Hoyt. Rebecca is very lucky considering the impact, so let's focus on that, for your daughter's sake."

But her mother wasn't about to let it go this morning. "I still can't bear the thought of you in the back seat of that man's truck for god knows how long, Rebecca—he nearly drove you into the river, what if—" Her mother sucked in sharply; she'd be close to tears now. "Why did he wait so long to call for help? Was it to sober up? While his own sister died in the middle of the road like some animal? You're my daughter and you were just left there, *unconscious*—"

"I've told you that is not what happened!"

"And that awful Kelsey Price... I still won't step foot in her little hair salon. How could she have thrown that wild party when her parents were out? How could she have let you get in that truck with that man—"

"Goodbye, Mother."

Becca shoved the keys so hard into the ignition she broke a nail. She leaned back, screwed her eyes shut, counted to twenty to calm her rattled breathing. Of course it was AJ Hill and horrid Mrs. Kilsworth throwing their weight around to take down the West Wilmer bridge—to make themselves seem important, to inject themselves into something that had nothing to do with them. Becca's stomach twisted remembering when she'd seen Mrs. Kilsworth in the store, and the grave concern that Mrs. Kilsworth had shown for Mrs. Dean, when she'd had nothing for Becca—not even the decency to ask how she was coping!

Becca yanked the mirror down, forced her face into a smile, brushed her long dark hair behind her shoulders so she could touch her earrings, small pearls. They'd been Phoebe's, pretty and perfect, just like Phoebe had been. Becca reached into her purse for her pills before pulling out onto the long dirt road to the highway.

Becca checked the time. If she was quick, she could drive by the factory parking lot, see if Grant had made it into work. He was working the day shift today. She'd figured out how to check his schedule online so she wouldn't have to bother him to ask.

What she really needed to figure out was how to fall asleep at night. How to get rid of the nightmares so she could stay asleep, or this app would have her parents forcing her back to therapy, she could feel it. Since the memorial was announced last month, her mother had been calling more often, there had been more invites to lunches and dinners, more unannounced drop-ins at her house, and Becca absolutely refused to go back. She was done with therapy and the nonstop talking and trying to remember absolutely everything when she remembered enough: Dancing with Phoebe in the living room. Grant grinning at her in the rearview mirror of the truck. The way he'd looked in his football jersey, his hair still sweaty from the game. She blushed, remembering, touched her cheeks. She could still smell his sweat if she tried.

"Be kind," Becca spoke to her face in the mirror. "You've been through a trauma. Be gentle."

She drummed her hands on the steering wheel, remembering last summer when a group of out-of-towner teens had come late one night to jump from the bridge. They'd been high on drugs and wanting to conjure some fatalistic meaning from the site of Phoebe's death, but then one idiot had gotten hypothermia and another nearly drowned and the sheriff got involved, and when Becca had called Grant to see how they should feel about strangers using their bridge like a stupid Ouija board, he'd hung up and hadn't returned her calls for months, sunken deep into one of his dark spots.

Well, she'd make damn sure that didn't happen this time, not with everything that was going on. The cruelty of the timing. It was a lot and he'd need her support, and she'd be there for him every step of the way. Whatever he needed she'd do, as she'd done for the last ten years.

They'd been like Romeo and Juliet back then, with their secret relationship in high school. They'd had to keep it to themselves because if anyone knew, it might lead to too many questions. About that night. About why they still couldn't tell anyone.

But it was ten years now, something the Deans were acknowledging very seriously with this memorial. And so Becca wondered if maybe a decade was long enough for her and Grant too. The guilt was crushing sometimes; how might it feel to unburden herself? No. *No.* Becca shoved the bad thought back into the recesses of her mind. She sat up, tightened her grip on the wheel. She had to talk to Grant, see how he was doing, see what he'd need from her.

Did my heart love till now? Forswear it, sight. For I never saw true beauty till this night.

She smiled.

TEN YEARS AGO

10:27 a.m.

Mrs. Nancy Kilsworth reluctantly handed the poor girl her English paper. Phoebe's dark eyes flitted to the corner and then back to her, surprised at first and then dismayed.

"It's just one assignment," Mrs. Kilsworth said, trying to sound soothing but firm; she was her teacher, that was all. "Shakespeare's a hard take, Macbeth *especially. There's always next time, Phoebe."*

"Okay." Phoebe's small fingers clutched the paper to her chest. "Thank you," she said and went back to her seat where she shoved the paper deep in her desk and then stared out the window.

Had she noticed bags under the girl's eyes lately? Mrs. Kilsworth wondered whether it was drugs. It was usually drugs. The thing with drugs, as she understood well, having been a teacher for twenty-five years already, was that they could ruin anyone's life, not just the ones you assumed would be the first to sink.

Mrs. Kilsworth sighed and let her ears rejoin the grating din of her class. She sighed again, because she just could not shake her concern. Something had changed with Phoebe over the last couple of weeks, since the beginning of the school year. She kept catching the girl staring out the window, preoccupied. And now this paper. Mrs. Kilsworth wondered if she should involve Ellen Dean. She'd never called a parent for a C– on an assignment before, but it had also been turned in late, and Phoebe had missed an entire section on yesterday's quiz. And she'd never had a student like Phoebe Dean before either, who got straight As and still sought extra credit. Who actually cared about learning, who actually asked smart questions, who actually respected Mrs. Kilsworth's thoughts on Macbeth. *Someone who spoke eagerly about college.*

Phoebe had even baked her cookies last year, to thank her for such an interesting semester, could you imagine! That had been a first.

Mrs. Kilsworth stood behind her desk, shaking her head. There was something exhausting about students with such promise starting to fall short, slipping into the dark clutches of god knows what.

"Come now, Nancy," she imagined her husband would chide. "It's just one assignment, one quiz. Can't be perfect all the time; that's too much pressure for a child. She should stop baking for her teachers and get out and live a little."

"Harold," she'd respond—flushed, because what the hell did he know about teaching, or how special Phoebe Dean was? "You don't know what you're talking about, so shut it and leave the worrying to me."

"Becca," she said to the class. "Turn to page forty-three and read the second scene aloud, with a little more feeling this time."

Her attention found its way back to Phoebe, who had a look of pure anger on her face. Mrs. Kilsworth startled and her hands flew to her mouth, knocking over her mug. Her cheeks burned; it was unnerving to see the girl's prettiness quite so twisted. She ignored the question that Rebecca Hoyt had just asked her, to better see what Phoebe was staring at out the window.

Her breath caught as Phoebe turned back to class, her face relaxed again. Phoebe smiled in her direction in such a calm manner that Mrs. Kilsworth wondered if she'd imagined the whole thing. But no, she knew what she'd seen. Phoebe Dean had been quietly furious at something outside.

Mrs. Kilsworth stood, her knees cracking, and barked, "Silent reading until the bell," as she walked over to the window herself. What kind of a teacher would she be if she didn't know what was going on with her best student?

The high school sat in the middle of nowhere, a squat beige building surrounded by razed fields, the dilapidated water tower in the distance. The clouds were dense and ash gray; that storm was indeed moving in. She'd have to leave straight after her last period, no chitchat in the teachers' lounge today.

Mrs. Kilsworth pushed her forehead hard against the glass, trying to spot something, anything. Some students on free period stood in clots outside. Some sat cross-legged on the brittle yellowing grass; some leaned against the colorless cement wall smoking; some—she turned her face after a whistle blew—ran practice drills of some sort far to her left.

The parking lot was full and quiet, but in the crisp pre-fall morning, exhaust fumes snaked into the air at the very back of it. Mrs. Kilsworth slid her glasses on and peered out.

Her jaw set and she nodded curtly to herself. She brushed her hands along her skirt, chastising herself for not assuming that—of course the saying was true—where there was smoke there was going to be fire. There, hiding in plain sight, and certainly skipping class and that very important math test she knew was happening that very minute, was Grant Dean, constantly checking his watch, clearly waiting very anxiously for someone.

GRANT

After the way his morning had begun, Grant was all edges. Things were shifting in their house; his mother was bringing things up that normally stayed buried between them. Phoebe's accident. His father. The facade they'd built up through the years—that practiced, indifferent dance they did—was fracturing.

Grant tried to stay focused on his work, on the chicken parts swimming by on their rickety belt, but today the rippling of heads and beaks and wings seemed like a dismembered poultry version of that classic *I Love Lucy* episode he knew his mother loved watching.

His mother. His parents.

His father. His father. His father. Grant rubbed his bare wrist roughly. He was having trouble reining in his thoughts, as if maybe they were taking pleasure in torturing him.

His mother and father had been next-door neighbors separated by five acres of cornfields. They had fallen in love at twelve, married at sixteen, their bleak surroundings no match at the time for their young love and the future they'd build in the house that his father's family had owned for over a century.

But like their youth, their love aged, and by the time Grant came along, it was hardened by the pressures of adulthood and its suffocating responsibilities. Maintaining their ancient home in the ever-worse winters; near-empty bank accounts with limited options for work; having no real escape from within their four uninsulated walls.

Morris did what he could, where he could; he worked with his hands, he tended to his garden, he tried to seem content.

But it was never enough; he felt stuck.

Grant was just a toddler, and Phoebe an infant, when Morris Edward Dean died in his sleep one humid August night. And although Ellen rarely spoke of Morris, his oppressive presence never left their home. Morris lingered in the photos she would grab from the wall when a stab of grief struck; in the worn wooden furniture he'd built in the small shed Ellen eventually bulldozed with no explanation to Grant or Phoebe, her face tear-soaked and strained as she supervised from the back porch. Morris existed in the old books he had collected, something no one would think to do in West Wilmer, which made them prized even if they were never once read.

The idea that Grant would never live up to the ghost of this great man was spoken aloud only once, and so long ago that he could shrug it off like a bad dream when he felt like pretending that his life hadn't started out so unfairly, that maybe it hadn't always been destined to end up this way.

When Grant was seven years old, on what would have been their father's thirtieth birthday, their mother, for the first time since her husband had died five years earlier, decided it was time to celebrate him.

"You look just like him—" she told Grant in a voice he'd never heard before. It sounded like an accusation, like he'd done something wrong. She was drinking gin, which she never did, and she was mostly ignoring Phoebe, which was also unusual.

The three of them were eating birthday cake on a quilt on the lawn, which should have been thrilling in its novelty—his mother, by that time, had fully embraced her role as long-suffering widow and was not one for fun—but the evening was scaring Grant. It had started to rain but their mother had no intention of heading inside, smiling at him with her mouth, her eyes so very small and angry.

"You look just like him. But you are nothing like him. Why couldn't you stay out of trouble? It exhausted him," his mother slurred, and Grant recoiled as if struck. "The night he died, do you remember? You broke something in his shed, and you couldn't stop crying about it when he found out."

Grant shrugged, but his lip was twitching the way it did before he'd cry, and Phoebe, barely five, started whimpering, but their mother just stood, wrung out her apron in the still-pouring rain, and looked at them both in silence before she walked into the house and went to bed. Grant cleaned the crumbs from Phoebe's face with the hem of his rain-soaked shirt and then held her tiny hand as they went into the house and up the stairs and he eased her into her bed.

Grant cried himself to sleep that night, trying to understand what his mother had meant. Was he drawn to trouble? Was his father's death his fault? How could he amount to a man he had no memory of—how could you compete with a ghost?

The next morning his mother behaved as if nothing had happened, but there was a subtle shift in the kitchen as she hummed softly at the stove, making their pancakes extra fluffy, as her gaze lingered longer and longer on Phoebe. She twirled Phoebe's soft hair and kissed the top of her small head.

"You'll start piano lessons in Lyons," Ellen said to her, smiling. "Your father's grandmother was talented. It must run in the family."

As the years dragged on, from the outside things may have seemed as normal as life for a family who had lost their father at such a young age could seem. Grant's mother would attend his teacher meetings and ask the right questions that proved that, yes, she was concerned that Grant was easily distracted, that his grades were slipping, that maybe he could use some structure and encouragement, but then she would just shake her head at him in the car and never mention it again. Whether she just didn't care or couldn't be bothered, he wasn't sure.

She'd attend his football games and cheer at the right moments, but she never really watched him. Not when she had Phoebe beside her to talk to, to check in on, to dote on by playing with her hair.

As his mother passed time in a haze of indifference toward him, she sharpened her focus on Phoebe. Phoebe, who was so easy to talk about when people asked; Phoebe, who had been such a happy baby, who never got into mischief, who was her pride and joy. The accolades were endless, as if Phoebe alone could soak up their mother's first terrible loss.

And Phoebe played her part, easy and amenable and engaged, maybe because she understood that she could help ease their mother's suffering, or maybe because the role had been placed on her at such a young age that she didn't know any different.

Until she did.

Grant found Phoebe in the barn late one afternoon, several months before her accident, scribbling away furiously in her journal.

"Phoebe." He snapped his fingers to get her attention. "Can't you hear Mom from here? She's yelling for you—you're going to be late for some church thing."

"I'm not going to that."

"Right." Grant laughed easily, his hand already back on the door to leave. "You better hurry, she's on a real tear."

Phoebe looked at him from her spot in the dark corner, and even in the dim light he could tell she'd been crying. "Tell her I'm not going today. Just make something up, you're good at that. Please."

"You tell her." Grant then stepped closer to his sister. "Why are you crying?"

"I'm fine." Phoebe wiped her eyes. "It's just Mom."

Grant crossed the rough barn floor to where she sat. "What happened?"

Phoebe took his hand and let him pull her up before walking into his chest and hugging him. "Nothing happened—I'm just tired. Of piano, of tutors, of her watching me. You know how she is."

He snorted.

"I know it's worse for you." Phoebe leaned back and smiled sadly at him. "So we have to stay focused and we'll be okay when we both get out—can you imagine how demented she'd be with just one of us here?" She paused to catch her breath. "So, it's just us, like it's always been. Right, Grant?"

"Just us," he repeated.

"Promise me." Phoebe spoke into his chest; he could tell she'd started crying again.

"I promise."

He should have paid closer attention to the pressure Phoebe was under, to the times that she would look at him from across the kitchen table as if to say *save me* when their mother's beam was too intense, peppering her with too many questions about her exams, about what church group she'd be teaching that summer, about what dress she'd be wearing to the school dance and how she'd do her hair, that it looked best in a ponytail even if Phoebe didn't agree.

Grant did feel bad when this happened, which was all the time, because he did love his sister—they were on an island together in their insufferable home—but selfishly, the dynamic had worked for him. And so Grant would just roll his eyes at Phoebe, pretend he was suffering along with her, but he did nothing to break up their mother's harsh focus, because it meant that all of the bad choices he was drowning in could continue going unnoticed.

But now, looking back, he wished he'd known how serious Phoebe had been that day in the barn; how consumed she would become, with not just leaving home, but leaving home with him, the two of them together.

Just us, and we'll be okay.

How far she'd be willing to go to make sure he kept that childhood promise.

BECCA

Becca's life had been cleaved in half: before the accident, and after. Pre and post. Then and now. Rebecca Jane Hoyt was the same physical person in surroundings and body, but everything else about her had changed that night. Everything that was important, at least.

She'd recognized the change as soon as she was discharged from the hospital after nearly three agonizing weeks of blood tests and collapsed veins and reset bones and nurse rotations. On the drive home, as her parents' nervous energy filled their car, she noticed that everything she saw and felt and thought seemed slightly altered. A bit more subdued, a bit less bright.

Had the fields always looked so desolate and bland? Had time always passed so slowly? Had life always felt so fragile? Would she ever be able to move on from the accident intact?

Things aren't actually different, it's just a new lens that you're using. It's probably guilt, Dr. Murphy had said with a pleased nod. *Survivor's guilt. And guilt can be a very strong emotion. Just allow yourself time to process things, Rebecca. Be kind to yourself. Be patient with yourself. All of your thoughts and feelings are valid, so really feel them. This is a normal response to a very traumatic event.*

Becca still hadn't been able to get hold of Grant, so she'd decided that she'd visit the bridge on her second break to collect her thoughts. On the drive there, she noticed that people were already posting signs, announcing to their neighbors how they'd be voting next week. Becca slowed as she passed the fourth poster—KEEP OUR HISTORY: VOTE NO!—trying to understand how someone who probably hadn't been to the bridge in years could care enough to stick such an ugly thing in their yard.

There were no road signs or markings for the bridge, but the draw was magnetic. Becca drove away from town on the single-lane road without passing a single vehicle. She sped on, the caws of crows shrill overhead. When she reached the fork, when all that lay ahead of her was flat brown fields and the staccato of swollen decomposing fences, she turned left.

Becca pulled over onto the shoulder to park, gravel spitting under her wheels, tall grass scratching the metal body of her car. She hadn't been here in ages, but she did what she'd always done: walked halfway across the bridge to sit, dangling her legs over the rushing river. She inhaled deeply into her lungs the heaviness of being at the site of a tragedy. Phoebe's tragedy, *her* tragedy, not Rosie Wilson's. That woman had been old with dementia, it was certainly her time to go, so there was nothing really tragic about that. But she resented Mrs. Wilson for splitting this old scar open and drawing everyone's attention back to it. Keeping everything to herself was hard for Becca again, now that her biggest worry had crawled back and was perched on her shoulders. She was terrified that she'd soon burst and the words would storm out, too strong and willful for her to stop.

What would people think of her if they knew the accident had been entirely her fault?

Becca exhaled forcefully, trying to expel the guilt, and then rested her forehead against the cool guardrail, the same one that had stopped Grant's truck from flying completely off the bridge. "Thank you," she said, and then kissed the cold metal. This was something she did every time she came, because although her life and feelings were tangled and complicated, she was still very glad to be alive.

Becca hadn't brought anything with her today. She'd stopped that when the memorialized section of the bridge transformed from lovely tribute to something so horrid that you'd avert your eyes. Everything that had been stuck to the post had wilted and fused and bled into the ground, sprouting a carpet of pelt-less stuffed animals, rotting wooden crosses, and other decaying totems meant at one time to pay homage to Phoebe.

But today Becca was shocked to see fresh tributes when there hadn't been in years. A stuffed purple rabbit, three votive candles that had been lit and extinguished, Phoebe's blurred picture from the yearbook. Phoebe had never really left, for nearly a decade she had lingered everywhere, but it was like West Wilmer had just woken up and resurrected her entirely—remembering her, missing her, grieving her—thanks to this damn bridge and the memorial. The *decennial*, she corrected herself angrily, hearing Mrs. Kilsworth's gruff voice in her ear.

Becca strode over and snatched up the purple rabbit, leaving half its body still nailed to the post, hemorrhaging wet and dirty plush innards. Even though she had made mistakes, she was owed these things too. There were no memorials set up for *her* even though the night had happened to her, just as it had to Phoebe. And Becca had lost a lot too, maybe even more. Phoebe's big dreams had been abstract, whereas hers had been very real, and although both of theirs had been shattered that night, Becca still had to live day in and day out with her loss.

Becca clutched the soaked stuffed animal to her chest and returned to her car. She'd dry it out and add it to her box at home, along with the treasured pictures and rosaries and the many gifts Grant had given her over the years. They had to try very hard to keep their relationship a secret, but it worked that way, Grant always said, smiling at her, brushing her hair behind her ear gently, because it made it more special. It was hard, keeping it to themselves, but what was love without sacrifice?

Becca blushed, remembering when he'd called her his *lucky charm* that time she'd sworn he was at her house and so couldn't have taken a baseball bat to that man's car in the parking lot of Flo's. And his *sweet angel* the time she'd driven two hours to the casino to cover his debt before he got beaten up by security. Grant hated debt, and so of course she was happy to help. He'd bought her a dozen long-stem roses the next morning, which she'd pressed and put in her special black box.

She'd do anything for Grant Dean; she owed him that much.

When Becca woke up in the hospital, and the nurses told her that she'd been brought there in an ambulance, that she'd been in a very serious car accident, and they were so sorry to tell her that Phoebe Dean hadn't made it, she was stunned.

Later, Grant wheeled himself into her hospital room, all bandaged up and squinting through black eyes and wheezing in pain, just to make sure that she was all right. She was touched that, even in his state of shock and grief, he was still so worried about her.

"Hey," he said, his voice sounding hoarse. "We need to talk."

Becca's head was throbbing and she couldn't feel her left leg and the pain in her left shoulder was excruciating, but she nodded as best she could—they certainly did need to talk. To figure out what this accident meant for them, their carefully crafted plans, the ones she'd been dreaming of since she was a little girl, the ones they'd had to keep from everyone, because no one would have understood—especially not Phoebe.

JUNE

The knock startled June from a daze. She hadn't been quite asleep but she'd been staring so hard at the old white stove that she'd gotten lost. For how long? Minutes, hours, she wasn't sure. In the days since her mother's death, time had slid away from her sometimes, slippery as an eel. She'd been looking at the kettle after thinking she'd heard her mother down the hall, wanting some tea, but then she'd remembered that her mother was gone, and that was why she was sitting at the kitchen table like this, empty and heartsick and scared. Forgetting for a split second that she was all alone was a wickedness of June's own mind, and she blinked rapidly, to try to lessen the ache of that and also the feeling that her eyes were filled with sand.

June blew on her tea desperately, waiting for the knocking at the door to stop. *Please, leave.* She wasn't in the mood for a visitor. It was getting late. She was exhausted but also terrified of falling asleep. She'd been having such vivid dreams about her mother. Just that morning she'd woken with a start before the sun had even risen, swearing her mother was in her room, sitting on the edge of her bed singing to her as she had when June was a child. June had quickly reached for her—she'd wanted to feel this mother, the one she missed so purely—but as soon as she sat up her mother was gone, the room empty.

June shivered and got up to close the window.

The knock came again, this time like thunder. Persistent. June sighed, resigned herself, dropped the soggy tissues on the table and walked over to the door, unhooking the chain and opening it an inch.

She gasped and fell into the frame, slamming the door shut. Her mouth gaped and she tried to keep breathing, to keep her legs from buckling, to understand. She'd been struggling with sleep for weeks so she couldn't really trust her eyes. *That's right*, she nodded to herself frantically, this was just her tired mind playing tricks on her, her grief squeezing any remaining rational thought from her body.

After a heavy pause the knock came again, shaking the foundation of the house. June held her breath and opened the door very slowly, just a crack, and then another crack, and peered outside at the figure standing on her front porch.

"Hi, Juney."

June looked at him, frozen and dumb; was she asleep? She closed the door and then opened it again. She did this three times but every time he was still there, watching her in stony amusement, looming under the single bulb of the crumbling porch.

"Wyatt?" The name in his presence felt strange in her mouth, and she brought her hand to her lips because of it. If she tried, could she pull his name out—what would it look like in her palm? "Wyatt?" she said again, the double Ts rolling around like marbles.

"Juney."

June opened the door another crack. "Wyatt?" Her voice sounded so young to her ears; childlike. "Wyatt—oh god—I'm sorry, I'm so sorry. I hate to be the one to tell you this, but Mom just died. She's gone, Wy. Mom is gone."

"I know, Juney."

"What?" Her mouth made an uncomfortable sound. "What do you mean, you know? You know that Mom died? But how can you know that?" June rubbed the side of the aluminum door until it stung her palm. She did this to prove that she was in fact awake. "But you couldn't—you couldn't know that, because you weren't here. *You weren't here, Wyatt.*"

June was so confused she screwed her eyes shut as if to vanish, to remove herself from the front porch so she could properly consider what was happening. She opened them slowly one at a time. He was still standing there. Wyatt. *Wyatt.* "Wyatt?" June couldn't stop saying his name. He had saved her from a rabid dog once; it had left him with fifteen stitches, she could see the white scar under the collar of his sweater. "But she died four days ago. At 8:08 p.m. It's been four whole days since she died, Wyatt. She was yellow."

June was silent on the way to the hospital, holding her mother's limp hand. It struck her then, looking through the eyes of the paramedics, who hadn't been with them over the many months of slow decline, that her mother wasn't really there. She was skin and bones and thinning gray hair and loose yellow skin from her pickled, cancer-riddled liver.

June found the yellow hard to look at, it was such a sickly hue, but understood the significance of it. Her mother's body could no longer contain its sadness and had finally burst, spilling out and coloring her skin as if to say: See? Look at all the suffering I've endured; look at how it's transformed me.

"If you knew, Wyatt, why didn't you come home before, or to the funeral today at least? No one showed up, except Mrs. Lloyd."

"No one, huh." Wyatt's face contorted in the shadows of the porch but then he smiled sheepishly. "Nothing I can say to that, I guess. But I'm here now."

June kept opening and closing her mouth like a fish out of water, trying to grasp that her big brother was in fact on her doorstep. Here. "Why are you here now?"

"You should have told me it was getting so bad." Wyatt stepped forward but didn't cross the threshold. He was taller than she remembered, and much thinner. Both facts struck her as being profoundly sad.

"I should have told you?" A hysterical laugh wedged up between her ribs like a fist. "I would have loved to have done that—tell you how bad it was getting—but how? I didn't know where you were, so how could I have told you how impossible it was getting? Where have you been all this time, Wyatt? With not one word, not even after Dad left. He never came back either! He left us with debt, did you know all about that, too?"

"June, it's freezing out here, can I come in?"

June hesitated. There was something in his eyes. Had they always been so black?

"How did you even get here?" She tried looking over his shoulder, hoping he had a truck or a car, something worth selling, but it was too dark to see and he was dirty. He must have taken the bus and then walked to the house.

"Does that really matter now that I'm home?" Wyatt tugged at the hem of his aging woolen sweater, one she recognized suddenly as having belonged to their father. June felt tears in her sore eyes and swallowed a thick, aching lump. Had Wyatt been living on the streets? Could he have been nearby all this time? Was being homeless a better life than the one within these four walls with her? June opened the door wider for him—it seemed the least hard option—and when he slipped by she felt a chill clinging to his clothes.

"Wyatt—tea? There's chamomile." She was pleased she kept his favorite on hand, but the casual request disoriented her further. "The kettle is still hot I think."

June shut the door slowly and waited for him to sit in the cramped kitchen. She slid into the chair across from him at the table and studied him through her blurry vision. Her big brother. With his dark hair and dark eyes, his razor-sharp jawline, Wyatt had aged just how she'd pictured he would. He looked exactly like their father.

Wyatt stared back at her silently, unblinking, his face streaked with dirt.

June dropped her eyes to her lap nervously. "I don't really know what to make of this—you showing up here. I'm confused, I don't know what to say. I'm in shock I think, I'm sorry." Her instinct to apologize to him drained her further. "It's been ten whole years, Wy—*ten*."

"Not quite ten yet, but a whole decade does have a nice ring to it, doesn't it? Don't tell me you're not happy to see me, Juney."

"I am," June said quickly. She had wanted this—for him to come back so she wouldn't be alone—but now his dark eyes were watching her so intensely it made her uncomfortable. "I am glad you're back, but, Wyatt..." June's voice trembled. "Where have you been?"

GRANT

Despite the endless blast of air conditioning above him, and that he'd given in and taken some of his stronger pills, the ones he saved for especially bad days, Grant was sweating.

Things had continued to not go well. Just a few minutes ago, Grant had stopped in the hallway outside the factory break room and overheard a couple of the guys talking about Rosie Wilson and the bridge. About the upcoming vote. About the pros and cons, how they'd have to change their routes to work, but they could maybe swim in the river, something no one had done in decades. They didn't mention him directly by name but when Grant walked in to grab a stale donut, they immediately stopped talking. Every single one of them. Someone cleared their throat, someone else coughed. Grant stood there awkwardly in a silence that was unnerving and critical, and then smiled dumbly at the floor and left before someone could ask him what he thought, or how he'd be voting. Or said, *Hey man, what happened that night with your sister, really? Half an hour, really? Were you just in shock?* Or if there was someone who was angling for his job, or just thought the very worst of him: *Half an hour, Dean? Did you wait that long to sober up? Is that why they never pressed charges? You've got a horseshoe up your ass, you lucky sonofabitch.*

Grant had then hurried back to his section of the factory, recognizing that tensions continued to thicken at work. And he was already on thin ice with his foreman, after a fight with a new hire two weeks ago.

The new guy, Brandon, AJ Hill's younger brother, had eyed him all shift and was waiting for him in the parking lot.

"Dean." Brandon called him over. "A memorial, huh," he said, reeking of booze. "Ten years and still no one really knows what happened that night. How'd you get so goddamn lucky?"

Brandon swayed on his feet and Grant forced a smile. "Lucky? Lucky that my little sister died? Real nice, Brandon—you sound just like AJ. He always thought I was lucky, but am I still playing football? No. So, lucky? Christ."

Brandon spat on the ground. "No way it was just an accident. A deer? Fuck, man, no chance it was an accident, not with you behind the wheel."

Grant reared back and punched Brandon square in the jaw.

The next day Brandon was fired for drinking on the job after an anonymous tip to their foreman.

Grant sat down and focused hard on the moving belt, trying to calm down. He looked around the floor quickly, to see if anyone was watching him, or whispering about him, and then he saw her.

He gasped. She was there. Phoebe. She was sitting on the belt swinging her legs, she was twirling around the metal support column, she was spinning on an empty stool, reaching for him on every turn, her long black hair whipping around her face. Swings, roller coasters—she'd been afraid of heights, of anything that swung her into the air.

Let's save it for the birds, she'd squealed at a county fair once, after he'd convinced her to ride the Ferris wheel with him. *It's not natural for us to be up here like this.*

But you'll have to get on a plane, to really get out of here, he'd said.

We—*when* we *get out of here.* She'd been nervous and out of breath. *You and me, leaving on a jet plane, don't think we'll ever be back again.*

Grant stared at the dirty factory floor. Was he going crazy? He grabbed his leg, dug his nails into the thick mesh of scar tissue and then looked around the factory again, to see if anyone had noticed him losing his mind.

He stood now so his thigh wouldn't seize up. He tried to forget Phoebe and went back to searching for parts of the chicken that couldn't be sold and hadn't been caught by the mechanical sorters. He felt the job suited him—being surrounded by things that no one had any use for, and very few people he could disappoint.

"Grant." Reggie Nash came up to him. "I was just thinking—remember that sick pass? Against East Keane? Remember that night?"

Grant swiveled his stool to avoid Phoebe on the belt, stationary and mouthing *you promised you promised you promised* with lips that were crusted with dried blood. He snapped loudly at Reg: "No—why the fuck would I remember that?"

Reg shrugged. "Right, it was a long time ago." And then he dug into the pocket of his coveralls and handed him a flask. Grant took a long swig, his throat numbing comfortably.

"Let's go to Flo's tonight," Reg said. "Don't say no, you need to get out."

"Flo's?" Grant raked his hand through his hair, thinking of that dive bar and those people who might not be able to look him in the eye, not with this vote coming up, not with Sunday. "Not tonight."

"First round on me. If it sucks we'll leave. It's Flo's or nowhere. We can't drink in my garage tonight—Heather will kill me, man."

"Fine," Grant said, looking around before taking another long swig from the flask. "We can go to Flo's."

Reg leaned against the bar beside him. Flo's had been steadily filling up, and over the past hour a handful of people had come up to ask Grant what they could bring on Sunday, or to apologize that they couldn't make it but to please pass along their condolences to his mother.

It was very late and he knew he should leave, because the more people drank, the more they started to stare, to whisper about him. To remember. And it was just a matter of time before someone came up to ask him something he didn't want to answer. But the whiskey was dulling his head and he welcomed it. So instead of getting up to avoid a confrontation or a pointed question from someone who felt fearless and emotional about something that had nothing to do with them, he knocked his glass on the bar for another. "No ice this time, Mick," Grant said, the words pleasantly hard to string together.

Mick threw a dirty towel over his shoulder. "Always good to see you guys here."

Reg saluted him and Grant managed a smile now that he'd lost count of his drinks and knew more would be coming. "Anything new, Mick?"

"Not a thing." Mick filled his glass to the brim. "How you doing with everything, Dean? Seems Sunday's the only thing anyone's talking about. Real thoughtful of your mother to remember Phoebe this way—can't be easy on her though."

Grant fixed his teeth into a full smile that would hurt his face if he were sober. "Sunday should be nice."

Mick cleaned the rim of a glass slowly. "Saw Kelsey Price walk in an hour ago, and Trey's somewhere in the back. Real high school reunion tonight." Mick started wiping the bar. "Took my mother to the cemetery this morning to visit my pop's plot and nearly drove straight into June Delroy on the way home. I offered her a lift but she said no. Who wants to walk on the side of the highway like that?"

"I pass her place to get to my in-laws. Never seen a car in the driveway." Reg laughed. "Don't blame her for not wanting to get in the car with you, though."

Mick shrugged. "You hear her mother just passed? Think Wyatt'll finally come back?" Mick became serious. "Now that I've got boys myself, hard to make sense of that guy taking off like that." He nodded at Grant, waiting for him to say something, to gossip, to reminisce—Mick Dobson was nothing but a meddler—but the smell of dirty rags and bleach had started churning the whiskey in Grant's stomach.

"Wyatt?" Grant swallowed a mouthful of burning liquid. "Who knows about that guy—he'd been expelled and was in real shit with Randall Boyd. Owed him thousands." Grant sucked back every last drop of his drink. "Don't really remember, but I sure as shit wouldn't want to be in debt to Randy. Guy's still in prison, I think."

Grant could tell he was starting to sweat. It was grating on him—the crowd, the noise, the heat. He really should just get up and leave.

"Remember when Wyatt knocked Trey's teeth out when he didn't pay up for a little weed?" Mick whistled. "Ran off to Mexico is what I heard." He waved to someone who'd just walked in. "Maybe he went straight to Tijuana from Kelsey's party." Mick threw his head back to laugh but then stopped. "Sorry, Dean, didn't mean to bring that up."

Grant shook his head. "Don't think Wyatt was there. He didn't go out, not with us anyway. Too fucked up probably, or community service or something. Saw him picking garbage on the side of the road, remember?"

Mick let out a low whistle and moved down the bar to help someone else. Grant avoided Reg, who was throwing peanut shells on the floor, and instead leaned back on his stool, focused on the wall in front of him, and clenched his fists under the lip of the bar. There was a VOTE: YES! sign and then a picture of the bridge. How had this happened so quickly? Who could he talk to, to change their mind? Grant opened his mouth to yell at Mick to pull the flyer down but someone tapped him on the shoulder and he tensed. He watched a smile slink across Reg's face and his stomach flipped. He was far too drunk for a confrontation, and couldn't afford to get in a fight when people were thinking too much about him already.

The tap came again, harder, determined. Grant wiped the sweat from his forehead and turned very reluctantly on his bar stool.

JUNE

Wyatt leaned across the kitchen table and laughed, the sound strangled and forced. "Where have I been, Juney? Well, let's see: it doesn't matter, you wouldn't understand, it's hard to explain, it's none of your business. Just choose one of those."

"Wyatt." June flicked her wrist sharply under the table to loosen her nerves. "You've been gone for ten years and won't tell me where?"

"Well, the thing is, Juney"—Wyatt smiled at her—"I'm back now, so not sure why it matters?"

"Juney," she repeated softly toward her hands clasped tightly under the table. The childhood nickname she hadn't heard in years. "But you just left that night and never came back and never wrote or called or anything and I had to—" She tried not to use the words *deal with her*, because they were heartless, even though they were mostly true. "Mom was never the same after you left, so it matters to me, where you were—and what was more important than her? What was more important than our mother?"

"Well, Juney, she wasn't a very good mother, was she."

June inhaled, stung. "That's not true. She tried her best."

"Did she try her best? She ruined your goddamn life!" Wyatt shot up his hand. "Never mind. Can't you see that none of that matters now, Juney?"

"That's not my name," June said. It was their father who had called her that, and she didn't like the way it made Wyatt sound like him.

"Jesus Christ," he barked at her—a flare, before his face fell flat again. "Can't you see that none of that matters now, *June Alice Delroy*." Wyatt's tone was biting and reminded her of the difficult child, and then the troubled teenager, he'd been. She watched his dark eyes continue to flit rapidly across her face.

"Welcome home then?" June waved her arms at the window that needed to be replaced and the couch that was falling apart and the pipes she could hear emptying under the sink into a bucket. Her eyes filled with frustrated tears over everything he'd missed; over the burden he'd escaped.

"Mom asked for you right before she died," she said, hoping he'd feel regret. "You coming home was all she ever wanted. She didn't even fight the cancer; maybe she would have if you'd been around."

Wyatt stared at his clasped hands on the table and June released hers under it—she didn't want to participate in this nervous tic they'd both had as children, before everything fell apart. His skin was smooth and milky white but his fingernails were dirty; he always did love the dirt. "You blame me then, for all of this?" Wyatt asked. "For her cancer—really? What am I, fucking god?"

June squirmed awkwardly in her seat. "How can I blame you when I don't know anything? You just show up after our mother dies like something the cat dragged in—so tell me where you've been, and then I'll see if I blame you."

Wyatt smiled curiously at this but then turned his head to the small window. June noticed the faint outline of bruises on the back of his neck, under his long filthy hair. "Window's broken," Wyatt said. "I can fix that for you."

"You're going to stay, then?"

Wyatt swung his head from the window to look directly at her, but he was moving slowly and her heart skipped a familiar beat. Was he in pain? June looked harder, but the kitchen light was dim; so many bulbs had burned out that she hadn't had time to replace. "I thought maybe you'd hate me. Or be scared of me or something and want me to leave."

"No, it's fine—" June was overwhelmed and started crying, the kind that overtook her body and left her gasping for air. Wyatt reached across the table for her hands and she shook her head. *No*. He watched her, and then nodded, and then frowned down into his mug.

"You've been through a lot, I can see that." Wyatt smiled and his features softened, his expression now more the Wyatt she remembered, the big brother who could be kind sometimes, especially with her. And he was here now, and she wasn't alone anymore. Didn't that mean they could both start over? "But it was hard for me to come back here," he said. "With all of those rumors about me—" He stood abruptly, clumsily, jerking his hip into the corner of the table. He inhaled sharply, but kept his eyes down, avoiding hers. "I need some time before I can explain everything, so you're going to have to trust me. I'm tired now, I'm going to bed. We can talk in the morning."

"Wait—what rumors, what things to explain? Wyatt?"

But Wyatt left the kitchen without looking back. June watched him as he walked slowly down the hallway to the bathroom. She stood up on shaky legs, weak, desperate for her pillow and the faraway hope that she might sleep well tonight.

June stood at the sink where the mug Wyatt had used lay in a broken heap. She noticed something under one of the shards of ceramic. She used her finger to brush it aside, careful not to cut herself, and saw what she thought was a fingernail. She held it up to one of the lights that still worked. It looked rounded, like a small claw. Just her tired mind playing tricks on her.

She left the kitchen thinking about Wyatt and those rumors. He had taken off that night because of their father, but it didn't stop people in town from whispering about him. Making things up about him. Saying that he was spinning out of control, that he was a bad seed without morals who'd felt no responsibility to stick around anymore. That Wyatt had abandoned her, leaving her behind to pick up the pieces of her broken family.

The rumors were loudest in the first month after he left, but they soon faded; eventually everyone forgot about Wyatt entirely. But in the beginning, of course June noticed that people would stop talking when she rounded the aisle in the grocery store, or when they stood behind her in line at the Dairy Bar.

"Wait—Grant..." June had called after Grant a couple of weeks after Phoebe's death, when she was still taping up missing person flyers in town. Grant turned so reluctantly she knew he wanted to ignore her.

"What the fuck do you want?"

Grant's lack of manners felt so intimate to her that June blushed. "I'm sorry," she said, desperate and broken. "For Phoebe. For your loss. I can relate—I mean, we have something in common, the same night even."

"We do?" Grant snorted. "Except my sister is dead. We just buried her. My mother is such a wreck she can't leave her bedroom, can't handle a funeral. And your brother probably skipped town for a good reason, so we have absolutely nothing in common." Then he turned and sprinted off.

June rubbed her palm along the leg of her pants until the friction calmed her. She walked down the hall to her own bedroom, noticed as she passed the bathroom that the water was running. June touched the door gently, felt it purr under her fingertips as she imagined Wyatt drumming his hands on the sink like he used to. She suddenly recoiled, and then shrank back into the safety of the dark hall.

The Wyatt who had just shown up wasn't quite the Wyatt she remembered. He was cagey and his eyes were cold and calculating. Why had he waited until both of their parents were gone to come back?

It wasn't lost on June that she'd only been a teenager when he left. Did she really know what Wyatt was capable of back then?

Or now?

GRANT

"Hi."

Grant dropped his chin to his chest and groaned inwardly as he finished turning around.

"Hi, Harley," he said, weary.

Harley didn't smile. "Been a long time." Her mascara was smudged and her eyes were unfocused. She held up an empty glass with a damp paper umbrella in it. "Buy me a drink?"

"Didn't think this was your kind of place." But Grant turned and yelled to Mick, "One of whatever Harley Mitchell's drinking on my tab," and then turned back to his dead sister's best friend, whose mood he couldn't gauge.

"It's Harley Dews now—has been for five years, you know that. I tell you every time I see you. Just because you never showed up to the wedding doesn't mean it didn't happen. I *did* invite you."

"Couldn't get it off work, so I'll have to always remember you as Harley Mitchell."

Harley took the drink from Mick without taking her eyes off of him. She teetered on her heels, making him frown. She wasn't sober, which meant she could be volatile, and Grant was out of patience.

"I saw you sitting here so I thought I should be polite and come over. Me and Kelsey wanted to get together tonight to, you know, remember her, to remin… *reminisce*—" Harley hiccuped and looked down at her feet for a long moment. When she looked back up she had a glistening sheen of sweat on her forehead. "We do it every year."

"That's nice of you."

"Still can't believe it happened. Still miss her so much, you know?" Harley took a sip of her bright red drink. "Your mom asked me to give a speech on Sunday but I don't think I can do it. Would be too hard. Do you think it's good to keep talking about her, or does it make it worse? I still miss her all the time. And now that old woman…" She shook her head and, to Grant's horror, started to tear up. "I don't even know what she'd want me to do—she was my best friend, and I don't know what she'd want me to do about this stupid vote next week. That stupid old woman, making us all remember like this again."

Harley looked at him and he forced a smile. "But Phoebe loved the bridge. She loved watching the river from up there."

"She did?" Harley tilted her head. "I don't remember that."

Grant placed his hand on her upper arm to steady her. "She'd really hate for it to come down. The history of it—remember how much she loved history?"

"She did love history." Harley nodded slowly, spilling her

drink on the floor. "She loved school and she loved reading and she loved the fair—and you, she loved you the most." Harley gave him a funny look.

Grant lifted his empty glass to Mick, who was at the other end of the bar. He'd now sweat entirely through his shirt. Mick held up an apologetic finger for him to wait and he tried not to climb over the bar to grab the bottle himself. He turned back, praying that Harley wouldn't still be standing in front of him, drunk and intent on remembering things he'd spent the last ten years trying to forget.

Harley hiccuped again. "If Kelsey hadn't thrown that stupid party she'd still be here, and you..." Harley took a step backward, her finger in his face. "You were too drunk to drive, she was yelling at you not to—"

"No she wasn't." He cut her off.

Harley snickered, her head bobbing profusely, drunk and emboldened. "You dragged her out of the house screaming—"

Grant sprang up and she stumbled backward into someone. He grabbed her by the arm. "If that's true, if she was *screaming*, why did you let her leave with me? You wouldn't do anything to hurt her, would you? Since she was your *best friend*."

Harley's face paled and she yanked her arm from his hand. "You're an asshole."

"It's hard to remember something from so long ago. Don't beat yourself up about it." Grant sat back down on the stool as Harley rubbed the spot where he'd grabbed her. "It's always good to see you, Harley. Say hi to Kelsey for me."

Harley frowned, her lip shaking as if she might actually start to cry, but then she huffed and turned and got swallowed up by the crowd.

Grant exhaled through gritted teeth and watched a young woman in a gold tank top and low-slung jeans sidle up to Reg and say something in his ear. Reg laughed and shot a look Grant's way, eyebrow cocked. Grant shook his head hard. All he wanted to do was get even more wasted, then have Reg drive him home where he'd blissfully black out—no Harley, no accusations, no sirens in the distance, too late. No nightmares about those eyes, those dark eyes looking at him in wild, confused fear.

"Dean," Reg said, draping his scrawny arm around his shoulders. "This is Cherry like the fruit, and guess what? She's a big fan of football."

"Fuck, Reg," Grant hissed under his breath as the door to the bar swung open again and Becca Hoyt stormed in. Long dark hair, a leather jacket, those goddamn bracelets she never took off. Purpose in her eyes. Had she come here looking for him? Shit. He should buy her a drink and pull her aside so they could talk in private.

He willed himself to do the right thing, to deal with Becca before things got out of hand, but instead he thought: *Fuck it.* He plastered on a sly smile as the woman in gold slithered over beside him.

"Grant Dean," he said, taking her hand.

"Oh, I know." Cherry giggled.

Over the woman's bare shoulder, Becca was close enough that he saw the confusion settling in on her face.

"Cherry, it's so loud in here, why don't we go to your place?

My car's just outside—yes I'm fine to drive." Grant crossed the room with Cherry on his arm, and stopped in front of Becca. Her mouth was open and she was glaring at him. "Becca, I hate to do this but I have to drive Reg's cousin home before she gets in trouble." He smiled at Becca and then brushed her hair gently behind her ear. "Listen." Grant leaned close to whisper, "Harley and Kelsey are here and they're feeling nostalgic, so be careful what you say. I'll call you first thing tomorrow morning." He kissed her softly on the cheek.

As Grant walked to the front door of the bar with the woman whose name he'd already forgotten, he tensed, feeling Becca's eyes boring right into his back.

BECCA

She sat on her couch in her living room and poured herself another glass of white wine. She was permitting herself a third because it had been a very bad day and there was nothing she could do to relax. She'd dressed up and done her hair and driven to Flo's to see how Grant was doing, and he'd humiliated her.

She'd stood there stunned, blood draining from her face, feet stuck to the beer-stained floor of that awful bar, getting groped and bumped into, and watched him put his arm around that woman and then leave. Without buying Becca a drink, without asking how she was doing, without apologizing for not returning her calls.

Reg's cousin? Was that even true? Had he left with that cheap woman to have sex with her? Right in Becca's face? Her pulse was hammering in her chest. She touched it, afraid she might be having a heart attack.

Becca sipped her wine and scrolled mindlessly through

Facebook, read some comments about Mrs. Wilson and the vote—seemed people were already heated. She read a few back-and-forth arguments, then posted that she'd be MIA over the next couple of days, that it was such a hard time of year for her, remembering. As the likes started popping up on her screen, they didn't make her feel any better, and so she slammed her laptop shut.

Becca pulled the box, an heirloom passed down from her grandmother, out from under her coffee table and sat with it on her lap. She touched the cool black lacquer, then opened the lid and watched the ballerina twirl. It was old and the music was out-of-tune and high-pitched. She'd gotten angry not too long ago and thrown it across the room and so the entire lid was split, one corner broken off; the dancer's skirt was torn, and the spring was rusting. Becca wanted to cry because the box looked creepy and not beautiful like it was supposed to. She closed it and shoved it away from her. She was too wound up to go through her many treasures, like her hospital bracelet and the pieces of her bloody gown. They deserved more than that.

She knew it was wrong but she blamed Phoebe for her dreadful mood. Dead Phoebe who was still more important than her. Perfect Phoebe whose dark shadow she might never be able to escape.

But Phoebe had had a real vicious temper, did the town know that? Phoebe had been possessive of her brother, did the town know that? Always cajoling him to do the right thing and forcing him to study and *be better, be better, be better* when he was perfect just the way he was. No one knew that more than Becca did.

Becca was feeling desperate to talk to Grant, to have him hold her and smooth her hair and tell her everything would be all right, but Grant was busy with some stranger and she wasn't really allowed to speak to him unless he permitted it. It was one of their rules. Becca glared at the ceiling of her living room. She owed Grant a lot, but sometimes the burden of keeping everything to herself was suffocating.

She tried her deep breathing exercises because she was losing control of her thoughts, and they were not good ones for her to be having. But it didn't help. Becca started pacing her small living room. She thought about Sunday. What should she expect at the Deans? Would there be a blown-up photo of Phoebe on display? Which one would they choose? When Phoebe's hair was longest, nearly to her waist and so black it was almost blue? Becca touched her own hair; she was due for a touch-up. Maybe Julie could fit her in at the salon this weekend. Maybe she'd go a bit darker herself, for fall.

Would people cry? Would they dare to ask her what had happened that night? *What happened at Kelsey's party? Who was at the party? We heard there was a fight.* As if anything that had happened in that house mattered, when they'd all been laughing and dancing and having fun. It was when they left and Phoebe had lost her mind that everything went downhill.

Would people want to share their favorite memories? The time Phoebe won the state spelling bee with a raging fever from the flu? The time Phoebe helped that homeless man get a job at the auto shop by driving him there herself and helping with his interview because he couldn't read, and someone from the city paper had written an article about her? About how bright the future looked with people like Phoebe Dean in it? How could you narrow down just one special memory of the town's sparkling fucking treasure? Phoebe would never let Grant have a girlfriend, did the town know that?

Becca checked her phone again, but still nothing from Grant. She scrolled back and counted ten unanswered calls and twice as many texts. She dialed again but got sent straight through to voicemail. His phone seemed to be off now. Becca frowned at the metallic sound of his voice asking her to leave a message. Maybe his battery had died.

She finished the wine in her glass but corked the bottle before she let herself pour another. She knew she needed help. She'd ask Rusty to get someone to cover one of her doubles this weekend. She'd get her nails done. Blue polish, the really light one. Phoebe's favorite color—the one she'd been wearing the night she died. She was sure Grant would think that was sweet.

She would also accept her parents' lunch invitation, because if she brushed them off again, they might force her back to Dr. Murphy. She would do anything to never go back to that man, who she hadn't seen in years, and who she certainly did not miss. He'd never understood a thing about her, even after the four years of sessions she had to endure. He might have played the part, with his wool trousers and mousy receptionist, but that was just for show because it had been a waste of time. She didn't need a therapist; it was just that her parents were simple and she was complicated.

Dr. Murphy spoke very softly: "Your parents tell me you've been having nightmares again?"

"I'm not, I'm fine."

"They said they can hear you screaming at night, Rebecca. That you're screaming: Grant, help us. *What does that mean to you?"*

"I don't know! Or maybe it means Grant, help us, *because we were in a serious car accident and needed his help?"*

"And what can Grant do to help you? What else are you seeing in these dreams? Sometimes our unconscious mind works at night to make sense of things that are too hard to process when we're awake."

"Grant saved my life that night."

"You mention Grant with fondness." Dr. Murphy smiled. "Last month you told me that he pulled you from the burning car before his sister, that he chose you over her. Those were your words."

"So?"

"But the truck was never on fire, was it, Rebecca? That never happened, did it? Try to remember. Take your time."

Becca shook her head quickly, eyes watering, frustrated with herself. It was hard for her to know what was true and what wasn't, and her mind wasn't helping at all.

"All right. And what about his sister, Phoebe? She's the one who has passed on—how is processing that lately?"

"It's hard to process."

"Would you like to talk about Phoebe today?"

"What do you want me to say that I haven't already said a hundred times? It's horrible that she died like that, it was awful. There was so much blood and she was just lying there, and I

could see her teeth—" Becca sucked in, tried to push the image away. "But Phoebe wasn't as perfect as everyone thinks. She hid it but she had a real temper, especially when it came to her brother. No one would ever be good enough for him according to her. Wait—my dreams? Are my parents allowed to tell you things like that? Isn't there some doctor-patient privilege thing?"

"You're getting upset, let's move on," Dr. Murphy said, making languid loopy notes on the page, eyeing her above his leather-bound notebook. "Your parents tell me that you've been taking things again. Are you ready to talk about that today?"

"They—what?"

"They found a box under your bed filled with things that don't belong to you, Rebecca."

"That's a complete invasion of my privacy, and those were gifts! They don't know everything about my life because they're impossible to talk to. Can't you see that they're smothering me? How could I have told them about Grant and me, that we loved each other, that we had real plans, that we were going to leave town?" She was on the verge of tears. "They would have freaked out! They would have never understood, they would have locked me up or something. And besides, that's completely private! You can't tell anyone what I just said, can you? About Grant and me—swear it."

Dr. Murphy sat back in his chair. "It's quite privileged, which I continue to reassure you almost every session. But you've been down this path before with these fixations, where you create meaning and take things that don't belong to you to reinforce them. Would now be a good time to talk about AJ Hill again?"

"No!" Becca roared, her ears burning. "Because that was a complete misunderstanding! We dated, my parents thought it was moving too fast, that we were too young, and they didn't like his family, which is awful of them. My parents wouldn't understand true love if it showed up at their front door! But it's been over with AJ for a long time." She calmed herself by pulling at the loose fabric under her seat. She inhaled; exhaled. Be kind, *she thought,* be kind.

Becca's phone rang on her coffee table. She fingered the gold chain around her neck, listened as the stack of bangles chimed. She checked the time; it was nearly 1:00 a.m.

"Debbie?" Becca answered her older sister's call, disappointed it wasn't Grant but relieved that it wasn't her mother for once. "It's late, what if I was sleeping?"

"I hear you're not sleeping much, and I promised Mom I'd check on you—"

Becca groaned and heard the wail of a baby crying. "God, Debbie, I'm fine."

"Mom and Dad just care about you. Why can't you let them do that?"

"Because I'm an adult? Because I don't need them breathing down my neck? Because I don't like being treated like a child?"

"Mom told me that you want to go to this memorial thing at the Dean home."

"Yes—and?"

"To their house? Isn't it time to let this go? Why would you want to be around him after everything he's done?" Debbie asked. "Ten years would be a good time to finally move on, Becca."

Becca laughed into the receiver. "Okay, Deb—when you barely survive a car crash, then you can let me know when the appropriate time would be to move on. And I think I'm doing pretty well considering I nearly died that night. *Died*, Debbie."

"Okay, then." Debbie sighed. "I told Mom I'd call. She's worried about you, so I called. Can you please think about Sunday? About whether it's the best thing for you right now?"

"I'm fine," Becca said. "Give that baby a big kiss for me."

She hung up and put her wineglass in the sink. Her eyebrow twitched as she remembered her palms being sliced open by thick shards of glass as she crawled from the truck toward Phoebe. Phoebe's face, the blood, the white of her jawbone showing through her skin like a cracked egg. Grant—she couldn't see Grant but she could hear him screaming. She squeezed the side of the sink.

Becca set her phone down and stared at her tired face in the dead screen. She was worried about Grant, she really was, but she didn't like the nagging feeling that he'd lied to her at Flo's. That he'd pushed her aside. That he was avoiding her. Not after everything they'd been through, and certainly not when she could sink them both.

TEN YEARS AGO

2:34 p.m.

Becca Hoyt had just overheard in Spanish class that Kelsey Price was throwing a party, and she was determined to attend. She was still grounded for life basically, because of the misunderstanding over AJ, but her parents were taking Debbie to look at a new car, so Becca knew she could sneak out without them noticing.

She leaned against her locker, smiling to herself. She'd never been to one of Kelsey's parties, and she was excited to go. She'd grab something from her parents' liquor cabinet so she didn't show up empty-handed; they'd never notice anything was missing.

"Hey, Becca?"

Becca turned unwillingly to the sad voice behind her. Harley and Kelsey were at their lockers across the hall and she was trying to hear what they were whispering about. "What is it, June?"

June's face was paler than normal. "Have you seen Wyatt?"

Becca was annoyed because she'd been interrupted, and now Harley and Kelsey were walking away and she hadn't heard what time the party started. "Didn't Wyatt get kicked out of school?"

June looked down at her scuffed sneakers. "I thought I saw Wyatt's car in the parking lot. Maybe he came to talk to the principal or something, about coming back so he can graduate."

"June." Becca felt that pang of sympathy she always did when June was seeming extra lost, but she was far too busy for Delroy family drama right now. "I haven't seen him, but if I do, I'll let you know. I have to run, okay? Have a good weekend, see you Monday!"

Becca left school, noticing how the clouds rolling overhead were now a very angry gray. The air was thick and smelled like it was going to storm. Damn, *she thought, rain would ruin the plans she had for her hair. She chewed on her lip, trying to decide if she should wear it up now. She stopped halfway across the parking lot when she noticed Grant leaning against the fence at the back of the field, sweating and checking his watch. She waved quickly so no one would see. He looked up in her direction and caught her eye, but then got into a speeding car that barely stopped long enough to let him jump in.*

Becca spun around to see if anyone had noticed her waving to Grant, but the lot was already clearing out. She smiled to herself; their secret was still safe.

Grant had never really had a girlfriend before, at least no one long-term, and everyone wondered behind his back if it was because of his sister. Becca heard the way they gossiped about him sleeping around, and how Phoebe couldn't stand it. How she'd hide the girls' shoes and clothes so they'd never come back. Phoebe was a prude who insisted that Grant focus only on school and football and whatever other things Phoebe demanded of him.

What kind of a dysfunctional codependent relationship was that? It was true that Grant and Phoebe were very close—or at least they used to be. Always eating lunch together, driving to and from school together, sitting together in the hall when their free periods lined up. But lately they were growing up and apart—and, well, Becca didn't want to blame herself for this wedge, but if the shoe fit. Becca smiled and smoothed her hair. She'd been waiting for this for as long as she could remember—since she was a little girl really. She'd filled diary after diary with plans for her and Grant Dean. She'd take back everything that had happened with AJ if she could, and she was grateful that Grant didn't hold that whole misunderstanding against her. He was wonderful, he really was.

Becca climbed into her car, determined. She was going to walk into that party tonight with her head held high, and she and Grant were going to talk. Really talk. It was time they told everyone. That he was about to quit the team. That they *had real plans, that they were in love. That the only person he'd be leaving town with was Becca.*

That there was nothing anyone could do to stop them.

WYATT

A door opened so slowly he might have been imagining it. Where was he? He was inside but something was wrong; it was too empty and cold. He remembered then, knocking on a brown door. June. His little sister. Juney. His old house, the shower, cold water; his old bedroom. Wyatt relaxed somewhat, sank back into the lumpy mattress of his old single bed. Still formless and heavy, he could feel it everywhere. That dark stormy night. Running in the rain. Eyes filled with fear. He snapped his own open, drawing the truth back inside himself with a yawn. He could not reveal too much too soon; he had to think of June, who had been through so much. He had to be careful with her.

Wyatt sensed his body. This was something he'd had to start doing recently. He had a headache but it was manageable. He rubbed his temples, touched a scab that seemed to be healing. He dragged his tongue around the inside of his mouth, tasting dirt and iron but his teeth were all intact; that was a good sign.

He knew June had noticed his emaciated frame, his bloodshot eyes; he'd have to tell her that he didn't have much time. But not yet. He couldn't risk scaring her and being forced to leave, not when they both knew how much she needed him. He'd keep his condition from her for as long as he could, until all of the pieces were in place and she was strong enough to hear it.

Wyatt saw a small window, a closet, black walls. The door continued to creak open and now weak light spilled in from the hall.

He could make out the silhouette of June's thin body, standing in the dark doorway, motionless. He'd just fallen asleep, and being woken so suddenly made him confused, as if he were underwater and had to claw his way up to the surface for air. It also made him angry. Hadn't he told her he was tired? Hadn't he told her not to disturb him, that they could talk in the goddamn morning? Hadn't he asked her to trust him? Didn't she realize how hard it had been to return to this dreadful house, with its dreadful memories? Sure, June was suffering, but she didn't have a clue what he'd been through, or what he was going to have to do now.

He couldn't let the others keep going like this, their lives so unconstrained, so unaffected. He would drag them back down to the ground kicking and screaming—or worse if he had to. He had nothing left to lose, and as they say, desperate people are capable of desperate things, and there was no one more desperate than him to be set free.

The truth would do that; it would release him. It was time. His time.

Wyatt's chest felt raw. He loosened his hands; they'd been

in tight balls beside his legs. They were caked with dirt and a couple of his nails were broken, ripped and jagged, as if he'd been outside digging.

The window and curtains were open, the moon an orb suspended in tar.

He lay still and tried to wait patiently for June to speak. He wrestled with the burning of his rage as it heated his bones; suppressed the urge to scream at her and ask what she was fucking thinking waking him in the middle of the night when he'd told her how tired he was.

He had told her that, hadn't he? He tried to replay their conversation but it was hard to draw on; his mind was a yawning black hole.

Wake up, he thought, *wake up*.

June changed her mind and started closing the door.

"June?" Wyatt's voice was thick with sleep, like cotton balls—could he pull one out? She stopped with the door nearly closed, night refilling the room, the moon brighter by contrast. "What do you want? I'm tired."

The door clicked shut softly. Wyatt could tell by the shadow inked on the floor, spiked fingers scrabbling for him from under the door, that she stood in the hallway still.

"June." Wyatt unhinged his mouth angrily. "*I can see your fucking shadow.*" He shook his legs, tried to loosen sleep's grip on him, tried to wake himself up some more. "You're freaking me out—did you have a bad dream?" He was really heated now, his blood was starting to simmer, bubble. He rubbed his arms so it wouldn't boil over and make a mess. He stood up, railed against the dizziness, and was very loud: "June, goddamn it, what do you want?"

"I'm just glad you're back."

June walked off and he heard the click of the door to her own bedroom. He blew out through grinding teeth; the endless tension left a deep ache in his jaw. He lay back down and closed his eyes and tried to fall back asleep, though he was too wound up and his mind started to race, and he chased it, all the way until morning.

JUNE

Two Days before the Phoebe Dean Memorial

A soft, almost imperceptible thud. June flung her eyes open, instantly alert. She held her breath, tense, but the sound didn't repeat. Outside it was nearly dawn, a thick gray film spread against the glass.

She'd slept a bit, fitfully, but after weeks with none, sleep in any capacity was a small win. She thought immediately of her brother, startling herself. Wyatt. Wyatt was home. She pictured him lying in his old twin bed, separated from her by just one thin wall. June placed her palm on it, flat, but it felt hot and she pulled her hand back nervously. Had he set a fire, was he back for the insurance claim, did he think their mother had savings, did he owe someone money, did someone owe him; how much, how much, how much?

Sometimes Wyatt would be flush after claiming he'd won at

cards, or found a job that paid him under the table. He'd bought her a book about birds once, and a silver ring as a months'-late birthday gift. Both were tucked under her bed now, the only nice things she had to remember him by. But money had been a constant sore spot between Wyatt and their father, who'd obsessed over it: why Wyatt had it, or why he didn't; who Wyatt owed, who owed him.

But when asked, Wyatt would just smile that glib smile and never tell their father anything. Not about the job or what he got up to or who he spent time with, which only enraged their father further. That smile had grown more crooked in the weeks and days before he left. It was the loss of control perhaps, that was the worst part for their father—the fearless contempt from his own flesh and blood.

"Why can't you stay out of trouble?" their father soothed, his chin resting on laced fingers at the kitchen table. The juxtaposition of such a casual stance with the fury that he spewed was always frightening. June had her bedroom door open a crack, just enough to see and hear, but not enough that she couldn't shut it quickly, lock it, drag her chest of drawers in front of it, to brace for the inevitable blast.

"Answer me, son, goddamn it."

"Can't believe everything you hear at that shit bar," Wyatt responded with a smile. "Flo's—really? You're going to believe a bunch of drunks over your own flesh and blood?" Wyatt's tone was mocking, parroting the phrase their father so often used to try to hurt him.

Their father snorted, pushed his chair back from the table with a screech. "Too good for that place, huh. Too good for us?"

"Hank—"

"Shut up, Birdie. Listen to me, son. We aren't like that family, we don't get second chances. So cut him loose, Wyatt. Or the golden girl, or whatever it is you're up to. Keep your name and theirs out of people's mouths. Nothing good will come of it. Nothing."

June sat on the side of the bed and rubbed her eyes. She remembered the thud then, that weak smacking sound, and crept to the window. She peered through the curtains at the sun rising like yolks over the back fields. She unlatched the window, slid it open and looked outside. It was then she saw the cardinal lying on the ground. It moved slightly—not dead then, but badly injured from flying into the glass. She leaned out the window, her toes nearly off the floor, to touch the bird's head. It was tiny, like a marble, and its feathers were impossibly soft. June rubbed the body with her finger as it lay on the ground. She didn't want it to freeze, so she brought it into her room, holding it in the palm of her hand and marveling at its beautiful wings, and round eyes, and how weightless a living thing could possibly be; how still, how light. June knew some people thought cardinals were spirits of the recently departed, there was a page on it in the book Wyatt had given her. She wasn't sure if she believed this to be true, but her mother's was the first body she'd ever buried, and she didn't want to take any chances. The bird lifted its head slightly as if hearing her thoughts.

"Mom," June whispered to it. "Momma, is it you?"

The bird didn't answer.

June stroked the small body nervously, and it twitched once and then was so still she knew it had died. She might have felt its life float up and away.

"Bye, Mom," June said softly, just in case. "I'll come visit you soon. With Wyatt."

The bird's legs stiffened and June's heart clamored up inside her chest. *I don't know why he's back*, she wanted to explain to the bird; *the timing is cruel*, she wanted to admit. But sometime in the middle of the night, as she'd tossed and turned and fretted, she had resolved to find out from her brother. She hated secrets, she always had; they were dark and insidious and sometimes lethal.

June walked carefully with the bird's body in the palm of her hand to the small bathroom down the short hall. She drew the yellowing plastic shower curtain aside, and the hooks creaked loudly along the metal rod. She crouched by the tub and lay the cardinal by the drain and then wiped her hands quickly along her pajama pants. She'd wait until Wyatt woke and ask him to help her bury it in the backyard under the maple tree. It seemed a fitting spot.

June's heart raced when she thought of her brother sleeping in his old bedroom, in his old bed. It was unsettling—him showing up like that in the middle of the night, looking like a vagrant or escaped convict.

She sucked in her breath. Could that be it? Is that why he'd never come home? Had he been in prison, and had he somehow escaped? He'd be smart and wily enough to do it.

"Prison is better than what you thought."

June turned to the voice coming from the darkened end of the tub. “It is?”

“You thought he was dead.”

“But being a criminal is better?”

She pictured the cardinal shrugging casually, with its tiny wings and lifeless eyes and slowly stiffening body.

June pulled herself up to stand at the sink. She was exhausted again, even with the couple of hours she’d slept. The lightness she’d felt minutes ago was seeping from her body in a rush, because now here she was in the pitch-black bathroom, talking to a dead bird with her stomach in knots about her brother—about where he’d been and why he was back now and what he’d been searching for on her face just last night at their kitchen table. Compassion? Absolution?

June shoved her forehead hard against the bathroom door. She refused to go back to how things had been when they were young—all that tension, constantly waiting for disaster to strike, all of Wyatt’s darkness and secrecy.

June had suffered enough, and so things had to be different now. And she was older; she could be strong, or at least pretend to be. She’d been pretending that for the last ten years. They could start over, she wanted that—an extra set of hands around the house, someone else moving within these cold walls with her.

And so when Wyatt got up, she’d insist that he tell her the truth. That he unburden himself of it all, whatever it was, so he could put his past behind him. A fresh start, a clean slate. For both of them.

This was her house now. No more secrets.

GRANT

Grant sat at the very edge of the stranger's unmade bed, head in his hands, the vice tightening like a screw. Phoebe wouldn't leave him alone. She stood there in the doorway, a slim silhouette in cutoff jean shorts with a bandage on one knee, hands on her hips, judging. He caught her eye, and she shook her head at him, disgusted.

How could you? she mouthed, blood leaking from her nose. *You monster.* She smiled at him slowly, wet crimson smeared along her upper front teeth. *Liar.*

What was she doing here? Had she seen him drive drunk from Flo's to this shitty basement apartment? Phoebe just didn't know how the world worked for people who weren't as righteous as she was; people who couldn't always find their way to do the right thing, who sometimes did the wrong thing. And hadn't Phoebe made mistakes? Of course she had. Sometimes she drank too much and smoked and had started threatening to betray Grant's trust.

But it's not tattling, Phoebe had said with frustrated tears, when she warned him that she'd tell their mother that he'd been fired from the Dairy Bar for too many light tills. *It'll help you, Grant. I want you to see that you don't have to do these things.*

Phoebe never did tell their mother why he'd been fired, and he knew he should have never stolen that money, but he'd been in a jam.

Grant touched his bare wrist absently, tasted bile, and willed her away. Phoebe tucked her long black hair behind her ears and slunk backward down the hall. He was pulsing now, bringing himself back to the dimly lit room. He smelled oily skin, and stale booze from overturned bottles on the stained brown carpet.

The woman sat up against the bare wall and lit a thin white cigarette. The smoke nauseated him, and he snatched it from her fingers and stubbed it out with his bare foot.

She side-eyed him and then smiled, her lips curling around the fresh cigarette she placed between her teeth. "They still talk about you sometimes, you know. You were a real legend I guess."

"Who does?" Grant asked. "Never mind..."

"At the high school. I work there." The woman blew a perfect smoke ring, and in the hazy slick of dawn he could see her mascara was smudged and that she had bad skin. "I don't do this often—sleep with strangers from bars."

"Me neither," Grant lied. Strangers were the only women he slept with now; no strings, no questions. When he was younger, Phoebe would lecture him for sleeping around, for jeopardizing his future for meaningless sex, for being unfocused. He knew that she worried that if he got serious with someone, maybe he'd choose her and stay back.

Grant eyed the messy piles of clothes on the floor, queasy, looking for his pants. "I have an early shift—what time is it?"

The woman leaned over him, the tattoos on her back unfolding across his lap, to dig beside the bed for her phone. "Not quite eight. You could come back to bed—"

"Eight? I'm already late then."

Grant could hear Phoebe whispering from somewhere down the hall: *liar, liar, liar*. He balled his hands into fists and shoved them hard into his eyes.

"I've watched videos of some of your games. My older brother was a couple years after you—Brian Litt? He says you could have been the best quarterback in the state. Broken records. That true?"

"Not really."

"You were a lot bigger then. He says everyone thought you were, you know, using. I guess everyone does that now, but not back then. Tsk, tsk. *Naughty*." She ran her fingers along Grant's shoulder and he stood up from the bed. "But then you really fucked up your leg in that accident, huh. Such a shame, missing out on college football. I mean, that's just sad, you know? Unlucky." She gestured to his thigh, dripping ash onto the bare mattress, but he was too hungover to be embarrassed by the patchwork of scars, by his reliance on pain meds, by those doping rumors and his dashed hopes of a football scholarship and a real future; how everything had been ripped away from him in an instant.

"And your sister, too—so pretty and smart, and everyone

says she was quiet but still real popular. And that lady from the grocery store? She has scars, I've seen them—least yours can be covered up."

Fuck. Who was this woman? How dare she? He rubbed his leg, felt the quilt of raised, ropy skin.

"Where's the bathroom? I have to go," Grant asked, ears pricked for faint footsteps in the hallway.

The woman pointed to the door. "Just down the hall, but don't be too long." She smiled around the cigarette again, and he wondered how loudly she'd scream if he dragged her off the bed by her hair. He unclenched his fist, released the image. "My friends still love the Wildcats," she said. "We go to all of the games. *Grant Dean, number eighteen*, right?"

He couldn't help but laugh harshly and she looked stunned. Maybe even afraid. Good. He stumbled down the short hall to a bathroom that was littered with ashtrays and overturned cans of hairspray. He cupped his hands under the leaking faucet, splashed cold water on his face and rinsed out his mouth.

He glared at his reflection in the mirror. *Grant Dean, number eighteen*, had to get to work at the poultry factory. *Grant Dean, number eighteen* hoped his car had enough gas to get him there. *Grant Dean, number eighteen* had driven drunk to this stranger's house just to avoid talking to Becca Hoyt, which now that he was thinking straight, had been a terrible idea that was going to cost him dearly.

Phoebe sat in the bathtub, hugging her legs to her chest; the bandage on one knee was neon green and peeling. She was laughing. The sound made him want to cry.

"Please go away," he said. "I can't handle this right now."

"Using? Grant—she means drugs you know, but that would be cheating and you'd never cheat. You'd never do something so risky to us." She drew the curtain and was quiet. He found the dead silence far worse than her laughter.

Grant made his way back to the bedroom that smelled of cigarette smoke and sex. He rifled through piles of clothes until he found his jeans, felt for his phone, saw he'd missed two calls from Reg, one from his foreman, and six from Becca. He turned it off.

He said nothing as he left the bedroom, and the woman called out that they should do it again, that she'd put her number in his phone, but he was already flying up the stairs.

Grant hadn't called his mother to tell her he wouldn't be home last night—that wasn't the kind of relationship they had—and so he had to rely on his slow foggy brain to retrieve it, the errand she'd asked him to do. He was already late for work, so he'd have to wait until his first break to head to the grocery store, where he prayed to a god he was fairly sure didn't exist that Becca wouldn't be working.

TEN YEARS AGO

3:10 p.m.

The ice burned the bare skin of AJ Hill's shoulder, but he held it there through gritted teeth and determination. He knew the scouts were already in the stands—he'd spotted their flashy cars in the school's parking lot. University of Alabama, Florida… hell, even Ohio. They may have come for Grant, but he could put on a show too. There wasn't some rule that they could only offer one scholarship per team, and he was practically killing himself by running track and playing football to broaden his chances. AJ wanted to get out of this town just as bad as anyone.

The mess with Crazy Becca was lingering close to a year later, and it still made his skin crawl but there was no good way out that he could see. People in his town never forgot shit so AJ had begged his parents not to involve the sheriff, who was his uncle Ricky, which made it worse somehow. But they hadn't listened. What did a restraining order against Becca say about him? He was a two-hundred-pound running back for the West Wilmer Wildcats, for Christ's sake. A restraining order said that he couldn't hold his own against a crazy teenage girl who had a crush on him. And yet they'd insisted, because their mothers had had their own feud in high school and his parents watched too much Dr. Phil *on TV, and they couldn't let go of the times they'd seen Becca watching the house, and then once, when she'd been over, she'd stolen something from his mother. Becca swore it was a misunderstanding, that she'd thought it was a gift AJ had left out for her after they'd had an argument. AJ didn't know what to believe, nor did he really give a shit. The entire situation pissed him off; what was the restraining order really for—his safety? Or to protect his mother's shitty jewelry that she left lying around?*

AJ wheezed through the discomfort and watched as Grant waltzed into the locker room as if he owned the place. "AJ," Grant barked without even looking over. "Don't make me look bad out there—better be on your feet."

He stiffened defensively but Grant had his head in his locker because Grant didn't care what AJ had to say. AJ watched him dress and wondered how it was possible that Grant was having the best season of his life. On track to break the state record for touchdowns, even with all the drinking and the partying and the girls.

AJ shut his own locker, and a smile grew as he imagined Grant Dean buying uppers or some shit in a disgusting alley. He wondered if Coach suspected the same thing he did. That would be delicious, actually—for it to all come crashing down.

He knew people liked the Deans well enough, because they'd been in town four generations and because Ellen was a widow. But Mrs. Dean just seemed cold and absent-minded to him; she was always last to pick Grant up from practice when they were kids. And anyways, how was being widowed any different than the many single moms in town, his aunt Kathy included? Left at twenty-two years old with one baby on each hip.

It didn't seem right, to sympathize with one and judge the other.

If Grant was stupid and lazy enough to cheat, Phoebe would lose her holier-than-thou head, that's for sure. With her perfect GPA and her hand always up in class and the fact that she volunteered at god knows what soup kitchen, and her big fancy dreams of medical school or whatever other school she'd set her sights on, AJ found Phoebe an insufferable bitch. How could anyone stand the judgmental smile she was always shining on everyone? Had Phoebe herself not come into the world at the very same rundown rural hospital he had?

"You coming tonight?" Grant asked, tugging his jersey on over his head. "Nine o'clock, parents are gone all night, apparently."

"Huh," AJ replied, squeezing the bag of ice, considering it. He hated these lame parties, and truthfully was worried Becca would be there and cause a scene. Becca didn't go out much, and her parents were probably keeping her under lock and key, but he still worried he'd run into her. Not that he couldn't handle himself—he could; he just didn't want a scene and she could be completely mental. He shouldn't have slept with her those few

times, because now he didn't know if she'd actually moved on or was just keeping her crazy under wraps because of the restraining order. He could have sworn last year he'd woken up to her standing in the doorway to his bedroom, but as soon as he'd turned on the lights, she was gone. "Where's the party at?"

"Kelsey's."

This perked AJ up. Kelsey lived not too far from the Delroys, on the outskirts of town. Maybe Wyatt knew something about what Grant was getting up to. AJ thought Wyatt Delroy was an okay guy, but there was no one else who got in half as much trouble. Uncle Ricky had let it slip after too many beers at dinner last month that Wyatt was close to a third strike, and who knew what his asshole father would do then. Uncle Ricky had said that the Delroy house was a powder keg about to blow.

"Yeah," AJ said now to Grant. "I'll be there. And good luck out there, we're all rooting for you, brother." He felt a smile stretch right across his face. He'd seen Becca's car parked down the road from Grant's house a couple of times over the last several months. Maybe she was circling Grant now and would really leave AJ alone. Maybe he'd even catch a break and barge into the bathroom while Grant was snorting lines or something, and that would be it for his football career, leaving the door open wider for AJ's own chances. Now that would more than make up for the last shitty year of his life.

AJ dropped the melted ice and started stretching out his shoulder. He should probably feel sorry that he was willing to drag a teammate down, but Grant was an asshole, and would do the same to him if given half the chance.

WYATT

Had he slept? He wasn't rested. He rolled onto his side to stare at the blank wall, trying to wade through the sludge in his mind. He touched the plaster, dug into it until the noise bothered his ears and the yellowing paint was loose powder under his fingernails.

Wyatt looked around the small room that sat at the very back of the house, forgotten, an apt metaphor that he swallowed bitterly. It had eroded into a junk room, with towers of cardboard boxes and broken lamps and other rejected pieces of furniture. They'd kept nothing of his; he'd left with nothing, he'd come back with nothing. It was all so bleakly poetic he cracked a smile.

Well, that wasn't entirely true. He hadn't come back with nothing. He'd come back with purpose, to really stir shit up. Wyatt could hear June moving in the room beside his, and he touched the wall again. He tapped lightly but she didn't tap back. He sighed and felt his breath rattle his ribs. He wasn't sure how

June would handle his past, the things he'd done, the things he'd been forced to do. What did June remember of him? That he liked to run; that he got high; that he'd sheltered her from their father, or thought he had. Or was it just dumb luck that their father had hated him more than her? He'd hated him more than anyone. Because Wyatt was growing up to be just like him, and being faced with that failure every day had eaten away at Hank Delroy until there was nothing left between father and son but loathing.

Wyatt stood slowly. The night clung to him and he was stiff and sore; it was getting harder to move in the mornings. He pushed his way through stacks of boxes to the closet, which smelled of mothballs and contained piles of coats and his father's old gray suit. He pulled on the cord for the bare bulb, but it didn't work so he stood on his tiptoes to reach the top shelf, his fingers catching on slivers of wood and then a pair of his old running shoes and then, in the very back corner, his old metal tin.

He sat on the bed and put on his shoes, wriggled his toes, tied them up. A lace broke in his hands, it was so hardened with age, and his resentment swelled. He opened the tin on his lap and rifled through the tidy rows of baseball cards. He tried to keep his hands busy otherwise they'd start to tremble and then shake, sometimes so violently he'd have to force them down at his sides so they didn't flap around until the sensation stopped. He was losing control of his body. It no longer scared him, but he could tell June wasn't ready to see it—and until she was, he would try to protect her.

This feeling—of thinking of someone other than himself, of caring for his little sister—was uncomfortable and made his skin itch, but he'd try. For June. To make up for leaving her back then, and for not returning until now.

Wyatt looked up suddenly as June appeared in the doorway, as though summoned, moving slightly from side to side on her feet.

"Morning, Wyatt."

He could tell she was nervous. He tried to smile at her. "Morning, June."

"What are you looking at?"

"Nothing." Wyatt dropped the tin to the floor, nudged it under the bed with his foot. "Did you come in here last night?"

"In here—your bedroom? No." June motioned to the tin on the floor. "How did you find those? They were at the very back of the closet. What were you looking for in there?"

"Nothing."

June frowned. She looked so tired standing there in the dark doorway, he wondered if she'd slept at all. "No, really, how did you know that tin was still there, Wyatt?"

"Just a guess." Wyatt shrugged and nudged the tin further under the bed. "Why did she keep it?"

"I did, I kept it."

"Why?"

"In case you came back. You loved those baseball cards." June was staring down at her feet. She was wearing their mother's furry yellow slippers, a Christmas gift from years ago when they still celebrated things like that. "Why did you come back right after Mom died? Where have you been for the last ten years? Why now?"

Wyatt looked to the window and the bright day outside.

"I really need you to answer me, Wyatt."

Wyatt felt the pull of the tin under his bed, wondered if she'd kept anything else of his.

June sighed loudly and he hid a smile. "Still nothing, Wyatt? Still not a single word about it? Okay, so look, you're going to listen very closely to me."

Wyatt knew she'd practiced this. Maybe she'd stayed up all night gathering her courage to talk to him this way, and that's why she hadn't slept. He should probably feel worse that he made her so nervous, but it was for her own good that he was keeping certain things to himself.

"Wyatt, I'm going to insist that you explain to me what's going on—where you've been and why you're back—or I'm going to tell the sheriff that you're here. I think he may like to know."

Wyatt threw his head back and laughed, delighted. "Cute, Juney, but you're not going to do that."

June gripped the door so tightly her nail broke, and she flinched. "I am going to do that, Wyatt."

There was a sound in the hallway that they both turned to sharply. "June?" Wyatt swallowed. "What was that?"

June shrugged. "Someone's at the door I guess."

The burn in the pit of his stomach crawled up to his throat. He hoped that June had kept some of their mother's pills; he'd take anything to get rid of the pain. He tried to adjust his face into a warm smile. "Just wait a second, June, listen to me." He pretended he was calm, that someone coming to the house before he was ready wasn't rattling him. "June, we'll talk, I promise. But whoever's at the door, don't tell them I'm here. Not yet. Maybe don't let them inside; say you're busy. Just make up an excuse for them to leave."

June opened her mouth to speak; he jerked his hand up to shut her up. "Just—for now. You have to trust me on this."

June's face was very pale. "But what if it's someone coming to pay their respects to Mom?"

"Say thank you and get them to leave. It's just for now. Please."

June looked over her shoulder to the dark hallway, and he flinched at a second and then a third knock on the door. Wyatt threw up his pinky finger; the cuticle was raw and bleeding. "Pinky promise?" He tried to laugh, but it came out as a wet snicker that made June frown again.

"Fine," she whispered, and left to answer the door.

Wyatt wasn't sure if he believed her, or what kind of excuse she'd be able to come up with—she'd never been a good liar—but there was nothing else he could do to keep her mouth shut, save tie her to a chair, which he swore to himself he wouldn't do.

BECCA

Becca leaned back, shocked, dreading this chore her mother had asked her to do. June's house was in such a state that it was hard to look at. Beige siding panels were hanging off, the roof was patched up but needed to be completely replaced, all the windows were framed by strips of peeling paint thick as orange peel.

She had stopped twice on the highway to turn around and go back to town. The second time she'd sat in her car long enough that someone had pulled up in a pickup truck to ask if she needed help.

"No," she'd said, waving them off. "Just trying to shut my mother up."

The old man had tipped his faded Coors Light cap and sped off, his truck kicking up a cloud of brown dust that stung Becca's eyes.

Becca sighed and knocked again and then lowered her fist

to her side. She hadn't been out this way in years, and had never really considered how poor June was when they were young. What she did remember from back then, which was very little, was that June had often had trouble at home, with her Dad at Flo's and her mother shut in her bedroom because of it, and her brother had gotten in a lot of trouble. Wyatt had been suspended from school for a fight at a track meet, she remembered vaguely. He'd put someone in the hospital.

She'd been to June's house just a handful of times, and once they'd found a small bag of pills in a metal tin in Wyatt's bedroom. They'd marveled at them uncomfortably, and then slid the tin back into his closet.

That was about all she remembered of June's family. But looking around now with more mature eyes, Becca wasn't all that surprised that June's brother and father had both taken off and never come back; there didn't seem to be much to come back to.

Becca clutched the frozen lasagna to her chest and knocked for a fifth time, groaning loudly at this excruciating obligation. Didn't she have enough to deal with? Wasn't she completely stressed with the memorial coming up and the fresh grief and guilt it had released? Not to mention the damn bridge no one could shut up about at work; there'd been an argument in the produce aisle this very morning! And then there was how Grant was treating her. She'd stayed awake all night replaying what had happened at Flo's, and she was pretty sure that he'd brushed her off, like she meant nothing to him. Like she was expendable. Becca shook her head, tried to focus on the task at hand. She couldn't remember the last time she'd had an actual conversation with June. Five years ago? Eight? They'd been friendly enough at school, but after the accident they'd drifted apart.

Relieved when there was no answer, Becca turned to go, but then heard faint footsteps beyond the thin door. She watched as the knob squeaked round and the door opened an inch, the rusting loose chain hanging above June's eyes, hiding them.

Sadness wafted from June like a bad smell. "Hi, June—I'm sorry to just pop by without calling first. Are you busy? If you're busy I can come back, but I heard about your mother and I wanted to come see how you're doing, and to pass on my condolences in person. Did my mom call you? She said she was going to call to find out the details of the funeral."

June didn't budge; her eyes remained hidden. "The funeral was yesterday—no one came."

"Wait, what? It was yesterday? And no one came—no one?" Becca flushed at the thought of June standing there all alone. "Well, that's awful." She paused to smile uneasily. "But I guess things have been busy around here, haven't they, with Sunday being so soon, but—I'm sorry, June, that's awful that no one knew about it. So, I just came from work and... I brought this for you." Becca proffered the now soggy cardboard box and tried to smile again at June, who frowned and then shut the door. Becca waited awkwardly. She heard the chain being undone and then the door opened, further this time, but still not wide enough to let her inside. She winced at June's half-hidden face. "It's lasagna, you can put it in the freezer if you don't want it tonight. It should last a couple of months in there. It's my favorite from the store, and I've honestly tried them all. I can't cook to save my life—never felt the need to learn, I guess, when I work at a grocery store." Becca knew she was rambling but June made no effort to speak or even move back another inch to let her inside, and she was now looking down at her feet in a pair of ratty yellow slippers. Her dead mother's slippers, no doubt. Picturing June sticking her feet into something worn by her mother who was now dead made Becca so uncomfortable she could cry. "I'm really sorry, June, it must have been hard to lose her like that. I know how close you were, at least when we were kids. Are you doing okay on your own?"

"I'm doing fine, you didn't have to come, but thank you." June raised her eyes finally. They were bloodshot and cushioned by dark bags.

"I know I didn't have to, I wanted to." Becca forced a wider smile. "I wanted to make sure you're doing okay, and tell you in person how sorry I am about your mother—such a terrible loss. So, are you managing okay?"

June looked over her shoulder into the living room, which was dark enough to be a hole. "I'm doing fine."

"That's good. Listen, since I'm already here, is there anything I can do?" Was June really not going to let her inside? Becca tightened her grip on the wet lasagna. "I have some time before I have to get back to the store. It's my break, I get a full hour, so I drove all the way out here to see you."

June ignored her, continuing to look over her shoulder, as if she were waiting for something to happen. "Like what?" June swung her head back to her now, eyes dull. "What could you do while you're here? It's been so long since I've seen you, Becca."

Becca kept smiling but her temples were tight; was she starting to sweat? “It has been a long time, and I’m sorry about that—”

“Sorry about what?”

“That it’s been so long, I guess—that I didn’t come earlier. But I’m here now, so I could, I don’t know, help you with the laundry? Make you a cup of tea? Gossip about things to take your mind off of this?”

June gave her a funny look and then sighed, as if she were about to perform a favor for *Becca*. “Sure, why don’t you come in, Becca, and we can have some tea, and we can gossip about things to take my mind off of this.”

“I didn’t mean anything—”

“It’ll be nice,” June cut her off. “And the kettle is already on. And like you said, you drove all the way out here to see me.”

“Okay, great.” Becca followed June into the small, very dark, very cold house. If the lights had been on she could probably have seen her breath. Was the electricity off? “I should have called when your mom got sick. I’m sorry I didn’t, but you know everyone is talking about the bridge—*again*—so I’ve been busy too, grieving Phoebe and the whole trauma of that night. I’d be a good person to talk to, if you want. About your mom and how you’re feeling. Complicated grief is actually a real disease.”

June waved this away with her hand and a strange sound that made Becca wonder if perhaps June was not quite all right.

The living room darkened further when the front door shut. Becca could barely see a foot in front of her, and the house smelled so strongly of bleach that it made her feel ill. June didn’t turn on any lights as they walked into the kitchen that was maybe even darker. The shades were drawn; there were a few candles lit. She could hear water running down the hall. Becca slid the lasagna onto the bare counter. "Is there someone else here?"

"No," June said quietly, opening the cupboard for two mugs. "Just me."

"But I hear water running—"

"Some pipes are leaking. I've been meaning to call someone." June lifted the kettle, poured the water, reached for the tea bags. "I can't offer you anything to eat; I haven't been to the store."

"Oh, that's fine." Becca's eyes had adjusted slightly to the empty kitchen, and she looked around at the old framed photos on the wall that were all off-kilter, and the small round table, and the piles of crumpled tissues littering the floor like dirty snow. She sat down carefully, tried to avoid stepping on one. "Why is it so dark in here?"

"Helps my headaches."

"You poor thing—you have to stay hydrated when you're crying a lot. Trust me."

June looked quickly over her shoulder as though spooked, to the dark hall that led to the bedrooms at the back of the house. Becca tried to see what June was looking at, but it was pitch-black. The running water stopped and June looked wearily at her. "What was that you said?"

"It's important to stay hydrated?"

"I thought you said something about Phoebe Dean," June said. "I saw Mrs. Dean at the cemetery yesterday."

"Mrs. Dean was there with you? But you just said—"

"No, Becca, she wasn't with me."

"She probably went to visit Phoebe ahead of Sunday—"

"That memorial is all anyone seems to care about again—ten whole years later." June looked away again, her attention drawn back to the pitch-black hall. "When I heard you knocking, I thought maybe it was Wyatt. That he'd come back now that I'm on my own, to help out around the house."

"That would be good; it does need some work. I think that window might be broken." Becca blew on her tea just for something to do. "That's funny because I was just thinking about Wyatt when I was standing on your front porch. Any word from him? The last time I saw him was at Kelsey's—you know, that night. Can you believe it's been almost a decade? It still feels so fresh—"

June sat up straight. "What?"

Becca took a sip and nodded solemnly. "I know, how can so much time have passed and it still feel like it was just yesterday—"

"No, what did you say about seeing Wyatt?"

"Oh—yeah, he was there I think."

June leaned forward. "You think, or you know?"

"It was crowded—but I think I saw him there, outside smoking maybe? Maybe I didn't." Becca shrugged. "Maybe it wasn't even him? It was forever ago."

"I came to visit you in the hospital. Why didn't you tell me this?"

Becca swallowed a large mouthful of tea, irritated. All she was trying to do was help June on her one break. Had June even thought to ask her how she was coping? "You came to see me in the hospital?"

"Of course I did—you'd been in a car accident and we were friends. And I would have liked to have known that you saw my brother that night."

Why would I have even thought of it? Becca wanted to say, to wipe the confused look from June's sad face. *When I had enough to deal with?*

"I'm sorry that I don't remember you visiting me. Thank you for doing that." Becca cleared her throat. Why did June care about this—what difference did it make now? "I shouldn't have said anything about Wyatt when I really don't remember; it was so long ago now."

June leaned back again. "Because you were too busy caring about the Deans, just like everyone else. You always were obsessed with Grant; you filled a hundred diaries about him when we were kids, remember? You'd keep track of every time he looked at you or smiled at you or—"

"We were just kids." Becca shifted uncomfortably while June sat very still in her chair, staring.

"Do you know who I saw yesterday morning raising money for the Deans? It was on my way home from my mother's funeral that no one came to." June didn't wait for an answer: "The Hill twins. AJ and Linda live down the road now, in the Albertsons' old place." June smiled strangely at her; Becca's heart started racing. "Remember AJ Hill?"

"Yes."

"Do you keep in touch with him?"

What on earth had she said to change June's mood so drastically? *No good deed goes unpunished*, Becca thought bitterly, and shifted in her seat. She heard pipes spluttering again down the hall, and what she imagined were mice or rats rustling in the ceiling, their tiny claws scratching above her head. Suddenly Becca felt, as she tried to understand what she'd done to deserve this nasty treatment from June, like she was about to snap.

TEN YEARS AGO

5:18 p.m.

Harley Mitchell fixed her bangs, knocked a second time, and waited as Mrs. Dean walked through the living room.

"Hi, Harley," Mrs. Dean said. "Phoebe's out in the barn."

Harley smiled, confused.

"I'm serious, she is." Mrs. Dean turned her around by the shoulders. "She's been out there studying all afternoon—been doing it for weeks actually. Quieter, I guess."

"Oh, okay." Harley checked her watch. The barn was at least a five-minute walk and Phoebe hated being in there alone. "I'll go find her out there then. Thanks, Mrs. Dean."

Mrs. Dean called after her: "And if you see that son of mine, you tell him he needs to fix the cellar door before it starts to rain!"

Harley rolled her eyes. She didn't know how Phoebe or

Grant could stand their mother. Ellen Dean seemed like a woman who was stuck and didn't care to do anything about it. She didn't bother dyeing her grays and still wore her wedding ring for Christ's sake!

She hopped back down the front steps, cursing Phoebe under her breath. Harley hated the damn barn and hated that Phoebe was all the way out there and not in the house waiting to be picked up, like a normal person. Phoebe was always marching to the beat of her own drum, not really caring how her behavior affected other people. But she sure demanded a lot, didn't she? Everything had to be beyond reproach, or she'd freeze you out. When Kelsey had let it slip that they'd stolen lip gloss from the pharmacy a couple months ago, Phoebe had ignored them both for a whole week.

What was the point in becoming anything you wanted to if you didn't have any fun in the process?

Harley checked her watch again. Kelsey would be pissed if they were late to help set up, and she wasn't in the mood to deal with that either—she had enough on her mind. She'd been best friends with Phoebe since they were babies, brought home from the hospital three days apart, but she was getting tired of hearing how worried Phoebe was about Grant; about his lack of ambition or focus or whatever it was she'd whine about that day, going on and on about how he was letting her down.

Phoebe was smart—couldn't she see that Grant was going to make up his own mind? Maybe it would even be good for Phoebe; let her relax a little, let her focus on herself again. The fixation with keeping Grant on the right track wasn't really helping anyone, was it? And who's to say what the right track really was? Was West Wilmer really all that bad?

Harley half jogged through the Deans' back fields. The tall dying stalks were sharp and scraped at her skin like claws. She heard the barn door slam shut, echoing loudly through the early evening air.

"Phoebe?" Harley called out, disturbing a flock of crows that were so close to her she ducked. "Phoebe, is that you? We're going to be late."

"Sorry" wound its way over to her. Harley lifted her hand to wave and watched as Phoebe came into view. "Sorry," Phoebe repeated, but she walked slowly, her silly journal by her side but nothing else—no stack of text books, no SAT preparation exams, no backpack.

"What are you doing out here?" Harley asked, annoyed. Her jeans were now soaked at the cuffs and her arms were stinging. She tried to catch Phoebe's eye. "Seriously—what's going on with you? I thought you hated it out here alone."

Phoebe passed her by without stopping. "Come on. Like you said, we'll be late. Kelsey won't like that and I don't want to deal with her tonight, do you?"

"Hey," Harley said. "I'm serious, why are you out here like this? Shouldn't you be studying?"

Phoebe raised her face to the sky. "Definitely going to rain," she said. "Did you go to the house first?"

"Yes."

"Was Grant there?"

"No. Maybe? I didn't see him."

"How has he seemed lately to you?"

Harley stopped walking, shielding her eyes from the setting sun. "What do you mean?"

"Does he seem different to you?"

"How should I know how he seems?"

"I see you talking to him at school. I just wondered if you'd noticed anything." Phoebe kept walking. "I have to run into the house before we go. I'll be quick," she said, speeding up. "Grant put a lock on his door—can you believe that? And he came home late last night totally wasted, left his shirt on the stairs like he didn't care if he was caught. Like he doesn't care about anything anymore. He was with a girl, I could hear them in his bed this morning. Trey was having people over last night—didn't you say you were going to drop by? Did you see Grant with anyone?"

"No, I don't think so." Harley's stomach twisted. "But is it really that big a deal—"

"He has just one chance," Phoebe said over her shoulder, "to get out of here." She looked away. "Have you heard what they're saying about him now?"

Harley's mind raced; there were many things that people said about Grant Dean, not half of which were true. "No—what who are saying?"

"Never mind." Phoebe walked ahead to the house. "I just really need to talk to him—tonight."

BECCA

"*No*," Becca answered June, not caring how harsh she sounded. "*No*—I do not still keep in touch with AJ. I haven't spoken to him since high school. Actually, I'm not sure why you would bring this up; it's mean."

"Mean?" June smiled thinly. "Why were you even there that night, Becca—did you go to that party to find AJ? I was surprised to hear that you somehow ended up in Grant's truck—"

"Grant offered to drive me home, he was being nice." Becca ripped the corner of her thumbnail off. She shouldn't have come here. June clearly wasn't up to having visitors so soon.

June stared at her. "Grant? Being nice to you?"

"I was at the party with Grant," Becca said, and stopped herself from explaining further. "It had nothing to do with AJ. You know that ended long before that night."

June patted her gently on the hand and looked at her with pity. "Right."

Becca stared at her. Sad, lonely, pathetic June! June, who had probably never even had a boyfriend! Who was June to judge her on her past relationships, mistakes or not?

"We were together, me and Grant," Becca snapped, the words tumbling out of her mouth. "But we were keeping it to ourselves, because we were going to leave town. He was going to quit the team for me. He was going to leave everything for me."

June giggled, and Becca fell back against her chair as if slapped. June covered her mouth with her hand and then leaned forward slowly, studying her. "Oh, you're being serious?" June sounded incredulous. "Okay, Becca, you and Grant Dean were going to leave town together."

Was June Delroy *making fun of her*? Becca ballooned with rage at her mother for suggesting this visit. "Yes—we were" is all Becca could rasp out without screaming.

June smiled at her oddly and then lowered her eyes.

Becca stared unblinking at the top of June's head as she continued looking deep into her mug. Could June not bear to look at her? Becca stiffened in her chair. *She* was the one sitting here in a cold dark kitchen, after coming to bring June food on her only break; *she* was the one coming to check in on June when she was barely hanging on by a thread herself.

"It was because of Phoebe." Becca exhaled the truth. "It was all because of her." Becca wanted June to look up, to hear what she was saying, but June didn't raise her eyes from her mug.

"Phoebe was so possessive of Grant; no one was ever going to be good enough. She was completely obsessed with him leaving town with her, this silly plan they made when they were just kids!

But she could be a real bitch—she threatened me you know, to stay away from him. She threatened me that night!" Becca deflated in her chair, panting with the release, glad of the shadows now, hoping June couldn't see how alarmed she was that the secret she'd kept for ten years had marched right out of her mouth.

"Phoebe threatened you? How?"

"Well, no, not really," Becca said quickly, picturing Grant's face, their pact. She gave a little wave of her hand as she swallowed down her pride for him, again. "I'm exaggerating, it wasn't that bad. We were all really drunk, having fun, it was nothing." Becca stood and screwed her hands together behind her back until they stung. "But look at the time, I should get back to work and you probably want to rest, so I'll get going, but it's been nice catching up."

Becca banged into the chair beside her because she still couldn't really see, and then fumbled to the sink and placed her mug inside the yawning hole. The flame of a nearby candle flickered and she saw that the sink was filled with broken dishes and streaks of dark liquid.

She spun around, desperate to leave this sad, creepy house. She walked quickly as June followed her through the darkened living room to the front door.

"I'm sorry again—about your mother," Becca said hurriedly.

June nodded but remained silent.

Becca stepped out into daylight and blinked so her eyes could adjust. She heard the chain being slid back on before she walked to her car. She sank down in the driver's seat, fumbled with her keys, hit the gas so hard her tires squealed.

She shouldn't have told June all that she had. Not that June would have anyone to tell. But if it ever got out somehow—about the relationship they'd kept secret all these years and why—Grant would be livid.

JUNE

As Becca's car screeched out of the driveway, June went to find Wyatt. There was an indentation in his bedroom door that she didn't remember being there before. She paused and looked at it closely. Had he punched the door? Was Wyatt angry with her? June drew in her breath nervously and knocked.

"What?"

"Can I come in?"

"Seems like you do whatever the fuck you want, regardless of what I say."

June rested her hand on the knob, hesitating, hating that she felt so uncomfortable in her own home. She braced herself and opened the door into a swell of thick gloom. The thin curtains were drawn, the light shining through was weak, yellow. The room reeked of sweat and dirty track jerseys. It was amazing, June thought, how quickly his bedroom had reverted to the one she'd grown up with, as if he'd dragged his teenage bad habits back home with him.

Wyatt sat on the side of the bed, facing the closed window, his back to her. He didn't turn but spoke angrily to the bare wall: "Are you fucking serious with this shit? I told you not to let anyone inside, and then you let Crazy Becca of all people in? And then talked about me?"

June could see the tense knobs of his spine through his shirt.

"I wouldn't test me, June, if I were you."

She crossed the floor to open the curtains but Wyatt grabbed her hand to stop her; his sharp fingernails pierced her skin. "Ouch." She drew her hand back quickly. "Why does it have to be so dark in here?"

"I have a headache." Wyatt's dark eyes flared up at her from where he sat rigid on the bed. "So? What the fuck else did you say about me? Why did she come here—are people looking for me? Do they know I'm back?"

"No one is looking for you or knows you're here, but I heard you in the bathroom, which made me look like an idiot lying to her like that." June frowned. "She just came to pay her respects to Mom."

"Don't lie to me."

"I'm not. She brought lasagna."

Wyatt squeezed her wrist until she yanked it away. "Stop that—you're hurting me. I swear I didn't say anything; it was Becca that said she saw you that night, at that party. Do you know I ran into Mick Dobson leaving the cemetery yesterday? He asked if I wanted a ride, also asked if you'd come home yet—*with his tail between his legs* were his words—now that Mom was gone. That he hadn't seen you since that party. I didn't think much of it—it's *Mick* and I'd just left our mother—but that's two people, Wy. What were you doing there? You left here because of Dad, but why did you go there after?"

Wyatt visibly blanched and looked away from her.

"Just tell me, Wyatt, so we can put it behind us—"

"I said I need a little time."

"You also said that it was hard to come home because of the rumors, so please just tell me the truth—how can we move on if I don't know—"

"A few fucking days, June! I said I just needed a few fucking days!"

June started rolling her eyes but quickly stopped. Wyatt was becoming very agitated and it worried her. Was he high? It would explain his mood swings and how thin and sickly and jittery he seemed. "Wyatt. Don't think I can't tell that you're avoiding my questions—that party, at Kelsey Price's, why did you go? I'm remembering now that Grant had come by the house a few times; did you go to see him? Dad said—"

"Dad said what, June? That I was worthless? That I was an embarrassment? That I would ruin his good name?"

"Wyatt, please—you can tell me, I just need to know so we can move on without—"

"Without what, June? Baggage? Is that all I am to you?"

"No, of course not." She shook her head, frustrated. His questions were confusing her. "Don't you want a clean slate?

When Becca said that she saw you, and I know I saw you with Grant at the end of the driveway a few times, I just thought—"

"You just thought?"

June looked to the window. She realized he was enjoying this and it made her want to cry. "Were you selling Grant drugs, Wyatt? That's what Dad thought he'd heard, and I thought maybe it was just a rumor—"

"Jesus Christ, stop talking about Dad!"

Wyatt stood from the bed and smiled down at her in a way that made her want to sink to the floor. "You're like a regular Nancy Drew, aren't you—digging into my past, talking about me. But do you think that's smart, Juney? To defy me? When I've told you not to tell anyone I'm back? That I just need a few fucking days? Why is that so hard for you to understand?"

"Can you sit down, please, you're making me nervous, Wy—"

"Aw, but this is the most fun I've had in a while." Wyatt raised his hands above his head to stretch. His tattered shirt lifted above the waist of his dirty jeans and June noticed his sharp protruding hip bones and a series of fresh bruises.

"Wyatt." She reached for him. "Your stomach, what happened—"

Wyatt swatted her hand away, jerked his shirt down. "Nothing."

"I thought I heard you leaving in the middle of the night—"

"You didn't hear that."

"I thought I heard the window open."

Wyatt towered over her, intimidating, breathing heavily. "You didn't hear shit—and, Juney?"

She kept her eyes on his but her pulse was racing; his charged mood was scaring her. "What?"

"I told you I'd explain everything when I'm fucking ready. You can't even give me that? When I came back to help you? Do you know how hard it was for me to come back here? Do you even give a shit about that? I mean, holy fuck, this isn't just about you! Do you know what I know? Keeping your mouth shut about me being home is for your own fucking good."

June shook her head, close to tears.

"And so you're going to listen to me very carefully, because I am not fucking around anymore. Do not let anyone else inside this house. No one. I don't trust you not to slip up and tell people that I'm here."

"You don't trust *me*?" A laugh bubbled out involuntarily as June sprang away from him. "Me?" She crossed the room to the door. Wyatt cocked his head, amused. "You think you're so clever," she said, hand on the cool knob, feeling braver the closer she got to leaving his room, to leaving him. "But I knew you kept your stash in that baseball tin, and I knew you were selling, so I need you to tell me right now where you went last night and why you have bruises, why it looks like you're getting in fights again. And don't think to keep lying to me—this is my house now, so if you're doing something illegal, I have a right to know. I can't deal with one more thing, Wyatt—I cannot slide backward."

A slow, vicious smirk spread across Wyatt's face and she sucked in hard. That look, that hardening of features, she'd seen it a hundred times on their father—the fury that would slide across his skin like a roiling storm.

June hated herself for starting to cry in front of him. "You're scaring me. You look just like Dad."

"Dad?" Wyatt shook his head several times, softening. "I'm just tired, listen to me—I'm not doing anything that would get you in trouble. Please stop crying, I just need—" Wyatt's eyes grew wide and he snapped his head back like a spring. One hand flew to his face, the other reached out for her. "Tissue," he spoke, spitting wet. "June, hurry, my nose is bleeding."

June backed into the hallway, rushed to her own bedroom, scanned the tiny space for a box of tissues, found one that wasn't empty beside her pillow. She grabbed a handful and hurried back to where the curtains were now flapping wildly in the wind, the window open, Wyatt's room empty.

GRANT

The high-pitched trill of the checkout felt like a personal attack. The registers at the front of the store had been deserted when he came in, and he couldn't see them from here, but he prayed it wasn't Becca who was working.

Grant opened the door to the freezer and a wet cloud of condensation hit his face. He inhaled deeply, the icy air shaking him slightly out of the hangover that refused to lift. He'd climb in there if he could, and fall asleep between the frozen peas and corn and soggy TV dinners with bright gelatinous desserts—to forget, if only for a minute.

Grant slammed the door shut, winced, his pulsing headache increasing in tempo, and then pushed off toward the deli to grab what his mother had called ahead for, for his sister's memorial on Sunday. Only two days away now. Dread slid slowly down his spine.

"Can I help you?" the girl behind the deli counter asked. She had braces with yellow elastics and looked sixteen. Her nose was in a dog-eared copy of *Wuthering Heights* and she didn't bother looking up.

"Dean," he said. "Picking up an order for Ellen Dean."

The girl rifled through a spiral-coiled notepad, used a finger with chipped polish to find the entry. "The roast?"

"That's it."

She wrote in bubble handwriting that hadn't matured yet: *Dean picked up*.

Grant waited at the counter while the girl disappeared into the back. She emerged a minute later with a brown package that looked like a football. She handed it to him with her nose scrunched up. He didn't want to touch it, but took it from her anyway.

"Can I pay for it here?"

"Register's broken, has to be at the front," the girl said, back on her stool reading, forgetting already that he was there.

Grant walked on dead legs to the front. The sunlight screaming through the windows blinded him and felt like razors in his eyes. He dropped the bundle onto the conveyor belt and the cashier turned. His stomach heaved. He blinked rapidly, trying to will this entire goddamn nightmare away, trying to think.

"Grant?" Becca startled but then recovered with a weak smile.

"Hey—hi."

She stared at him.

"How are you, Becca?"

She shook her head quickly. "It's after lunch and you said

you'd call me this morning but you didn't." Grant could tell she was frustrated but he let her finish. "And you left me standing alone in the middle of Flo's last night. Was that really Reg's cousin you left with? Who was she really?"

"I came in hoping you'd be working," Grant said quietly and cleared his throat, which was suddenly tight. "Shit." He smacked his forehead lightly. "Shit, I bought you flowers but forgot them in the sink at home—I wanted to bring them to apologize for not calling you back. My phone's been acting up, I need a new one—I'm actually on my way to get a new one so this doesn't happen again. And you're right, I did say I'd call this morning but I've been busy running errands for my mom for Sunday, she's a real mess about it. But I am sorry about last night, she—Reg's cousin—she was getting a little out of hand and we didn't want her to get in trouble. You know how that place can be."

Becca crossed her arms over her chest and looked out the window into the parking lot. "Why didn't Reg drive her home if it was his cousin? Why did you have to do it?"

"Reg was waiting for Heather and couldn't leave—they're fighting again, so he had to stay. I hate that I left as soon as you came in. I wanted to buy you a drink."

Becca turned to face him but wasn't smiling. "Heather hasn't said anything about fighting with Reg. We volunteer at the animal shelter together you know."

"Maybe Heather is embarrassed? I think he's stepping out on her again, but that's just between you and me of course." Grant leaned closer to her, smiled. "You look nice today, Becca—is that new lipstick?"

"It is new." Becca chewed on her bottom lip for a second, watching him. "What kind of flowers?"

"What kind of flowers?" Grant winked. "Your favorite—roses, the light pink ones. What do you call that color? Baby pink? Those ones, a dozen. I drove to that flower market in Benton that you love."

"And you just drove that woman home last night? You swear?"

Grant nodded and Becca smiled. "That's sweet—you didn't have to do that, buy me flowers. And it's nice of you to look out for his cousin like that; she did look like trouble in that terrible outfit."

Becca continued to smile and finally took the package from his hands to ring it up. "You don't look so great, do you want something? I could make you a coffee, or a glass of water? There's a sink in the back, it's no problem."

"Oh, thanks—but I'm good." Smiling hurt his head but he was really trying. "And I came in to see *you*—how are you, Becca? Everything okay? You've been trying to get in touch?"

"Right. We should catch up, don't you think?" Becca said, leaning against her till, watching him closely again. "We should talk about, *you know*." She lowered her voice. "The bridge? Can you believe that dumb old woman? Now everyone thinks they can talk about it again. But we should vote, right?" Becca paused. "Maybe we should go together? And we should vote?" Becca raised her eyebrow, and then nodded at him, prompting.

"Against it, absolutely." He couldn't help but sound annoyed. "And you know we can't go together."

Becca pouted and looked away and Grant swallowed hard. She handed him the hunk of meat wrapped in a plastic bag. "But it's been almost ten years," she said very softly. "Don't you think that's maybe long enough?"

Grant's smile vanished. "Long enough for what?"

Becca wouldn't meet his eyes. "Long enough to keep our secret?"

He squeezed the bag so hard his fingers broke through the plastic. "I don't think I heard you right, because there's no way you would say something that stupid to me."

"I'm not *stupid.*" Becca's cheeks turned pink. "I thought that maybe since so much time has passed—ten years! And I'm just—" She bit her lip and he backed away because he didn't know what he'd do if she started crying in front of him, in public. "I'm having a hard time keeping everything in. I'm trying, Grant, but you don't know what it's like, the way everyone looks at me like that night didn't impact me, like I'm nothing."

Grant looked around the store to make sure no one was within earshot. He leaned across the conveyor belt until he was right in her face, but lowered his voice anyway. "Did you come to the bar looking for me last night? That's not what we agreed, Becca—we can't be seen together, you know that."

Becca's eyes widened. "But we haven't talked once since your mother decided to host this thing, and I've been trying to get a hold of you for weeks to see how you're doing, but you haven't returned any of my calls and I'm just really worried about you, Grant."

"*I'm fine.*" He said it too loudly and tried to catch himself, tried to smile at her, but Becca frowned and looked away from him again. "Becca, you're right and I'm sorry. We should definitely catch up, so let's do something next week—"

"No—*no*," Becca said, completely red-faced now. "No, it has to be before Sunday. I want to talk *about* Sunday. About how hard this is for us, how hard this is for *me*, to keep all of this to myself—"

"Keep what to yourself?"

"That we were *together*," Becca said, and then in a very small voice: "And that we've never been able to tell anyone about it."

"Fine." Grant raked his hand through his hair, spent and furious. "Coffee. I'll text you. But let's be clear, and I'm not sure why we're even talking about this here—Becca, if people thought there was more to that night than me just driving you home, that we were actually together and keeping it from Phoebe, that would look bad. And why would that look bad? Look at me. I'm asking you a question, Becca." Grant watched her mouth start to quiver. He could see the tears in the corners of her eyes. "Answer the question, Becca."

"They might think we're lying about other things that happened that night," Becca said quietly. "Because everyone knew how possessive Phoebe was of you, how she didn't want you with anybody—"

"That's enough." He stopped her. "And if anyone ever started to question what we said happened, who would that be very bad for?"

Becca dropped her chin and whispered so softly it was more sound than word. "Me."

"That's right—you. But who's been protecting you this whole time?"

"You have."

"And why is that, Becca?"

When she looked up, all of the blood had drained from her face. "Because you love me," she whispered.

"Because we love each other. But no one can ever know we were keeping this from Phoebe."

Becca nodded and wiped her eyes, and so Grant straightened, relaxed his shoulders. He smiled down at her, patted her on the shoulder. "That's my good girl."

JUNE

Wyatt might have fled his room to avoid their conversation, but June wasn't about to wait around for him to slink back with more evasion and more secrets, so she stormed right past her cleaning closet and out the front door.

It took her over an hour to walk to town, but each step felt lighter than the last. Wyatt had been back just one night but was already taking up so much space in the house that she felt propelled to move, to distance herself from the games he was playing.

June thought about what Becca had said—that she might have seen Wyatt at that party. And Mick Dobson had said the same thing when he'd pulled up beside her on the highway. Wyatt had avoided the question in his room, had maybe even looked guilty. But it felt absurd, didn't it? Their father had been drunk and out of control that night ten years ago, swinging at Wyatt with a baseball bat, accusing him of being a lowlife drug dealer and screaming that he was dead to him, that Wyatt wasn't welcome in this house anymore. Something in Wyatt had snapped, she'd seen it on his face, but June had never considered that when Wyatt had stormed out the front door and into the pouring rain, he'd run off to Kelsey Price's. Run to a shelter or the bus stop or stolen a car, maybe, but a high school party?

June had never thought to ask anyone if he'd been there, and of course no one had offered that information to her. They'd not even considered it—that she might like to know. After Wyatt left, most people had wanted her to avoid talking about him altogether. It made them too uncomfortable to be faced with her suffering, so how dare she mention him, really.

But why had Wyatt gone to the party? Why stop there before leaving to god knows where? Who had he gone to see? June's mind was trying to make connections, but nothing was clicking. After this long, perhaps it shouldn't matter, but it did to her. Wyatt was being cagey; was it because of that night? The accident? Did Wyatt know something about it? Did he think she couldn't handle the truth, that she was weak?

Had she not lost him, and then their father, and then their mother? Was she not a survivor?

She would keep asking him until he gave in; she would prove to him that she was strong enough to hear anything he had to say. She would prove it to herself.

June reached McCray's Co-Op, with its buckets of rakes and colorful watering cans and a foldout table with small potted plants, all sitting outside as if the store was bursting at the seams, though she knew there was an entire center aisle that was empty.

She pushed on the door, tinging the bell, and the smell—of fertilizer and flammable plastic—reminded her of her father. He was always tinkering with something in the garage and he'd bring her here sometimes, just the two of them, and take her for ice cream afterward at the Dairy Bar. She touched her throat, felt her light pulse; sometimes the good memories, though rare, were hardest to bear.

"Morning!" Mrs. McCray called from the back of the store.

"Shovels?" June asked, hoping old Mrs. McCray wasn't having one of her off days.

"Second aisle, be right out."

June passed the power tools and mouse traps and hammers and found a bin of trowels that could work to dig a hole under the maple tree. She had fond memories of that tree and wanted to bury her bird properly. She grabbed one and turned, and let it drop to the ground in surprise.

"Oh," June said, bending to retrieve the trowel. "You startled me, I didn't know anyone else was in here."

Grant Dean squinted at her as if he was confused by what he was seeing, and then ran his hand through his hair. "June." He turned from her to study a section of lightbulbs. "I was sorry to hear about your mother, my condolences."

"Oh. Thank you."

June hadn't seen Grant in a long time, and he looked gaunt and shifty. It was afternoon but she could smell whiskey on his breath and wondered if that could explain it. "And my condolences to you," she said to fill the silence. "For your sister's memorial coming up."

Grant picked up a yellow box and turned it over carefully in his hand to read the back. "The memorial is important to my mother, to remember her officially."

"It's all anyone's talking about, the whole town must be planning to go—everyone misses Phoebe still. Even after this long."

June watched Grant clear his throat. "I guess they do."

"Actually..." June said, clutching the trowel, trying to seem less nervous than she was, but was this not the perfect opportunity to ask about Wyatt? Grant had been there that night, everyone knew that. Maybe they'd seen each other, maybe Wyatt had even told Grant something that could help her now; and the more she knew, the less he'd be able to keep from her. "I'm glad to run into you. I know it was a long time ago, but"—June's pulse was loud in her ears—"Becca said that she saw my brother that night at Kelsey's. Did you talk to Wyatt there? Did he tell you where he was going? Or has he ever reached out to you? Have you ever heard from him?"

"Wyatt? Didn't see him, but it was packed, could have missed him I guess." Grant smiled at her. "Why would he reach out to me? We didn't know each other."

"I saw you come by the house a couple times."

"Did I? We had some classes together—Social Studies maybe? But no, I definitely haven't heard from him. Like I said, we didn't know each other. Have you heard anything?"

June considered this. "No, nothing."

Grant snapped his fingers. "You know, I think I was over

once for some study notes, and he told me that things at home were getting tense."

This surprised her. "Wyatt told you that?"

Grant nodded sympathetically. "That your father was—I'm sorry to say this—getting violent. *Volatile* is the word he used, I think. It must have been hard for him, to be scared all the time, to be living with that kind of fear."

"*Wyatt* told you that?" June stared at Grant, who stared back at her. "But he was so private, and you just said you didn't know him, but he told you that he was scared? I don't think Wyatt was scared of very much."

Grant shrugged. "Everyone's scared of something."

June pictured her brother's piercing dark eyes, remembered the music he'd blare from his bedroom after he'd snuck out for the night. "Wyatt was expelled, why would he be studying? Unless he stole the notes or something. Did he steal them? Was he selling exams?"

"Who knows." Grant's jaw tensed. "It was ten years ago—why would I remember what he was doing?"

"I know you were at the house a couple of times at night. I saw you at the edge of the driveway—"

"At night with no streetlights out where you live, how could you know for sure that it was me?" Grant turned the box over in his hands again. "Wyatt was involved with some bad people—owed them a lot of money."

"So you did know him."

"No—but we live in a small town so I heard what people were saying about him, and they were saying that Wyatt owed a lot of money to some bad guys in the city—but who really knows, it was years ago… This damn porch light." Grant sighed. "My mother's been nagging at me for weeks and there's a broken door, and a broken railing, and she just will not let it go." Grant looked up from the box. "What's the trowel for?"

"Some gardening."

"Well, I have to get going—"

"Becca came by the house earlier today. That's when she told me about Wyatt being at the party."

"I just don't remember, I'm sorry."

June shrugged as casually as she could. "Becca's quite worked up about Sunday, about your sister, about the whole thing."

Grant raked his hand through his hair. "Well, it never really goes away. You probably understand that."

June watched him curiously for a second. "Becca said that you were together back then."

Grant smiled but didn't say anything.

"Becca said that you didn't want your sister to know about it. She got pretty upset, said your sister threatened her."

Grant cleared his throat while he continued to stare at June, like he was frozen. She waited for him to deny it. To laugh it off. To make fun of Becca, who'd been obsessed with Grant Dean since they were in grade school. Who'd sworn she was in a serious relationship with AJ Hill until AJ's parents took out a restraining order and everyone started calling her Crazy Becca behind her back. June waited for the denial, but Grant just lowered his eyes from hers and then turned the box over in his hand again. And then turned it over yet again. "June, if you knew what a toll this weekend is taking on my mother—she can barely get out of bed if I'm being honest with you... So I'm going to ask you to keep this to yourself. For my poor mother's sake. She wasn't the biggest fan of Becca and I don't want to add to her grief right now. If my mother knew Phoebe was upset that night—"

"Wait—so it's true?"

"It's complicated." Grant's temples tensed. "But I'm sure that you get me wanting to protect my mother, and you know how fast gossip spreads in this town. And you know Becca, she's imaginative."

June shook her head, confused. "I don't understand—"

"When Wyatt took off, and he said he didn't want anyone looking for him, and it came out that he was in such deep shit... I'm sure you'd do anything to protect your mother from hearing those things about him, wouldn't you? If she were still alive?"

June cleared the tickle in her throat, flicked her wrist twice. "How do you know Wyatt didn't want anyone looking for him?"

Grant finally put the box back on the shelf. "He never came back, did he?"

June flinched. "What does that mean?"

"Nothing," Grant said. "You probably don't want to hear these things about your brother."

"But you keep saying that you didn't know him—"

"Are you fucking deaf? Did you not hear the rumors? How scared everyone was of him? How desperate he was to pay off his debts? How dangerous he could be? Trey landed in the hospital because of him, and I'm sure there were others! Look..." Grant tried to smile but looked a little crazed. "Look, it doesn't matter anymore—Wyatt's gone and what he did or didn't do is gone with him, so just leave it alone. I really have to run, I can't have my mother wondering where I am. She worries about me."

Grant turned on his heel and left.

"Didn't have what you needed?" Mrs. McCray called after him, but Grant was long gone.

June walked to the front of the store, nearly dazed by their exchange. It had never made much sense to her that Becca had been at the party that night and then ended up in Grant's truck. Why would Grant have driven Becca home, when as far as June knew, they barely knew each other?

But thinking about it now, even June had been aware back then that Phoebe had a real thing about keeping girls away from her brother. About wanting Grant on the straight and narrow. So if Becca and Grant *had* been together back then, would June have even noticed?

What if Becca and Grant had been afraid of what Phoebe would do if she found out about them? How far would Phoebe have gone for her brother? How far would Becca and Grant have gone to protect themselves from her?

And then Wyatt's voice in her ear: *See, Juney, that's the thing about lies. They're like string—once they start unraveling, you're fucked.*

TEN YEARS AGO

6:15 p.m.

It was going to be one of those nights, Kelsey Price could feel it. Maybe because the storm was supposed to break and everyone in town could finally shut up about the damn weather. Like they'd never had a thunderstorm before! She rolled her eyes and uncapped her lip gloss. She applied a few coats until her lips looked shiny and wet. She smiled brightly. She'd just had her braces off and knew her teeth looked perfect. She brushed her hair. The last party she'd thrown had been lame, but this time she'd bought extra vodka, extra rum, extra gin, even convinced Trey to sell her two jugs of his moonshine.

"Kelsey, we're heading out—make sure you lock up!"

"Bye," she yelled, craning her neck to the open bedroom door. "Have fun!"

Kelsey opened the drawer of her vanity, searched for her

blush, looked in the mirror for the clock on her bedside table: 6:15 p.m. Her parents were nothing if not punctual, leaving for their monthly date night at the tavern the next town over, having promised to spend the night at her aunt's rather than chance getting stuck in the storm.

Kelsey smiled again because she wouldn't have to kick anyone out this time, not with her parents not expected back until the morning. No—this time the party would be memorable, she could feel it.

A tree branch slapped against her window and she jumped in her seat. She stood, straightening her denim skirt just as two headlights wound up the long driveway to her house.

She bounced on her heels. The girls were late, but she'd let it go; she didn't want to ruin anyone's mood. Tonight was going to be perfect. The guys had won their first away game and everyone had played well, especially Grant. He really was having a good year—scouts coming already. It was a big deal, and everyone was excited about it. Everyone but Phoebe, who seemed perpetually distraught lately.

"Do you know who he's seeing?" Phoebe had asked Kelsey two weekends ago over milkshakes at the Dairy Bar. "I know there's someone. He's out every night and then late for practice. I talked to his coach, tried to explain that he's just under a lot of pressure, but he can't keep getting away with it. He'll get cut, and then what?"

"No offense, but is there a girl in town your brother hasn't slept with?" Kelsey asked.

"This is different. He's not himself. He won't talk to me."

"Maybe it's just the pressure, like you said, or maybe he just doesn't care as much as you do—"

"He does *care. But if he's actually doing what I think he might be—" Phoebe sucked in, and Kelsey tried not to groan at the melodrama of it all.*

"You guys are the worst sometimes," Kelsey said as lightly as she could. "The rest of us are praying to barely graduate and all you ever talk about is leaving town, and stressing over every little thing Grant does—and honestly, Phoebe, could you both actually leave your mother behind?"

Kelsey had been on the Deans' porch the other day and overheard Phoebe and her mother arguing. When Kelsey had asked her about it, Phoebe had just shrugged it off as being nothing, but it had been unusual, to hear Ellen Dean raise her voice like that at her perfect daughter.

"You couldn't both leave her," Kelsey said to Phoebe again. "Could you?"

Phoebe had frowned at this and then stuck her nose back in her textbook, twirling her highlighter like a baton.

Kelsey raced out of her bedroom and threw open the front door. "Bitches!" Kelsey laughed, but then clamped her mouth shut. "Wait, what's wrong, what's going on?"

Harley had her arm around Phoebe, who was mumbling: "It's not a girl. Well, it is a girl, but it's not just a girl. It's a girl and it's Wyatt Delroy. I found it in his room, I found it, he's going to ruin everything we've planned, everything I've done for him, because of Wyatt Delroy." Phoebe was slurring, holding out a half-empty bottle of vodka.

"You found that vodka? And what's this about June's brother?" Kelsey snatched the bottle before Phoebe let it drop to the floor and break. "Didn't Wyatt get expelled, like for good? Why would Grant be hanging out with him?" Kelsey asked this because Phoebe was staring at her, but she didn't care if Grant was getting high; she did however care very much that whatever had been brewing between Phoebe and Grant not explode at her house tonight. "What did you find in his room, Phoebe? What girl?"

Phoebe looked at her coolly, head tilted, her long black hair swept perfectly over her new leather jacket. Kelsey could almost die of jealousy; the jacket was so perfect. "He's going to ruin everything, Kelsey, and for what?"

"Come on," Kelsey shushed. "It's going to be fine; you'll sort it out. Right, Harley?"

Harley looked horrified. "Absolutely."

"Whatever it is, it'll pass—"

"You don't understand," Phoebe muttered, and then she left the doorway to make her way into the kitchen. "No one does."

"What the fuck?" Kelsey hissed to Harley when Phoebe was out of earshot. "She's wasted, is she going to cause a scene? She's been spiraling about Grant 'being distracted' for weeks, so if there is some girl, that girl better watch her back."

"The stress, maybe." Harley stepped inside. "She was out in that creepy barn when I picked her up. Like, by herself."

"She was?"

Harley nodded.

Kelsey shut the door. "I'm sure she'll be fine; we'll deal with it tomorrow."

"I think Becca's car is at the foot of your driveway. She's not allowed to come inside, is she? If he's going to be here?" Harley asked.

"Absolutely not." Kelsey groaned. "I sort of regret it now, this party. Things feel off, don't you think? And the storm—karma maybe, like something really bad is about to happen."

JUNE

June went to the cash to pay, trying to forget the terrible thoughts she'd just had about Becca and Grant and Phoebe. Thinking the worst of people was no doubt Wyatt's influence.

"Morning, Birdie."

June tightened her grip on the trowel. The adrenaline she'd just felt talking to Grant like that vanished, leaving her tired and exposed. "Afternoon, Mrs. McCray," she said. "But it's June. Birdie is—was—my mother. Did you take your medication today?"

"Don't need that stuff," Mrs. McCray scoffed. "Now, how is that son of yours, dear? Any word on where he gone off to? He loves those dinosaurs, that what the shovel's for? To dig up some bones in the garden?" Mrs. McCray chuckled to herself.

June pocketed her change. "Actually, Doris, Wyatt has come home and we're all so relieved. It was just one big misunderstanding."

"Told you he would, didn't I?" Doris McCray clasped her deeply veined hands together. "You don't be listening to what anyone says. We know he's a good boy."

"You're right, he is," June said and walked out the front, the bell jingling as the door shut behind her.

On the rundown single block of Main Street, June sat for a minute on the only bench. She watched a few people walk by, heading into the diner, the laundromat; a couple of aging construction workers ducking into one of the many empty storefronts plastered with FOR LEASE and FOR SALE signs.

June wasn't ready to go home yet. She still had to think. She was certain she'd made Grant uncomfortable with her questions, and she thought there was a good chance he'd been lying about his relationship with Becca, which could mean that he was lying about Wyatt.

June smiled politely at a passerby, who barely looked her way. Being in town, talking to people—even if one of them was old Mrs. McCray at the hardware store—was such a drastic change from being stuck inside her house listening to her mother crying or whimpering in pain. June sat forward, realizing with a start that she hadn't thought of her mother in nearly an hour, nor had she thought to clean anything that day.

She wondered if Wyatt might be proud of her for engaging with people, for talking to Grant that way, asking him those very direct questions, nearly prying—so unlike her! She realized that Wyatt was probably back home by now waiting for her, maybe wondering what was taking her so long. Maybe even concerned about her.

It had been so long since anyone had thought about her at all.

This feeling of being seen fueled June as she stood up and walked toward the hair salon on the corner. She'd pop in to see if Kelsey Price was working. She hadn't talked to Kelsey in years and they had never really been friends, but maybe Kelsey could at least confirm whether or not Wyatt had been at her house that night. The way Wyatt was behaving, so stubborn and closed-lipped, June figured the more truths she knew about him, the harder it would be for him to keep avoiding her questions. And then they could start over; maybe buy a car and come back to the hardware store together for the tools they'd need to start fixing up the house. She smiled, picturing them removing the junk from Wyatt's bedroom so they could repaint it whatever color he wanted. June would help him get comfortable at home, and then once his slate was good and clean and he was ready, he could re-settle back into town, free from his troubled past. He could get a job—she knew they were looking for help at the auto shop. This was another thing she'd mention to him when she got back.

June paused at the door to the salon, remembering Wyatt's warning that she wasn't to tell a soul he was back until he was ready, and sighed. No one would even think to ask her about him—not back then, and certainly not now with the haze of the precious memorial smothering the town.

She opened the door and wrinkled her nose at the smell of burnt hair and cheap bleach. Kelsey Price was in the back corner sweeping, but looked up when June walked in, waved politely, and set her broom against the wall. She crossed the floor with a look of mild curiosity, probably wondering what on earth June Delroy was doing in her salon. Kelsey, who was maybe still sad sometimes missing her dead friend, but had a life that had continued forward, with three kids and a business in town; Kelsey, who had grown and changed and progressed whereas sometimes June felt like her own life had stopped that night ten years ago.

For weeks after the accident, June lay awake at night, desperately wishing for Wyatt to slide the window open, climb back through like he had dozens of times before, and drop quietly to her floor. He'd never say anything—he was never one to explain himself, a confidence June wished she had, but he'd pull her quilt up around her chin and kiss her forehead, never knowing if she was awake or asleep as he did it.

June had barely followed the story of Phoebe's car accident in the paper—there had been too much going on at home—but months later, when the initial shock wore off, her mother began spewing a lot of vitriol about that goddamn family, *the Deans.*

June came to understand that her mother blamed Phoebe for her family's pain, which June found unfair—after all, the girl had died tragically—but as the years crept on and the rot spread in the Delroy home, she started to wonder if there was more nuance to it than she had originally thought. About the attention Phoebe got when Wyatt got none. About her family's loss being ignored; her family being pushed aside like they didn't matter.

"Hi, Kelsey—I was just next door at McCray's." June held out the trowel awkwardly, but then smiled, thinking how pleased her mother would be for asking around a little, for making Grant, of that *goddamn family*, uncomfortable in the process. *Cheers, Juney*, June imagined her mother saying, raising her glass high, that sparkle she'd once had in her eyes, before it was extinguished completely. *Looks like you've got fight in you left.*

"June." Kelsey offered a sympathetic tut. "I'm so sorry about your mother. How are you holding up?"

"I'm managing," June said. "Oh, I'm not in for my hair. I saw Becca Hoyt earlier and then just ran into Grant at the hardware store, and it got me thinking back to that night—you know, the one at your house?"

"Sure—you and me both." Kelsey leaned back against the mirror. "Ten years! But still so hard, and now this awful thing with Rosie Wilson—she was just in getting her hair done last week. Sweet woman, but I can't imagine what she was thinking—of course I'll go next week to vote. That rotten thing should have been taken down years ago; you know I refuse to drive over it."

"Right, but about that night. My brother, Wyatt—do you remember him?"

"Wyatt?" Kelsey nodded. "Sure I do."

"Still no word from him, which has been hard with my mother and everything. You know I'm on my own now, so I wish I could find him, and like I said, Becca came by the house to pay her respects, and she said she saw him at your place that night. And so did Mick."

Kelsey's eyebrows raised slightly. "My place?"

"Your parents' place—do you remember him being there?"

"Oh, June," Kelsey sighed deeply. "I wish to god I'd never

thrown that stupid party—if I hadn't, Phoebe would still be here. I'd take it back if I could. I think about that sometimes still, that I'd do anything to take it back."

"But did you see him?"

"Who's that?"

"*Wyatt.*"

"Oh, right—Wyatt, let me think." Kelsey fluffed her bangs with her manicured fingers. "No, I can't say that I remember him being there, but he wouldn't normally come to those things, would he?"

"Right." June deflated. "He wouldn't." Had Becca been mistaken? And Mick?

Kelsey scrunched up her nose, and then said: "But Phoebe was talking about him." She nodded slowly, thinking. "Phoebe was definitely talking about him that night."

"Phoebe was talking about Wyatt?" June's stomach sank slightly. "Do you know why?"

"It's all such a blur now," Kelsey said, shrugging. "I really don't remember why."

June's confidence was slipping and she wanted to get home. She hadn't known that Wyatt even knew Phoebe. Or what Phoebe might have been saying about him. "What about Grant and Becca?" The smell of peroxide was making June feel faint.

"Grant and Becca? Well, Becca was in the truck when it happened; Grant was just driving her home. Talk about being in the wrong place at the wrong time."

"But were they together?"

Kelsey looked confused. "Yes, in the truck."

"No, were they dating?"

"*Dating?*" Kelsey laughed. "Haven't heard that one before, but no, definitely not. Phoebe did think Grant was sleeping with someone, thought the girl had been there that morning in his room, and she was upset about it."

"Could it have been Becca?"

"June." Kelsey looked at her like she was crazy. "After what happened with Becca and AJ, there's no way. I may have had my own suspicions about Grant, but it wasn't Becca. That girl was just in the wrong place at the wrong time. Whoever says otherwise is lying."

WYATT

They were the only ones in the parking lot, it being nearly too cool to eat anything frozen. The squat Dairy Bar sat on the side of the highway, its turquoise sign hung off-kilter, at the same angle it had ten years ago. The small window for placing orders was open today, but would soon be boarded up with plywood and closed for the season.

Silence flooded the car as June pulled the keys from their neighbor Evelyn Lloyd's ancient Buick, killing the engine. It had been his idea to ask to borrow the old bag's car, to shut June up about having to walk everywhere. But even still, June stared ahead through the windshield, refusing to look at him.

"Christ, I'm sorry, okay?" Wyatt groaned. "How many times do I have to say it? I didn't mean to upset you by leaving my room like that. I just needed some air so I went for a run, and wasn't it my idea to come here to make it up to you? And didn't you say: *Funny, Wy, I was just thinking about ice cream earlier*?"

Wyatt did feel bad that he couldn't control his temper and that his lashing out was scaring June, but the stress of dealing with her was causing his condition to worsen, and so he really needed her to listen to him. But she wouldn't, would she? June had gone into town while he was out to ask about him, when he'd explicitly told her not to. He'd been practically menacing about it and she'd still done it, and now she was asking how he knew Phoebe Dean and what Phoebe Dean might have been saying about him back then.

It was a real fucking fine line he was toeing: being pleased that June was getting stronger, getting out of the house, showing a little life in her eyes, but then having to rail against her constant, relentless, goddamn prying because of it. And it was all for her own good! Something Wyatt had told her a thousand goddamn times since he'd been back. *Just a few days*, he'd say, to which she had started rolling her eyes—rolling her eyes for fuck's sake! Like they were goddamn children!—which made him rage more, and there he was on that razor-thin line again, the one he was teetering on so perilously it was making him sicker.

June was talking so softly he had to squint to hear her. This caused his headache to worsen and his mood to be practically rabid.

"I said, tomorrow we're having that funeral, Wyatt."

"June—stop this."

"I walked two hours into town for a shovel. You're going to help me bury it tomorrow. It's the very least you can do."

Was June completely losing it? He didn't have the energy for this. He held his palms out and tried to keep calm. "Fine, okay?

We'll bury your bird tomorrow, but can you hear what you're saying out loud?"

"Cardinals are the spirits of those we've recently lost—did you know that? I'm not sure if I believe it, but she did fly into my window the day after I buried Mom, so I want to do the right thing."

Reclaiming his good name and turning the tables on the others was costing him so much more than he'd thought it would if his sister was about to lose her goddamn fucking mind. Wyatt sighed. "Fine. Please drop it."

June watched a truck pull in ahead of them. She reached for the door handle and he held out his arm to stop her.

"It's so windy out," Wyatt said. "Let's stay in the car where it's warmer until they leave."

June turned the car back on. "Fine."

Wyatt cranked up the heat until he could smell it. The chill from the house wasn't letting up, and he was constantly shivering and grinding his teeth. Sometimes he shook so hard he worried he might break a bone.

The truck doors flew open and two young girls tumbled out, pushing and shoving and shouting at one another. The father, a tall thin man wearing grease-stained coveralls, turned and waved and June waved curtly back. She spoke to the steering wheel: "Want to get out and say hi?"

Wyatt slid down further in his seat and shook his head.

June squeezed the wheel and was quiet a while. "You sure?" she asked, breaking the long silence. "You know who that is, right, you do recognize him? Or did you forget?" June waved again as the man and his kids returned, clutching paper cups and bags of burgers to their chests and climbing back into the truck. "It's AJ Hill—you ran track with him. He lives down the road now. Wyatt, are you hiding from AJ?" June's knuckles had gone white. "Are you in trouble again, Wyatt? Grant said you were in debt, that you owed a lot of money, is that why you left town? Do you still owe them? You can tell me. Maybe I can help so you don't have to hide—"

"Grant said all that, did he? I wouldn't listen to one goddamn word that asshole says. Shit—" Wyatt felt his nose itch and then ooze with warmth, and he opened the glove box, hunting for something to use before he bled onto his clothes. "Is there tissue or something, shit—" Wyatt pinched the bridge of his nose and tilted his head back, blinking rapidly at the dented ceiling of the car while June hopped out and rushed to the counter.

She raced back with a fistful of rough paper napkins. "Another one?" she asked, and he nodded, feeling light-headed and hating the warm slick of copper in his mouth. "That's a lot of blood, Wyatt—are you sure you're okay?"

He heard the squeal of tires as the truck pulled away. Wyatt sat up slowly and watched as the exhaust fumes cleared once the truck hit the highway. "I'm fine, I think it stopped." Wyatt balled the bloody napkins and dropped them at his feet. "I feel like a chocolate shake. What about you?"

"You're fine?" June looked at him, worried. "But your nose is bleeding again, and you have bruises, new ones. What's going on with you?"

He cleared his throat. "I'm not sure."

"It's getting worse though?"

"I think so—maybe."

"Should you see a doctor?"

"June..." Wyatt gritted his teeth so hard a molar cracked. The *prying*. "Sure." He said it to shut her up, but maybe it would be better if June focused on his nosebleeds and headaches and deteriorating health and not on the ins and outs of his relationship with Grant Dean. Or Phoebe.

June smiled but she looked so weary; was that his fault? "I'll make some calls, try to get you an appointment. It's probably nothing, you're probably just tired. Do you want to stay in here while I get out? You said a chocolate shake, right?"

He couldn't stomach the earnestness on June's gaunt face, the hope she had that she could help him. "Thanks, yeah—just in case it starts bleeding again." Wyatt ran his tongue around the side of his mouth and nearly gagged; he was unfixable, and he was running out of time.

June walked to the counter. When her back was turned, Wyatt reached down for one of the napkins he'd used. He unfolded it; the red was so unbelievably bright he blinked. His hand shook as he brought it to his mouth. He spat weakly and then crumpled it up and shoved it into his pocket. He leaned back and closed his eyes to stop the dizziness until June made her way back to the car.

Wyatt smiled as she handed him the shake. The waxy cup sweated in his cold hand. He pulled on the straw and tried not to visibly retch as the thick cold cream mixed with the fresh blood in his mouth from where he'd just lost a tooth.

BECCA

The knock on her car window shocked Becca awake in the front seat, and she bit down hard on her tongue. She screamed inwardly, trying to pull herself back into the memory she'd just had; of when she and Grant had been in love and he'd saved her life.

Becca's hospital room was dim, and after Grant wheeled himself into it, he slumped down in his chair beside her bed. "We need to talk. What did you tell the sheriff?"

"I don't really remember what happened." Becca winced around her swollen, fleshy tongue. "This is so bad—oh my god this is bad—but what happened?"

Grant peered at her through eyes that were black and swollen but still alert. "What do you mean?"

"I can't remember much." Her hands were too bandaged to

wipe the tears from her eyes. "Phoebe was lying there, oh god it was so awful, and you were by the side of the bridge, did we...?" She sniffled, embarrassed at how she might look to him. "Did we slip on the road because of the rain?"

The injuries covering Grant's body were hard to stomach. He was a mosaic of blood and cuts and bruises, and so she focused on his eyes, which were searching her face. He was so terribly worried about her, she could tell. "Yes, the roads were slippery, Becky—"

"Becca."

Grant winced. "God—these drugs are really fucking me up, but you're saying that you don't remember what happened? Are you sure? This is important."

"I woke up in the back seat and Phoebe was just lying there on the road. She looked—" Becca screwed her eyes shut, pushing away the awkward positioning of Phoebe's small body, her mangled face, her white jaw, all that blood, so much blood. "And you were screaming and then you were crying."

"I saw you in the truck. You must have hit your head and blacked out—what did the doctors say about that? About you not remembering, did they say you might never remember?"

"Yes." She nodded; it made everything hurt.

"So what did you tell the sheriff, then?"

Becca tried to smile at him. She knew that under his injuries he was still so handsome, so perfect. She'd loved him since she was a little girl. "He came in when I was sleeping, so I haven't said anything." The morphine was making her so dizzy and confused, but then she did remember something: sounds, anger, fear;

she pulled at them like threads. "Wait—you were shouting." Becca blushed, forcing fresh blood to the open cuts on her face. "You were shouting at Phoebe—was it because of us? She told me to stay away from you, she threatened me—"

"Phoebe threatened you because of us?" Grant was getting frustrated, but she didn't know what to say to make it better. "What do you mean?"

"I was nervous to be at the party with you and I drank too much. I'm sorry that I told Phoebe about us, it just slipped out," she said. "I told her about our plans. I'm so sorry, I swear I didn't mean to."

Grant winced again and she wished desperately to take his pain away.

"But we can still go, Grant, there's no one holding us back now. This accident was awful but we survived, maybe it was a sign that we can still be together, leave—"

Grant shook his head so abruptly that it made him wheeze. He squeezed his eyes shut, wincing. "Becca, this is very important—do you really not remember what happened? This isn't some joke, is it—you were in the back seat of my truck when we left the party."

"That's right." Becca remembered he'd tilted the mirror to look at her. "You were driving me home, but your sister, she told me at the party to stay away from you, that you two had plans, not us, and then you were shouting at her in the front seat. It must have been because of us, because you were choosing me over her. I'm so sorry she's gone, Grant, but it was an accident, a terrible accident, and we can get through it."

Grant closed his eyes. His temples bulged. Blood leached

slowly through the large white bandage on his forehead. The loud beeping of the machines concerned her gravely; could her heart burst talking to him like this?

"AJ," Grant said, his eyes still closed. "AJ was there. Is it really over with you two?"

"That was over long ago," Becca whispered, horrified. Was this a test? Was he testing her? "AJ didn't mean anything; you and I are together now, we have a future, I love you—"

"Right." Grant looked down at his hands in his lap; one was bandaged completely, the other was black and blue. "I can't think straight, I might still be in shock. But you're right, you're right about Phoebe, she was shouting in the front seat. And it was about us. About you and me leaving, like you just said."

Becca tried to nod, but pain shot from her neck to her waist. "Now we don't have to hide anymore."

Grant stared down at his bandaged hands for a long time. Becca could hear that his breathing was shallow and uneven, but she waited patiently. She'd waited for this her whole life. Eventually Grant looked up to meet her eyes, and she realized he was crying. She watched the tears stream silently down his face. He was so sad, so wrecked. But she would fix him, she could do that; she wouldn't abandon him now.

"Phoebe was very drunk." Grant spoke in a weak, distant voice. "She'd been upset lately, frustrated with me—us—and didn't know her limit."

Becca willed the throbbing and nausea away so she could focus on how this felt, being so close to him, so intimate. Through their trauma, their souls fused together.

"I'm sorry that you can't remember what happened, that must be awful. But you're right, Phoebe was screaming in the front seat—but, Becca, she was screaming at you, not me. I was trying to calm her down and get her to understand. About us, like you said, about our plan to leave. But she wouldn't listen, she could be so stubborn, and she just lost it and started grabbing at you and you tried to stop her, and you shoved her so hard—" Grant looked away from her with a strangled choke. He was easing her into the truth, to soften the blow. His kindness in this moment was something she'd never forget. "You shoved Phoebe into me, and I lost control of the truck."

Becca inhaled sharply; so this had been her fault.

The sheriff appeared in the doorway then, hat in his hands. "Ready to give your statement, Miss Hoyt? If you can manage it, can we talk out in the hall alone?"

Becca looked around, terrified. Could she be charged with a crime? For causing the crash? Should she ask for a lawyer, would there be an investigation? Could she go to jail? Was this manslaughter? Murder? Her life was flashing before her eyes. She should call her father; he'd know what to do.

"Look at her, Sheriff, she's in a lot of pain, let her stay in here. And anyways, we're not suspected of anything, are we?" Grant asked. "Because I hit a deer." He was staring down at his hands again. "I couldn't see it because of the rain; it just jumped in front of me and I lost control of my truck. It was an accident, just a horrible accident. I didn't mean for this to happen."

The sheriff cocked an eyebrow. "There was considerable damage to the front fender."

"It was a stag," Becca said, reaching for Grant's hand; he tensed but then relaxed and smiled at her. "It was a huge stag. I saw it too, Sheriff," she said. "It came out of nowhere and Phoebe wasn't wearing her seatbelt."

The sheriff put his cap back on, adjusted it slowly. "You're lucky, kid. With your breathalyzer being done so late, you made it just under the limit. Is that why you waited to call the ambulance? To sober up? It could have saved your sister's life if she'd been brought in right away."

Grant let out a sickly choking sound, and Becca felt furious at the sheriff for what he was implying. "How could you possibly know that?" she asked.

"Just doing my job." The sheriff frowned. "Let's see." He opened his small notepad. "You left Kelsey Price's house, dragging the deceased, who was agitated." The sheriff looked up, eyed her. "No mention of you leaving, Miss Hoyt."

"Phoebe was drunk. I was just helping her to the truck and Becca's house is on the way. We were driving her home," Grant said.

The sheriff sighed. "You left Miss Price's house around 1:20 a.m. and the bridge is a ten-minute drive, but the ambulance wasn't called until 2:01 a.m. Can you explain that gap, son? That thirty-minute gap?"

Becca tried to sit up but couldn't, and fell back in her hospital bed. "He was sober, I swear. I was with him all night, he had one beer, maybe two. I'll sign an official statement, anything you need." Grant placed his bandaged hand gently on her thigh; she smiled quietly to herself. "We were all knocked out and I was the first to wake up. That explains the gap.

Grant was passed out in the front for a while. I saw him the whole time."

The sheriff looked from one to the other. "It would be a serious crime if you were lying about any of this. Minors or not. A very serious crime." They both nodded solemnly. "Fine," he said. "If you remember anything else, let me know."

The sheriff left and the small room continued with its monitors and beeping and sterility and Becca watched as Grant dropped his chin to his chest.

"Thank you," she said. "For saying that about the deer, for protecting me."

Grant didn't raise his head, but when he spoke, he sounded cold and detached; she knew he'd started to grieve. "My sister would be alive if it weren't for you."

"But it was an accident. I didn't mean for this to happen," Becca whispered, tears stinging her eyes. "And I know we can get through this together—"

"No, not together. This was your fault, so I need time to process this alone. But I know you understand that we have to keep what really happened to ourselves."

"But—" Becca started to cry. How could she be losing him like this? "But what about our plans? Our future?"

"Listen to me—if people knew we were keeping things from Phoebe, and how angry she was when she found out about it, they might think we did this on purpose. You understand that, right? They might think that we wanted this to happen."

Becca opened her mouth but no words formed.

"I know you'll never forget what I just did for you. That

I lied to the sheriff, that I kept you out of jail. If it ever comes out that we were together and that you caused the crash and then lied about it, you'll go to prison. For killing her. For killing Phoebe."

Becca tried to swallow but found she couldn't. She was reeling at trying to understand the magnitude of what Grant had just done for her; how much he loved her.

She smiled weakly at him from her hospital bed, although he continued staring down into his lap.

"Thank you," she whispered. And then she repeated the words he'd just said, the words that would bind them together forever.

I'll never forget what you did for me.

GRANT

Grant stared hard out of his bedroom window to avoid thinking. About Sunday. About June Delroy asking him questions he didn't want to answer. About Becca starting to open her big mouth. He'd kept Becca hidden but close for a reason, and if she was straying from him, and about to ruin the punishing balance he'd worked so hard to maintain, he wasn't sure what he'd have to do. Grant's insides continued to corrode as the shred of control he'd held onto the last ten years came undone.

He rubbed the back of his neck to shake the feeling that someone had been in his room again. He'd been finding cigarette butts on the driveway recently, and neither he nor his mother smoked.

Outside, the fields and trees and sky were colorless, a ghostly white. The old barn was still off to the side of their property, like a speck of dirt in the corner of his eye. The slanting roof, the wooden boards that were no longer red but weather-beaten, neglected.

His mother had sworn repeatedly to tear it down but had never followed through. Because it had meant too much to Phoebe, he assumed.

Grant's shoulders tensed until they ached, as he tried to force back the memories that the sight of the barn had unleashed. Memories of when they were children and would spend entire weekends out there reading comics and devising plans to run away—to the city, to the moon, to anywhere far from here. Phoebe would draw maps on the wooden walls in chalk; excited, hopeful. As long as they were together, without their mother and the poison in their house, they'd be okay.

But aren't you afraid, he'd asked her once, *to leave home?*

Of course I am, Phoebe had answered. *But I'd rather be afraid somewhere out there, trying. And besides, I'll be with you.*

And then another rush like a wave, bearing down hard, of when they were older—a rare night that Phoebe had gone out with him.

They lay on their backs, legs propped up on the rough barn wall, and laughed, feverishly and uncontrollably, until the very last minute that they could sneak back into the house.

As they hurried from the barn, the sun was starting to rise, and Phoebe grabbed the back of his arm and said: Wait, Grant, let it break some more.

And he waited because she asked him to, and they stood in the field that was wet with dew, with grass up to their waists, until dawn broke and bled from red to orange to yellow. Phoebe smiled at him and then took his hand so they could swing their arms like when they were children.

In their contented silence walking to the house, in their clothes from the night before, Grant looked at Phoebe and wanted to ask her about the time she was six and she'd pocketed a pack of gum from the store.

Their mother had found the gum later that same night while doing the wash, and marched straight into his room, shaking him awake.

"So now you're a thief." She spoke in that measured tone that always scared him more than when she yelled. The tone that said: I know who you are, you can't hide from me.

"What?" Grant tried to sit, tried to wake up, tried to brace himself. "Mom, I didn't take anything—"

His mother tossed the foil package on his chest with a cruel laugh. "And a liar too."

"But I swear that's not mine. I didn't—"

"I asked you for the money but you said no."

His mother whipped her head around to where Phoebe was standing in the doorway. "Hush, Phoebe, it's late, get back to bed."

Phoebe tried to stand tall in the shadows of his moon-drenched room. "But Grant didn't take it, I did."

His mother turned slowly from Phoebe to him. He hoped she couldn't see the pounding of his small heart. "Grant made you do this? Made you steal?"

"No." Phoebe shook her head quickly, voice quivering. "Grant didn't know, I swear."

"Well." His mother left his bed and took Phoebe by the shoulders, pointed her gently back to her room. "Covering for your brother won't get you anywhere."

"But—"

"Get back to bed, Phoebe. Now."

Their mother woke them both at dawn the next morning, to drive them in loaded silence to the store. By the time they arrived, they were both in tears as Grant, aged eight, had to walk in alone to apologize to the manager for something he hadn't done.

It was the way the sun rose that morning, Grant figured, that made him remember that childhood cruelty. His mother had found the gum in Phoebe's pocket but would never believe that he'd had nothing to do with it.

Had that been the moment things solidified for them—he wanted to ask his sister as they held hands through the vast back fields. When he was eight years old, and Phoebe was six, and she'd decided she'd never get in trouble again for fear of him being blamed. That they would never truly be themselves, or seen—either of them. How unfair was that? Grant wanted to say to Phoebe. But he didn't bring it up because he didn't want to ruin the moment. He wanted to cling to it for as long as he could, for the last ever five minutes that they walked together, hand in hand, smiling quietly.

Grant knew that once they shut the front door, their mother would likely wake and accuse him of being a terrible influence. How dare he corrupt his little sister when she had exams coming up? What was he thinking, dragging her out with his degenerate friends?

And they'd both take the stairs to their rooms in silence, the lightness of their walk, of watching the sunrise together, evaporated.

Or worse, their mother would wake and say nothing to them at all. Accept their sneaking out, their transgression. Stand in the doorway of her bedroom, arms crossed over her chest, and nod at them, dismissing them without protest. A reaction he would normally be grateful for, but there was a new undercurrent between his mother and his sister, now that she was so close to leaving.

Something he couldn't quite put his finger on; was it tacit approval? Would his mother rather he drag Phoebe down than let her leave?

Was she really that cruel?

That morning was the last good memory he had of Phoebe, before things changed. Before Phoebe started spiraling, spending nights out there in the barn alone, pacing the old horse stalls, writing fanatically in her journal, trying to figure out how to fix him, how to get him back on track. The more he flailed, the harder she tried to save him, like he was some equation that she could eventually solve. Like he wasn't just a regular kid from a regular town who didn't know any better, who was seventeen years old and struggling with the crippling weight of the pressure to do well in school, do well on the field, be something worthy of her efforts—when maybe he just wasn't capable like she was of carving a different path.

Phoebe had been growing more frustrated with every fight, with every rigid conviction that *he was better than this*; but how could she have known that? What had she seen in him that he couldn't any longer?

He felt the familiar aching in his chest, the quickening of air in and out of his lungs. *Phoebe*, he thought, and then said it aloud: "*Phoebe.*" Because he didn't want to forget the feeling of her name in his mouth.

"Yes?"

Grant looked quickly over his shoulder, frightened, but his bedroom was empty. Just the small desk in the corner, his bed, his closet. He strode nervously across the floor to fling open the closet door. It banged against the wall, but the closet too was empty. Phoebe was not crouched in the back corner, long bloodied hair dripping across her face, ready to spring out and accuse him of being weak, of being a coward and a liar, of always taking the easy way out, of letting her down.

Grant shook his head and screwed his eyes shut. He was really losing it. He sat on his bed, trying to get a hold of himself. He didn't deserve such a beautiful memory of his sister delighting in dawn breaking, a new day beginning. A brief respite from the load she'd carried. Not just for herself, but for him. No, he was worthy only of the memories that repulsed him, like the first time Phoebe had threatened him.

She'd demanded to go to a party with him at Trey Munn's place, a guy he knew she didn't like. He should have just said no, but another argument would expend energy he no longer had. Lately, Phoebe was exhausting him.

Trey had brewed vats of moonshine in the decrepit bathtub in the cellar, a new recipe that still tasted like lighter fluid but was bright purple this time. They drank out of whatever they could get their hands on—plastic cups, bowls, the caps of bottles.

Phoebe was preoccupied, fidgeting on the only couch in the living room. It was mustard yellow with just one cushion and stains that were hard to avoid. She didn't talk to anyone—it wasn't her crowd—but kept looking around as if waiting for someone.

She would get up to change the music sometimes, something that increasingly grated on him as he stood in the corner chatting idly with guys from the team, watching her. No one else seemed to mind though, not when it was Phoebe doing it. When Phoebe was doing it, it was clever, as if her presence alone elevated their own circumstances.

Late, when AJ Hill walked through the door into the sweating living room, Phoebe sprang up and pulled him aside. Grant stiffened, and watched them closely until he'd had enough. Then he walked up to them and shoved AJ so hard into the wall that he split his bottom lip. Phoebe was horrified.

AJ looked incredulously at his own fingers, shiny with blood. "What the fuck, man?"

"Get out of my sister's face."

"Me?" AJ laughed at him, blood dripping down his chin. "She's in my *face, asking a lot of questions about you. About your stats, if you're skipping practices, if Coach is still happy, if*

you're still going to get that goddamn scholarship. Just talk to your fucking sister, man. Leave me out of your shit." He stood tall, menacing and wild-eyed, but then seemed to decide against fighting the quarterback of his own team. "Asshole," AJ muttered and lumbered off.

"Phoebe, you have to stop this, you have to trust me," Grant hissed. "You have to stop this—please."

She ripped herself away from him and went to find something else to drink, and he let her go, trying not to make a scene. He knew she suspected he was keeping things from her—a girl, probably more—and was hell-bent on keeping him clean, focused. She'd never allow a relationship that could drive a wedge between them and chain him to West Wilmer.

Grant grabbed a beer from the rusting outside fridge and sat on the rotting porch until he'd calmed down enough to go back in to find his sister.

Despite the blaring music and the dense, pulsing crowd, Phoebe had passed out on the couch. Grant's car was in the shop, so he picked her up and carried her home. It was over two miles, but she was light and he was drunk. As soon as he put her down on their driveway, she fell to her knees and threw up and giggled, like her body was surprising her, even after all that moonshine and the relentless stress that came with trying to sculpt him into a better man than he was. Phoebe reached behind her without looking, her head slung forward, hand swaying in the air, and grabbed the corner of his jersey to wipe her mouth. She knew he'd be near her, and despite everything he smiled; his sister still needed him. Phoebe still needed him.

She angled her head. "I know what you're doing," she said. "I'll stop it if you don't, I swear." And then she vomited again.

That was the first time she'd threatened him, but not the last. He should have paid closer attention, considered what Phoebe was capable of in order to never leave him behind, to drag him forward—even if it meant he was kicking and screaming.

Just us, we'll be okay.

"Grant!" his mother called from downstairs. He closed the curtains, shutting out the barn, Phoebe.

His phone rang. He didn't recognize the number, thought maybe it was the pharmacy with his prescription refill. He had his hand on the knob of the bedroom door when he answered. "Yeah?"

"Mr. Dean—Grant Dean?"

He paused in the hallway, clenched his jaw. "Yes?"

"Great—hi. It's Lisa Stewart from the *Gazette*. I left a couple of voicemails and managed to speak with your mother yesterday."

Grant stopped at the top of the stairs. "Now's not a good time—"

"I'll be quick. My editor grew up in the town over from yours, so this is a bit of a pet project for him. I've been assigned a small feature on the West Wilmer bridge—"

Static surged through his ear. He pulled the phone away and then pressed it to his forehead. If he hung up, she'd call back, he could tell. "Okay?"

"Great—so there's a vote being held next week—"

"I'm late for work."

"Just a sentence or two on how you feel, and how you'll be voting?"

"No sentence. And against it."

"Can I ask why? I could make it anonymous."

He doubted that. "My sister, Phoebe, I'm not sure if you know—"

"Wouldn't be doing my job if I didn't know. So tragic, I'm sorry—"

"Yes, well, she loved it up there, so taking it down feels wrong."

The scratch of pen on paper. "And, about the night she died, there was a span of about thirty minutes—"

Grant hung up as he walked into the living room.

"Here," his mother said from behind him.

Through the living room window, he watched a black crow land in the tree outside. Grant turned to face her and she drew her robe around her waist. The bluish skin of her bare ankle peeking out from above her slippers disgusted him.

She blinked slowly; he noticed that her eyes were watering. "Here," she repeated, walked closer to him, fingering the edges of an old picture frame. "You look just like him. Can you take it to the cellar?"

Grant swallowed. It was in the hardness of her voice, and the way she was looking him directly in the eye. *I know you*. Perhaps she savored it, this hateful spite, and brought it out when she wanted to feel something other than her grief.

He waited for her face to blank again, to become expressionless, and thought back to ten years ago, when his own mother hadn't picked him up from the hospital.

Grant had sat on the hard plastic bench outside the hospital for an hour, and then two, the realization slowly dawning on him that his mother was not coming despite knowing he'd been discharged—he'd heard the nurse place the call.

It had been an unseasonably warm day, and he'd stared at the sun hanging so low that it skimmed the horizon until his eyes burned, and he understood that although things had always been bad with his mother—terrible even—things would now be worse.

Grant took the photograph from her now. In it, his handsome father was sitting on the stoop of their house, grinning easily at the camera, a bottle of beer held casually in his hand. The trees on the property were shorter, but everything else was exactly the same as it was today. Except he was gone. And so was Phoebe.

His mother headed back to her room, dead silence trailing her. "Thank you."

Always with the pristine manners, the pleases and thank yous. Everything between them was a transaction; the coldness of their interactions was unbearable. He considered blurting it all out, just to get an honest reaction from her, but didn't. "I miss her too, you know," he said.

His mother flinched. And then kept walking away from him.

Grant moved down the hall to the cellar door. Each stair groaned under his weight. He watched the dust below his shoes being kicked to the bottom, settling. The cellar was low and unfinished, and when he hit the uneven floor, he could smell dank soil and the must of spoiled root vegetables—those centuries-old earthen smells.

He used the light of his phone to find the fraying string to turn on the light, but it just pulled and swung in the air; the socket was empty. Maybe his mother had removed the bulb on purpose.

The cellar ran the length of the house. The shelves propped against the dirty brick wall had once acted as a pantry, but were now bare but for the odd can, distended with age, long forgotten. Rusting, bloated surfaces from which spiders could weave their cotton-thick webs.

Grant reached the back corner with the growing stacks of pictures. He used his phone to look at the photo he held one last time.

Morris Edward Dean, husband to Ellen, father of two, who was now rarely mentioned or thought of, although his loss still lingered. Grant had been two years old when his father died and had not one single memory of him. Not an image or a smell; just a deep void and a limitless well of disappointment; that he was disappointed in Grant when he died, and that he would be disappointed in him now. Grant touched his arm, could feel the warm metal as if it were there.

Grant placed the picture on the pile, squinted. His breath caught. He bent over, touched the brown cover, the soft leather. Phoebe's journal. It had aged poorly and was now moldy and ripped. His mother must have sent him down to the cellar holding the framed ghost of his father so he'd see it. Leaving the journal in Phoebe's bedroom hadn't been enough; she wanted to make damn sure he was faced with Phoebe's absence, as if he'd ever been able to forget it. To torture him. But he refused to open it, to read what she'd written about him, to know all the horrible things she'd thought in the days before she died.

"Why are you still lying?"

Grant spun on his heels, dropped his phone, extinguishing the light, pitching himself into absolute darkness.

"You lied to Harley. And that woman on the phone. I hated the bridge. I was afraid of heights. Why are you so against taking it down?" Phoebe laughed, the childish burst echoing around him in the cave, tearing at his bare throat, his bare neck. "What don't you want them to find?"

"I'm sorry," Grant choked out, bending for his phone. "Do you know that? How sorry I am?"

"You're sorry?" Phoebe's small voice was close to him in the dark; if he reached out, could he touch her? Would he want to? "Sorry?" Phoebe repeated, but her voice had changed and was now filled with wet; she coughed, spluttered, was choking. "I can't breathe. Grant, I can't breathe. Help me. *Me*."

Grant reached frantically, blindly, into the void for her.

"Grant, I can't breathe, why are you standing there, who are you talking to? What did you do?"

He turned and fumbled his way to the bottom of the stairs, away from her voice, her fear.

"Why aren't you calling an ambulance? Help me. I can't breathe."

Grant flew up the stairs into the warmth and safety of the house. His breath was harsh and sharp and ached inside of him. He crossed the living room floor, flung the front door open, stumbled down the steps, bent over at the waist to try to catch his breath; screamed down into the dirt until he was winded and empty.

BECCA

Becca smoothed her hair and hurriedly climbed out of her car into the biting evening wind.

"You okay, Becca? Been sitting out here a while," Heather said. Becca had been volunteering with Reg's wife for a few years. "On the phone with your mother again?"

"Unfortunately," Becca answered. She felt groggy from the strange nap, and unsettled after remembering the hospital and Grant's promises. Or had they been threats? She blinked hard and kept talking so that Heather would stop looking at her with such concern. "Ever since Mrs. Dean announced the memorial, my mother cannot stop calling to talk to me about it. Just now she was wondering what she should bake for Sunday." Becca was glad the lies came easily. "I suggested she drop off cupcakes but she won't be staying; she's playing bridge with her sister that night, she lives in Benton."

"That's nice of her—I should bake something myself to bring."

Becca nodded and they walked together from her car to the

small animal shelter. "Hey, Heather? How are you—everything okay at home?"

"Everything's good—great, actually. Reg and I are thinking of taking that cruise we keep talking about."

Becca couldn't tell if Heather was being truthful or not. "You know you can talk to me, if you want. About anything."

Heather gave her a warm smile. "Sure, of course."

Becca smiled back. Maybe Reg was taking her on a cruise to make up for the cheating that Grant had confided in her about. "So, what's on the to-do list for tonight?"

"Someone dropped off a box of kittens infested with fleas, and all the temporary cages need to be cleaned." Heather held the door open for her. "Hope you brought your nose plugs."

They walked inside and were immediately hit with a flood of harsh animal sounds. It was chaotic at the shelter, but Becca liked that she was in a completely different world, somewhere where the sounds were so primal and loud that they emptied her mind of the things that were plaguing her. What she'd let slip to June, the intimidating look on Grant's face at the store, the unrelenting burden of that night; the secrets and lies. Becca closed her eyes and inhaled the chaos deeply, until everything melted away.

Avoidance, Dr. Murphy's voice whispered in her ear. "Leave me alone," Becca muttered under her breath. She was much more than a paragraph in a medical textbook; she was complicated. So what if she liked to escape sometimes? At least she was doing something useful with her spare time.

Trina, the vet tech, looked up briefly from the cluttered reception desk. "Evening," she said, and then went back to sorting meds for the animals. She'd say maybe one or two more words her entire shift. Becca didn't like Trina at all; she didn't ask Becca anything about herself, and Becca was a volunteer! You'd think it was the least Trina could do—ask how her day was, how the drive over was, what her plans were for the weekend, how she was coping with the memorial coming up. It was downright rude.

Becca dropped her purse in the tiny break room and then tied on her purple apron and walked back into the front, pulling on her plastic gloves with a satisfying snap.

A woman had entered the shelter and stood now in the front holding a gray carrier.

"Harley?" Becca smiled at her. "Hi."

"Oh!" Harley startled visibly. "Hi?"

The confused look on Harley's face ruined Becca's mood instantly; did she not remember her? After everything she'd been through? Becca had a mind to set her straight, but clamped down hard on her back teeth so she wouldn't.

That's my girl, Grant whispered in her ear.

Recognition dawned on Harley's face and she smiled thinly. "Becca—goodness—I didn't recognize you with your hair so long. And I had no idea you worked with Heather. She's never mentioned it."

"Coming up on three years volunteering here, but you're right, it's been a while since we ran into one another."

It hadn't been a while. Just a few weeks ago, Becca had helped load groceries into Harley's minivan while she held a shrieking toddler who wouldn't let go of Becca's hair. "It's nice to see you, Harley, you look great. What a cute little coat."

"Sweet, isn't it? Bit of a splurge, but look..." Harley peered through the carrier's metal door. "Sabrina hasn't been eating. It's been a couple of days and it could be nothing—but thought it best to bring her in. The kids would kill me if anything happened to the damn thing."

Becca looked to Trina for help with the now-hissing cat, but her head was still down, sorting pills, scooping them into their orange bottles.

Harley offered her the carrier with a thrust.

"A black cat named Sabrina." Becca shoved her hands into the deep pockets of her apron. "Cute."

"My oldest named her; she just loves that old show." Harley put the carrier down by her feet, impervious to the awful screeching sounds of her mangy pet. "Such a small world, isn't it? You working here—three years, you said? And I was just on the phone with Kelsey on my way over, and you'll never guess who went into her salon today."

"Who's that?"

"June Delroy. What a sad thing, her mother passing so young—don't think she was even sixty. Refused treatment, my mom heard, which makes it sadder still, but guess she didn't have much to live for. Now that poor girl's alone in that house."

There was something in the way that Harley was looking at her that began to worry Becca. "June went to get her hair done?" Had June repeated anything to Kelsey that Becca had said? "Good for June, to be getting out. I went by her place to pay my respects, but I didn't stay long. June was really tired, you know, a little *delicate*, so it was a really quick drop-in. We barely chatted."

"That's exactly what June told Kelsey—that you dropped by with a frozen lasagna. Nice of you to do that. I should bring her something myself, Kelsey said she looks real thin."

Grant's face flashed before Becca's eyes, and she was very worried now that June had said something to Kelsey. Becca looked at the cat in the carrier and wondered if Harley had come here on purpose, just to question her and make her uncomfortable. "June's really struggling—she seemed exhausted and a little out of it to be honest, which is normal with everything she's going through, but like I said, I didn't stay long, just dropped off dinner and had to rush right back to work."

"Poor thing. June told Kelsey that no one came to her mother's funeral, that it was just her alone at the cemetery." Harley shrugged. "I guess everyone's thinking about Phoebe and Sunday—Mrs. Dean asked me to speak at it, and I don't think I can but maybe I should. I don't know what to do about it."

Becca didn't know what to say, and Harley waved her hand in the air and went on. "Because I blame myself sometimes, for all of it. Oh, I know..." Harley waved her hand again. "Does that sound silly? But I do, because Phoebe was my best friend and I should have paid more attention to how unhappy she was. She was so upset that night."

Becca tucked her hair behind her ears nervously. "I don't remember her being upset."

That wasn't entirely true.

Phoebe spotted Becca and walked over to her through Kelsey's crowded living room. "Becca?" she said, smiling a strange, fore-boding smile. "You've been around him all night—where's my brother? I really need to talk to him."

Becca shrugged sharply, then hiccuped.

Phoebe smiled again, but the look in her eyes was searing. "It's important that I find him and I know you know where he is—so just tell me."

Becca swallowed, slightly rattled. "Upstairs."

Phoebe craned her long pale neck to look up at the second floor. "He's still hiding from me then."

Becca had already had far too much to drink but gulped back the rest of her flat beer; she was very put off by the charged mood Phoebe was in.

"You should know," Becca had to shout over the blaring music, "that I really love him."

Phoebe looked slowly around the packed living room before settling back on her. "You should stay away from him." Her eyes were like small lit fires on her beautiful face. "Okay?"

Becca was ruffled instantly, felt the heat of the crowd press-ing down on her, the beer thrumming loudly in her veins, embold-ening her. "And if I don't, Phoebe? What then?"

"He's my brother." Phoebe tilted her head, and even drunk she seemed able to see right through Becca. "I want what's best for him, and that means no distractions."

Becca's heart felt tight. "We have real plans, Phoebe."

"Do you?" Phoebe smiled, her hair falling so perfectly over her shoulders. "Well, so do we." And then she turned, and tripped up the stairs. Becca tried to grab her arm but missed.

She huffed, furious. She was at this party just like everyone else, and she did not deserve to be dismissed—not by Phoebe Dean, not by anyone.

Harley leaned forward and peered at her curiously. "Your earrings." She reached out to touch one. "They're pretty." Harley looked puzzled but then shrugged her shoulders. "Like I said, I wish I'd paid better attention to how upset Phoebe was. Maybe I could have fixed it. Stopped the whole thing from happening."

A dog started howling and Harley looked toward the back of the clinic.

Becca stepped away from her. "She seemed happy enough to me."

Harley took Becca's hand in hers and smiled sadly. "I'm sorry for what you've been through, Becca. That you were dragged into this—that must be awful for you."

Becca cleared her throat. The look on Harley's face was making it hard for her to keep biting her tongue.

Outsider. Harley's eyes screamed at her. *You're no one*.

"It's like a second tragedy in a way." Harley squeezed her hand gently and Becca tugged it away, shoved it deep into her apron pocket, started digging at her cuticles. "There was this terrible accident, and to just be so *randomly* driving you home?" Harley shook her head sympathetically, and when Becca didn't answer, she tilted her head like a parrot. "What's more tragic than you being in the wrong place at the wrong time?"

Not one of us. Never one of us. Nothing. No one.

Frustrated tears sprang to Becca's eyes.

It was all my fault, Becca wanted to scream, *and then Grant lied to protect me.*

I am someone.

"Hun, are you getting upset?" Harley clucked. "Shoot—it must be hard wondering why *you*." Harley opened her purse, rummaged around, handed her a wad of used tissues. "Phoebe would hate that this happened to you; she was always such a stickler for fairness."

We were together, you bitch. Becca wished desperately to be able to speak, to prove Harley wrong. *Grant was going to leave everything for me, you wretched cow. Football, his precious fucking sister, everything.*

I am someone.

Becca felt a tear slide down her face.

I am not invisible.

"Oh—Becca." Harley covered her mouth with her hand. "No one deserves what you went through. If you had just waited an extra five minutes or something, right? Taken a cab?"

Inside her apron pocket, Becca balled her hot hands into tight fists.

Don't. Grant's voice was slithering into her ears. *Do not say anything.*

O happy dagger, this is thy sheath.

Becca glared at Harley's overplucked eyebrows and the pimple on her chin. Harley, who drove a beat-up minivan. Harley, who had four feral children and a husband who hadn't graduated high school and only wore sweatpants. "We were a lot closer than you think," Becca exhaled in a thin stream. "Me and Grant."

Harley narrowed her eyes. "Kelsey mentioned that June said something like that."

Becca's stomach seized. "What did June say?"

Harley's smile froze on her face. "Oh, nothing really, just that June was asking about her brother—remember Wyatt?—and then something about you and Grant having a history, like before the accident. Honestly, nothing that made much sense, but we can't blame her. Like you said, June must be having a hard time dealing with the death of her mother—"

"Nothing that made much sense?" Becca thought her heart might explode. "How can you be so sure? Were you there that night with us?"

Harley's smile cranked bigger. "No, but no one knew Phoebe and Grant better than—"

"Phoebe attacked me, you know." Becca felt herself snap. "And we were together, me and Grant. We had real plans."

Becca watched Harley's face redden, pleased to have wiped the fake smile from it. But what was left behind was far worse, and Becca took a weak step backward, away. Because what was now plastered on Harley's face wasn't sympathy or warmth or compassion, but pity.

Pity.

Becca's insides curdled and boiled. She didn't trust herself not to say anything else she'd regret, and so she turned and stormed out of the shelter.

TEN YEARS AGO

10:40 p.m.

There wasn't enough booze in the house to lighten AJ Hill's foul mood. The party that he hadn't wanted to attend in the first place felt like a ticking time bomb.

Heather was trailing Reg around like a lost puppy. Becca had showed, something he was pretty sure went against the restraining order, but she hadn't noticed him, which was good. She'd been staring at Grant all night, which suited AJ fine. Let him *deal with her.*

Becca had probably always had a thing for Grant—King Grant—like half the school, but did they know what he was really like? AJ touched his lip that hadn't quite healed from when Grant had shoved him into the wall at Trey's house.

"Leave my sister alone!" Grant had shouted, as if AJ were hitting on her. Ha. Phoebe would probably die a virgin, she was so goddamn uptight.

Phoebe had grabbed AJ as soon as he'd walked into the party at Trey's, as if she'd been waiting for him all night. She was tipsy and firing off questions about Grant and football, about Coach, but also about money. If AJ knew of any pawnshops in the city and how they worked.

"Can you buy things back?" she asked.

"You need money?" he snorted. "Won't your scholarships cover everything?"

She looked away, shook her head.

"Those aren't places for someone like you, Phoebe—"

"Never mind," she said hurriedly as Grant stormed over, looking extremely pissed off. "It's research for an essay I'm working on. Just forget it."

Out of the corner of his eye, AJ saw Becca dancing in the corner of the room by herself. He watched with amusement as she reached out when Phoebe walked by her but was ignored, which made her angry. Something was definitely brewing between Becca and the Deans. Maybe Phoebe had warned her to stay away from Grant. There was a rumor going around that Grant had brought a girl home from a game last week and Phoebe had hidden the poor girl's shoes, so she'd had to drive home barefoot. AJ gulped back half of his beer. Not so perfect, was she?

Now AJ watched Phoebe, who was clearly wasted, stumbling to one of the windows in Kelsey's living room. It was dark and pouring rain, but she put her hands on the sill and looked outside for several minutes, and then looked at Grant, who was staring daggers at her from across the room.

Yawn. AJ needed another beer. He walked to the kitchen, nodding at Trey and a couple other guys from the team, and annoyed that every other piece of furniture had been moved into the garage. Where did Kelsey expect everyone to sit? There were at least fifty people already and it wasn't even that late.

The kitchen was crowded, but he squeezed through for a turn at the nearly empty keg.

He had to use the john. AJ left the kitchen and climbed the stairs, passing a couple that he didn't recognize making out, side-stepping empty beer bottles and a couple of cigarette butts. He walked down the hallway, and stopped outside the bathroom. He could hear shouting, and put his hand on the knob, but then the door swung open and knocked him backward.

"What the fuck?" he said as Harley rushed past him in tears. Grant was leaning against the sink, arms folded over his chest, red-faced and heaving so hard AJ wondered if he was high. "Everything okay in here?" AJ grinned.

"Fuck off." Grant slammed the door in his face.

"That's one upset girl, man—you fucking Harley now? Your sister's best friend? How you going to get out of that one?"

AJ snorted at the door, picturing Grant spiraling behind it. This was maybe even better than catching him with drugs. Because who knew what Phoebe would do if she ever found out.

WYATT

The Day before the Phoebe Dean Memorial

Wyatt's feet were soaked, but he left them slack in the water. The cold spread to his thighs, his waist. He didn't mind it, it kept him alert, the agonizing deep freeze overtaking his nauseating headaches, the rot in his gut, the knowledge that he was fading, fast.

He'd woken in the middle of the night, trembling, and had been unable to fall back to sleep. The tossing and turning had left him dizzy and then disoriented, as if he were drowning in his own bed, and so he'd waited until dawn and then run here, the door to the house creaking as he shut it, as if the house needed as much of a break from him as he needed from it. And if he was going to be uncomfortable and cold, he'd rather it be outside, where he wasn't claustrophobic or contained, where he didn't have to constantly fight with his sister, begging her to stop asking him things he knew she wasn't ready to hear the answers to.

Coming back to June had required more of him than he'd expected it to, or maybe he had softened. He snorted onto the water, a spitting bark, expelling the spineless thought that had wedged into his mind—June's influence, no doubt. He wasn't soft. But June had started standing up to him, even raising her voice to him. The color in her cheeks proved that she was healing, that she was getting stronger. Wyatt wasn't sure if he was a good person, but he did care about her. He loved her, in his own way, and he wanted to make sure she was really ready for the course of her life to be changed. Again.

No. June would say, lip quivering. *That can't be true, you're lying to me.*

But she'd know it was the truth when she saw it in his eyes. Eyes didn't lie; eyes couldn't lie. And she'd probably look sad and pathetic and Wyatt would rage inside, because although June was getting stronger, it was taking more effort than he'd expected it to and he was running out of time. But he would hold on for as long as he could—until he'd set his truth free. About what had really happened that night.

Wyatt craned his neck suddenly, toward movement he'd seen out of the corner of his eye, toward the bridge that hung high above him. Flecks of yellow crime scene tape were still nailed to parts of the railing. That wonderful old bat, Wyatt thought; she'd never know what her foolish accident had unleashed. Forcing everyone to think again about the bridge that he'd loved so much. There was something about being so high above such dangerous rushing water that had always thrilled him.

Wyatt smiled to himself in the shadows as he watched a

figure look down into the river near where he sat. He shrank back instinctively, but he was too well hidden for anyone to register it was him; no one would think he'd be down here. He knew no one thought about him at all.

But they would soon.

Wyatt had decided on his run here that it was time. That the memorial would be fitting—poetic even—for his big reveal. He'd left that night, and now ten years later he'd come back to fuck things up for the rest of them; that goddamn family.

Wyatt wiped the mud from his legs, felt a welt of a scab through a rip in his faded jeans. He had woken with new bruises and worried he was bleeding internally. He shrugged it off; he'd worry about it later. Maybe it was just stress—dealing with June was taking a lot out of him.

Wyatt scrambled back up the steep incline on leaden legs, wheezing and gasping for air, to the now-empty bridge. Whoever had been there was gone. Good. He felt a breeze, and shivered as he stood in the spot where it had all started ten years ago.

So, tomorrow. It was perfect.

They'd never see it coming.

GRANT

Grant had overslept after waking in the middle of the night, afraid, sure that he was being watched. The moon had been bright, the curtains open; shadows prowled in the corner, by the door, at the foot of his bed. He'd opened his mouth to scream out her name, and then closed it, shaking. He was losing it. Had things ever been this bad? Maybe in the beginning, but not since. Shouldn't they be getting easier, not harder? Was someone watching the house? Was he in danger? Did he need a gun?

He'd been restless the rest of the night, sleeping in fits and starts, sweating, tossing and turning, railing against the last couple of days and what the next couple might bring. Railing against reality. He'd finished all his stronger pills, weeks ahead of when he should have. And still, he was constantly rattled.

He couldn't bear seeing his mother that morning, so he skipped breakfast. He'd had no appetite lately, anyway. Just another thing that he'd lost.

Grant walked through the sun-drenched house, hurrying to get ready for work as best he could with nerves that were completely shot, then out the front door and down the stairs to the driveway.

He froze in front of his car. He blinked. He stared. He blinked again. Grant rubbed his eyes to erase what he was seeing, but no, there was indeed a bleached deer skull resting on the hood. It was old and worn yellow-white, something you might stumble across in the woods and lug home with pride; but here… He shook his head quickly. Was this really happening? He leaned over, hands on his thighs, staring unseeing at the ground, trying to think.

He'd throw it in the dumpster behind the factory, then he could forget about it altogether, force away the wave that was barreling down on him. Grant could pretend this was a mistake; after all, he pretended a lot. Maybe all he was was pretense: that he was normal, that he was deserving of life. Grant scanned the clear morning sky, searching for the eagle or vulture or other large bird that might have dropped the skull. He looked behind him to the deep woods and thick tree line, trying to spot the retreating vandal, the bear, the wolf.

He stepped closer to his car, clutching his keys in his fist nervously, as if the skull might leap off the hood and attack him. It stayed unmoving, blind with its empty eye sockets and black nasal cavity, chipped bone and cracked antlers, resting on his hood like it was an altar, demanding reverence. He stepped closer still and held his breath and used his finger to trace the scratches surrounding the bone in the cool metal of his car. There were several and they were intentional. Grant accepted that this was in fact happening, someone was trying to spook him, and he'd have to take care of it right away. He couldn't let anyone in town see the scratches and brazen vandalism and get any ideas; couldn't let the cancer continue its fatal spread unchecked.

Grant looked around again before he snatched the skull from the hood, and then dropped heavily into the front seat, tossing the skull in the back. He rubbed his hands on his pant legs as the sun beat down on his face through the windshield. Tomorrow was the memorial and things were spinning completely out of control. How would he get through the day?

He knew Phoebe was in the car with him. He could sense her judgment, it filled his lungs like air, but he couldn't bring himself to turn around or look at her in the mirror. He couldn't stomach her bloodied face, her cadaverous black eyes, her long wet hair.

"That's creepy," Phoebe said. "There's a price tag under the antler. Who do you think left it there? It's not as big as the one you hit, though. You did hit a deer, right? That's how I died?"

When Phoebe started giggling, Grant opened his mouth to scream but no sound came out.

JUNE

Evelyn Lloyd had asked for her car back, but they'd needed food, as June's appetite was improving. She'd been walking back from town for about twenty minutes, the bags of groceries growing heavy in her hands. The road snaked on ahead of her, gray lines disappearing over the horizon. She walked as close to the shoulder as she dared. She didn't want to slip and fall into the steep weedy ditch.

June heard a motor in the distance—or more like the chug of an engine. She looked both ways down the long stretch of dusty pavement, but they were empty. She kept walking, moving the bags from one hand to the other when one started aching. She'd thrown on Wyatt's knit sweater before leaving the house, but the cuffs were much too long and were getting in the way.

After another minute she could tell that the car was coming up behind her, and that it was in rough shape. She could also tell that it was slowing down. June appreciated this. The odd time that she'd been passed that morning, the cars had sped by her as if she were invisible. Once it had been a big growling pickup truck that was driving so fast she'd had to jump out of the way to avoid being hit.

The car came up behind her but didn't pass. June felt hot exhaust on the backs of her legs. She looked over her shoulder uneasily. The driver waved.

She stopped, confused, squinting through the streaky windshield into the front seat. And then walked over to it. "Wyatt?"

"Need a ride?"

"Where'd you get this car?"

Wyatt grinned, pleased with himself. "Hop in, you look tired."

June used her free hand to shield her eyes from the sun. "But this isn't Mrs. Lloyd's car."

"That's right, it's not."

June frowned at how rusty the car was, how the engine sputtered and choked, making it sound like the car was sick. It was a jerry-rigged pile of red pieces; the mirror on the passenger side was attached with a leather belt. "Is it even safe to drive this thing?"

"Old Evelyn wanted her car back and you said you were tired of walking into town. You said your feet hurt, that your legs ache in the mornings, so I found a car."

"You just *happened* to find this—"

Wyatt laid on the horn, startling her. She fumbled not to drop the groceries, but heard some eggs crack in the process. A group of crows—*a murder*, she corrected herself—burst out of the field beside her. June held her breath as she watched them soar away until they were specks, and then gone.

Wyatt reached across the front seat to open the passenger-side door. "Come on, haven't got all day."

"No? You really busy, huh?" June sat down reluctantly on leather that was hot and hard and split open like something had attacked it. On the dash was an old-fashioned lighter that would pop out with a glowing red coil. She'd burned her finger on one when she was six. "Do I recognize this car?" June asked suddenly. The car had a strange smell of corrosion.

"How should I know?"

June checked the back seat, but it was empty. She reached over her shoulder but there wasn't a seatbelt. She shut the door and Wyatt hit the accelerator. He had to push his foot all the way down for it to work. The waft of leaking gasoline made her dizzy.

"So?" Wyatt asked. "Am I helpful or what? You glad I'm back or what?"

June looked out the window as they drove, at the dead stalks of corn, the patchwork fields, the scarecrows flapping their tattered rags in the wind. "Did you steal this car, Wyatt?"

He shot her a look and then turned back to the road. He tapped his hands lightly on the steering wheel. His thumb looked bruised enough to be broken and he was missing the fingernail on his index finger, which needed to be cleaned and bandaged or an infection could take root. He kept flicking his eyes to the rearview mirror. He was restless. He was also very pale. She was finding bloodied tissues in all of the garbage cans and had found a fat molar in the sink that morning.

June worried that Wyatt was much sicker than he was letting on, and was keeping it from her. Would he do that to her? To re-emerge after so long, to give her hope for the two of them, only to let her down again? She focused harder out the window, tried to find something to distract herself: there, above the matchstick treetops on the horizon, a large bird in the cloudless blue sky. She studied it, the wingspan, the predatory nature of its deliberate, swooping circles. "Look," she said, pointing. "A turkey vulture."

"You still crazy obsessed with birds, huh?"

"Not *obsessed*—"

"From that book I bought you when we were kids? With all the stupid pictures?"

"Never mind," June sighed, her throat itchy like just before she'd start to cry. "How did you find this car then—did you buy it? With a credit card or something? Because you know we can't go into any more debt—I told you how much debt Dad left us with. No more debt, Wyatt."

"How many times do I have to say that I am not like fucking Dad, June. Jesus, don't worry about the car."

"Grant said you owed money to bad people, so if you're still in debt to them—"

"June!" Wyatt shouted, and swerved hard on the road. "*Bad people*? What does that even mean? I'll tell you what it means: Grant is a goddamn liar. And besides, what did our sweet daddy say about debt? Think, June."

June swallowed nervously. "That it never dies." She swallowed again. Wyatt was driving recklessly; would he run them off the road just to prove a point?

"Debt," Wyatt snorted, not letting it go. "All this talk of fucking debt. Think for yourself, Juney, think—did anyone come around the house looking to collect after I'd left? No? So please shut the fuck up and let me drive."

June's lip started to tremble, a flood of memories rushing at her—of the sheriff beating on their door in the middle of the night, explaining indifferently to her sobbing mother that Wyatt had been arrested again. This time for stealing stereos from cars. This time for minor assault after a track meet. This time for shoplifting. This time for possession; not enough to throw him in jail, but close.

"What kind of drugs?" her father demanded.

June was listening from behind her closed bedroom door, terrified.

"I'm not at liberty to discuss—"

"Just tell me, Rick. If this were your son, if this were Gabe—"

"Steroids. Speed. Cocaine. Weed. I know it means he'll be cut from the team. Likely expelled," the sheriff said. "I'm sorry, Hank, there's nothing I can do."

Her father broke the window above their door with his fist the second the sheriff drove away, swearing that he'd never let Wyatt live this down—not again. He would not let a no-good son of his ruin his good name. June recognized the cruel irony—that Wyatt would be cut from the very thing he'd been driven to love by their father. Running in the dark, along the highway, through the woods sometimes, to the bridge; electrified by the movement of his legs and the cars that would speed by him—the only thing, he'd told her once, that made him feel good to be alive.

"Wy, if there's money, we need it for our bills, to turn the heat back on—"

"Fine—I borrowed the car! Happy? It was just sitting there at the back of the lot. No one will even notice it's gone, and don't I deserve some fucking credit? Aren't I giving you a ride when you're tired? And aren't you feeling a bit better now that I'm back? Eating something? Leaving the house?"

"You're right." June nodded, growing heated. "I am getting out of the house, but what about you? You're still hiding from everyone! How much longer can you refuse to tell me what you've done—"

"What *I've* done?" Wyatt looked over and smiled at her; his mouth inching up slowly at the corners.

"And you're going to return this car." June's heart pounded behind her ribs. "Before anyone knows it's gone. And then we can forget about it—but that's your only chance, Wy. Please don't get in any more trouble."

"We'll see, Juney. And don't you worry, I won't be hiding anymore, very, very soon." Wyatt laughed and placed his hand on her thigh; it felt heavy as lead. "Soon everyone will think of me when they think of that night—and not that goddamn family. Isn't that what Mom called them? *That goddamn family*? Well, not for long. Do you know why, Juney? Because I'm holding something very valuable in my hands. Do you know what that is?"

She shook her head, afraid.

"The truth."

June woke to the beating sound of feathers flapping. She expected a flurry of wings on her ceiling or trying to breach the window, but only bright sun flooded her eyes. She blinked at the pounding in her head, confused. She pulled the blankets down, sat up groggily, surprised she'd been able to nap. Then she stood and stretched and shuffled to the door of her bedroom. June caught herself starting to hum. She stopped dead, touched her throat and then her mouth.

Humming.

She smiled as she shut her bedroom door behind her. The walls of the hallway were empty, and had been for a while. June wondered if her mom had put away some pictures somewhere. Maybe she could hang one. They'd had a dog for a few years when they were kids; June thought there might be a picture with the three of them—the dog, her and Wyatt—in it.

Wyatt looked up from the kitchen table when he saw her. "You slept again." He seemed proud. "You look better, you needed it."

"Again?" June self-consciously touched her hair and then the back of her neck, remembering waking on the couch that morning but not remembering how she got there. "We should go to the cemetery today," she said. "You still haven't been."

"Sure."

"Is there enough gas?"

"What?"

"Is the tank full?"

Wyatt gave her a funny look.

"The cemetery is in Lyons. It's a fifteen-minute drive."

Wyatt sat back in his chair, annoyed. "Okay—and?"

June felt a breeze and wrapped her arms around her body. She looked at the window above Wyatt's head to see if it was open, but it wasn't. She avoided her brother's watchful eyes, resisted the urge to step away from him to hide in the dark hall. "Is there enough gas in that car to get us there? Or did you return it already?" June spoke softly, nervously. Was it the grief, which never really left her alone, or maybe the brief nap that was confusing her?

"Sure, I'll play along—what car, June?" Wyatt sighed loudly at her. "Do you mean Mrs. Lloyd's piece-of-shit Buick? She wanted it back, that's what you said after we went for ice cream yesterday."

June bit her lip and spoke to her feet on the floor. "Right, nothing," she mumbled, scared now of the vividness of the dream she'd just had where Wyatt had picked her up on the side of the road. She exhaled shakily, dispelling the images, the feeling of the car behind her legs, the eggs she'd felt break in the bag, the argument with her brother that had felt so real. That beat-up red car she remembered now as the one Wyatt had driven when they were teens, something he'd been proud of, had taken care of. Sweat rolled slowly down her body. It was just a dream, that was fine; it was good she was sleeping more, that was good.

"Are you okay?" Wyatt reached up to draw the curtains,

darkening the kitchen, hiding his face in the shadows. "Headaches again? Maybe you should eat something, you look a little pale."

"I'm fine." June flicked her wrist. "Let's go see if Mrs. Lloyd will let us use her car again, then we can go."

June left the kitchen and the house without waiting for him to follow. She took the crumbling steps two at a time, refusing to touch her thighs that she swore felt sore, as though she'd already been walking for miles.

BECCA

Becca drummed her fingers on the linoleum table and kept looking to the door. She couldn't stop fidgeting. There was an elderly couple in the booth ahead of hers, cloud-white heads bobbing, whispering loudly. They were talking about her, she assumed, probably deciding whether to come pay their respects ahead of tomorrow, to ask how she was doing, to tell her that she looked good for someone that must be going through a hard time right now.

They hobbled over on their matching canes.

"How's your mother, dear?" the old woman asked shrilly.

"She's doing fine."

"We'll expect you all to come next week, and vote to take that godforsaken thing down," the old man said, spittle forming in the corners of his mouth.

Becca knew Grant's wishes and sat back. "And what if I think it should stay up? The history alone—"

"God help you then, if there's a third life lost," the old man spat, and he and his wife clutched each other's arms and shuffled out of the diner, continuing to whisper loudly to one another.

Becca tried to stop fidgeting. She checked the time again. It was nearly 11 a.m.; he was already half an hour late. She scrolled through her phone to read his text from earlier, agreeing to meet for coffee in town at 10:30 a.m.

The waitress walked back over, bored. "Want anything yet?"

"No," Becca said, more sharply than she intended. "No, thank you—I'm still waiting."

The waitress smacked her gum and folded a notepad into her apron slowly. "I'll be back over then in a minute. I'm sure they're on their way."

Becca stared out of the diner's streaky window, trying to hold back tears. The place was too hot, had they never heard of air conditioning? The cook was whistling off-tune in the kitchen and it made her want to scream.

She watched a car pull into the lot and sat up straighter, only to deflate when she realized it was Kelsey Price. Becca leaned back in the booth as Kelsey walked through the front door and up to the kitchen window. "Hey, Vernon, is it ready for me?"

Becca shrank back even further as Vernon handed Kelsey a brown paper takeout bag. "Tell Mark he still owes me from our last game of cards."

"I'll be saying no such thing!" Kelsey laughed, and then glanced over her shoulder, spotting Becca. Her mouth made a little O before she flashed a quick smile and crossed the room to the booth. "Becca, your ears must be burning something fierce, because June Delroy was just in the salon yesterday and didn't your name come up in conversation? And I know you saw Harley last night at the animal shelter. You ran out, she said, without even saying bye." Kelsey brushed her bangs off her forehead. "You doing okay?"

Becca checked her watch again, could feel the waitress eyeing them as she leaned against the counter between the container of striped straws and glass pie display.

"Doing as good as can be expected at this time of year. Just waiting for Grant, actually—we're meeting for coffee, to catch up."

Kelsey motioned to the empty seat ahead of her. "He running late?"

"I'm early."

"I won't keep you then. Don't want my lunch getting cold—see you around, Becca. Oh, maybe at the Deans'? It's tomorrow, you planning to go?"

Becca flinched but managed a curt nod. "Yes, I'll be there."

Kelsey looked as though she wanted to say something else but just left with a quick nod. Becca slid down further in her seat. Her neck was damp and her mind was racing so fast she couldn't grab hold of it. What did Grant think he was doing? Avoiding her calls and texts for weeks and then running out on her at Flo's and now standing her up. Embarrassing her in front of everyone in town. She'd told him it was important that they talk ahead of the memorial, and now she was sitting here looking the fool. Again. She slid her sunglasses on so the waitress, who was openly staring now, wouldn't see her eyes filling with tears.

Grant hadn't even bothered to offer an excuse. As if this

date with her hadn't even occurred to him. As if she hadn't even entered his mind. He couldn't even be bothered to come up with a lie. And she knew he was capable of lying; she'd watched him do it.

Becca stared into the lot as a few cars drove by, but none turned in. She felt her body stiffen, her heart race, her anger bloom.

Becca's parents watched her like she was a spooked animal they were scared to approach. She frowned down at her plate. She couldn't get the waitress's pitying smile out of her mind, after she'd finally given up and rushed out of the diner, paying for two coffees when only one had been touched.

Becca reached for the wine in the middle of the table. "I'm having a terrible day."

The chandelier was too bright. Had her parents changed the lightbulbs on purpose? Higher wattage for an interrogation? She wouldn't put it past them.

"Dad, I'm literally begging you not to look at me like that—stop staring!"

Her father tightened his crossed arms. "We just care about you, Rebecca, and we know how things can get, how fragile you—"

"Shut up!" Becca sprang to her feet, dropping her fork and knife. "If you could stop bringing it up, for Christ's sake. You'd think it was me who died on that fucking bridge!" The panic that spread across her parents' hapless faces was far worse than their chronic worry, and Becca regretted the outburst immediately. Her blood curdled as she watched them exchange a long look.

They hadn't yet forced her into a mental hospital and thrown away the key, but it was a fear she had, and so she swiftly regrouped. "I went to see June like you suggested, Mom." Becca sat back down carefully. "Poor thing, you were right—she's in rough shape and needed the company."

"Oh—you did?" Her mother's eyes widened. "I knew she'd love to see you. What did you take her?"

"Lasagna. The expensive one."

Her mother nodded thoughtfully. "Good. How is the poor thing coping? What a tragedy, to lose her mother—"

Becca speared a green bean. "I just told you. She's a wreck, which is normal. It's hard you know—grief, trauma." Her parents exchanged another look above their plates and Becca chewed aggressively on the mushy bean. "But do you remember her brother, Wyatt? I guess there's still been no word from him. What a complete mess over there, I mean honestly. The whole place is a disaster, lights burned out, freezing inside; it was like a big black hole—"

"Shame. And that Hank Delroy," her father tutted. "To just up and leave his family after the boy did. I will never understand what drives some people to abandon their children. Gambling though—that's what people were saying back then."

Becca sipped from her glass. "The house is creepy and June is very strange. Maybe that's why neither of them came back."

"Shush, Rebecca, that's a terrible thing to say. But it was lovely of you to visit her. I'm sure it brightened her day—"

"*Brightened her day*?" Becca slammed her fork down. "It was awful, and I should never have listened to you, but you're always on me, on me, on me, I could *scream*!"

"Rebecca, your mother and I think we should call Dr. Murphy—these outbursts, the not sleeping, the fixation with this Sunday and that man—"

Becca finished her wine in one gulp. "You voting next week? I saw Mr. McCray and Mr. Sampson yelling at each other in the produce section. Aren't they cousins? And what do they care about the bridge, anyway? Do they even drive at their age? Why does everyone get to vote when to most people it's just a regular bridge but to others it has so much meaning?"

Her parents had stopped pretending they were eating and were sitting back in their chairs, watching her closely, but Becca couldn't stop rambling.

Her mind raced, thinking. "Never mind the bridge, have you spoken to Debbie?"

Her parents said nothing.

"No? Well, I have, and Debbie's been complaining about how much Richard works lately. Sometimes he's not home until midnight and it's been going on for months." Becca cocked an eyebrow. "Debbie cried about it, and it's probably nothing, but *midnight*? He's an accountant, why would he be working such long hours?" She cut a piece of roast as she let this information sink in. "I mean, *Richard*? Sometimes it's the ones you least suspect."

She moved her eyes around her plate and then up to the hutch at the back of the room, with the good china and tiny crystal figurines, and then finally back to her parents, to the worry that was slowly sinking in as they thought about Debbie. "I'm sure it's nothing, but maybe you should call and check in with her."

Her mother frowned at Becca's father, who wiped the corner of his mouth with his napkin and then sighed. They nodded at each other.

Becca stood, desperate to leave, but thankful that her parents were nothing if not easy to manipulate. "Thanks so much for lunch. I can see myself out."

GRANT

He inched reluctantly into the lot of Allan & Sons Auto. It was empty but for a hoisted Honda, with a teenage boy underneath in denim coveralls and scruffy high-tops.

Grant had wrestled the whole way to the auto shop about driving the extra two hours to East Lansing, to get his car taken care of there rather than deal with AJ Hill. AJ, who had always been jealous and probably still held a grudge from high school.

But in the end, Grant had chosen haste. A quick drop-off during his last break, get a loaner, make it back to work. He'd be late, but he had no choice; these were things that had to be done to continue seeming as unruffled as possible. Though he was ruffled; he was very fucking ruffled.

Through the office's small filthy window, he watched AJ behind the counter on the phone. Grant killed the engine and AJ looked over. Their eyes met but neither smiled.

AJ left the office and shouted something to the boy, and then made his way over to where Grant had parked. He let out a low whistle. "Guess I know what brought you here."

Grant eyed the scrawny, bearded man standing in front of him. "Kids or something," Grant said. "Still a pain to have to get it fixed."

"See who did it?"

He shook his head and AJ nodded thoughtfully. "This happen a lot?"

"What? No."

"You sure?"

He stared up at AJ. "Yes—I'm sure my car doesn't get keyed up often."

AJ leaned down, traced the marks on the hood slowly. "Twenty-seven, huh? That's definitely what it says—there's a two and then a seven. You probably already figured that out, though."

Grant let go of the steering wheel so he could shield his eyes to better see AJ's face. "It's just some random scratches, man."

AJ stood back up, arms across his chest. "Maybe. Strange though, the timing."

Grant yanked the keys from the ignition and dropped them in AJ's hand. "Probably a dare or something—kids today, they've got no fear. Remember when we were that age?"

"Sure do remember." AJ stared at him. "You think it's a warning or something? Did you tell the sheriff? Ricky's real strict on mischief, wants to be nipping it in the bud."

Grant cleared his throat. "It's just a few scratches from some punk kids. Can you take care of it today or should I take it somewhere else? I have shit to do."

AJ leaned back down again, pulled studiously on his beard. "Marks sure look intentional to me, brother. Memorial tomorrow and all—do you think someone saw what happened that night with your sister? Always seemed a mystery to me. She was so on you back then, and then one night she's just gone, no more nagging you after that. So, you sure you don't want me to call my uncle Ricky? Would hate to see you being targeted after everything you've been through."

Grant stared, blinded, into the late afternoon sun, just as AJ laughed and rapped his fist on the hood. "Just kidding—you should see your face! I'll try to get to it tomorrow. And I have a loaner in the back with a full tank—Wildcats special."

Grant climbed out of the car and nodded at AJ, who was smiling strangely at him. "Is there paperwork or something?"

"It was my idea—the bridge. To take it down. Thought you'd like to know."

Grant blinked hard. "But *why*?"

"That thing's too dangerous. It's time. My daughters will be driving soon." AJ winked at him. "Can't keep having people dying on that thing."

The sun—it was a weight pushing down on Grant's shoulders. "I wish you hadn't. Phoebe would be devastated, man, honestly."

"Your dead sister would be devastated if it came down?" AJ nodded slowly, grease-stained fingers scratching his beard. "But she was afraid of heights, wasn't she? Would have avoided it then, right?"

Grant shivered, saw Phoebe sitting on the hood of his car, head tilted, watching him.

"Acrophobia," AJ went on. "Don't remember much from high school, but I do remember her explaining that to Linda. Linda's also afraid of heights; it made her feel better to know it was called something official. They were in Calculus together, remember?"

"He's right, Grant," Phoebe said, and he swatted at his ear. "You keep lying about me."

"You all right, man?" AJ asked, grinning. "There another reason you want to keep that thing from being torn down? Maybe some evidence of a real crime up there?"

Grant used the hem of his shirt to wipe the sweat from his forehead, then lifted his face to the sky. Behind his closed eyes, the sun burned deep maroon. "There something you want to say to me, AJ? Just fucking spit it out."

"Nah, man." AJ leaned forward, traced the scratches with his finger again. "Any evidence would be long gone by now, Ricky says. Guess Becca really saved your ass back then—but then again, you always were lucky."

"*Lucky*," Grant muttered under his breath. "Right."

AJ called behind him to the boy. "Curtis! Bring the junker 'round front for Mr. Grant Dean here. Maybe if you're lucky he'll throw the ball around with you, teach you some tricks. He's got a lot of them up his sleeve."

"I'll wait by the road," Grant said.

"Oh," AJ said, lighting a cigarette. "Thought you'd want to know, the vote is just a formality; that bridge is coming down either way. Council knows it's better than raising taxes to fix it, so guess your sister's going to be rolling over in her grave when she finds out."

WYATT

Mrs. Lloyd hadn't been home and June wouldn't let them borrow the old woman's car without permission. She had been close to tears at another day gone without a proper visit to the cemetery, an obsession she had that Wyatt couldn't understand. He didn't need to stand over their mother's dead body to know that she was gone. She wasn't here, wasn't that crystal clear? But June had rushed home ahead of him from their neighbor's house and slammed the door behind her.

Wyatt was irritated but also concerned. June seemed to be getting better but sometimes she'd slip backward. Maybe it was because she still wasn't sleeping; he could hear her moving around at all hours or going outside to sit on the back porch and stare off into the empty country night.

Aren't you cold out here? he'd asked her last night, but she'd flatly ignored him. *Fine,* he'd said, and gone back inside.

Wyatt finished his cigarette in peace and then went inside

to find her. She was in the last place he looked, the last place he wanted to be—sitting on the bed in their mother's room. The room still smelled, and Wyatt wrinkled his nose as he walked in. He left the door wide open because it felt like a crypt, and he didn't want to trap them both inside of it.

The room was sparsely decorated. One deep brown wooden dresser, two bowls of trinkets, three small oval picture frames that held three versions of the same generic model family. He supposed his mother had never gotten around to changing them out. Or perhaps there was never enough happiness around for her to frame.

A small closet, two bedside tables with heavy mismatched lamps. The window was open, the curtains pulled back, sun-faded yellow chiffon tied in sloppy bows. "Remember when Dad ripped the old curtains down in here?" Wyatt asked.

June stopped what she was doing to look over her shoulder at him. "She yelled at him not to come home until he replaced them." She half smiled. "So he nailed up an old tablecloth—that ugly one with the flowers—and said he could be resourceful when the alternative meant being away from her." June's mouth set in a thin line. "And then you left and he was never happy again. Neither was she."

"What are you doing in here?"

"Looking for something."

"Looking for what?"

"Some pictures, and a pair of gold earrings I thought I could sell. But I found these instead."

Wyatt leaned against the wall, watching her. "Found what?"

June turned back to the shoebox in her lap. "Why are your hands shaking like that?"

He hadn't noticed, and shoved them behind him. "Just tired. Are you wearing my running shoes?"

June tucked her feet under her and threw something at him that hit his chest and fell to the carpet silently. Wyatt stared at the empty orange pill bottle at his feet. "I tossed the rest," she said. "So you'll have to go back to whoever you used to get them from, if they're even still in business."

"I'm clean," Wyatt said, but June's eyes were wet. She didn't believe him. Why did this have to be so hard? "June—I swear I am."

"And what's this about, Wyatt?" June held out a fistful of letters. He took one from her and read it. Shuffled it to the back; read another. There were a dozen, paper so soft from being folded and unfolded so many times, all in the same sloping handwriting, all the same three lines:

I'm fine. Don't look for me. I'm sorry.
—Wyatt

He didn't know what to say and so he waited for June to speak.

June dropped the shoebox to the floor. "I've never seen those. Maybe she thought it would upset me, I don't know. Maybe she thought I was too weak, that I couldn't handle it. I can't exactly ask her why she kept them from me, can I? But you stopped sending them, I guess."

The letters weren't from him, and he could tell June knew that. Not his handwriting, not things he would say; he would never have apologized back then. Wyatt shifted his weight in the doorway, felt the cool rush of air from the window. He was about to get a nosebleed, could feel the tickle; but he waited, firmly planted on the threadbare carpet.

"It never made sense that you left everything behind—your clothes, the money you kept in that tin. What did you do for money after you left? You couldn't even come back for that? Leaving us without a word, worried sick, was more important?" June lay back on the bed and closed her eyes. "I swear this room feels different with her gone."

Wyatt coughed, but June didn't open her eyes even though the sound was loud and sickly. "Rooms can do that," he said. "Feel different. They can swallow you up."

"Riddles." June pinched the bridge of her nose before sitting back up on the side of the bed. "You and your riddles. Who sent her these letters? Who knows where you went? Mom must have believed them, or wanted to. Same thing I guess. Better than the truth maybe."

Wyatt felt the insides of his mouth, touched on the soft pockets at the back, the gummy tender holes where he'd lost two more molars in his sleep.

"What have you done, Wyatt? I can handle it, I'm not a little girl anymore." June looked straight at him, her eyes filled with tears. "Were you there that night? Did you see what happened to Phoebe? Did Grant kill her? Why couldn't you just stay and tell the truth? Why are you protecting him?"

June didn't ask, but he felt it in her eyes and in the space between them:

Were you involved?

What does he have over you?

"Aren't you clever," Wyatt said. "Relentless. Annoying, almost. But close, so close, Juney."

Wyatt braced himself for the endless barrage of questions, but to his surprise, June just sighed and looked to the open window. "*Soon, soon*, you keep saying. *Just wait, Juney, I just need a couple of fucking days, Juney*. I always thought you left because of Dad but now I'm not so sure. You had no money, no clothes, but you always were industrious, Wy. I do remember that. Do you know what that word means? *Industrious*?" June lay back on the bed again, closed her eyes. "I need a minute alone to think. This is a lot, your secrecy. I'm trying but you really are a lot, Wyatt. There's tissue in the bathroom for your nose; please don't get blood on the carpet, I just cleaned it."

Wyatt backed out of the room, glad to be in the cooler hallway. He touched his face, fingered the slick, tasted the copper. He shut the door and propped himself against it. His chest felt as though it was caving in. He could feel his ribs piercing his shirt. Wyatt bent over and gripped his head between his hands and opened his mouth, trying not to scream at the mounting pressure in his head.

His body was falling apart. He didn't have much time. He had to tell June the truth and he would, but right now he needed a shower, he needed water on him. He walked to the small bathroom, didn't bother with the light, turned on the shower, stepped in fully clothed, turned it to cold, let it wash over him; let it calm his failing mind.

TEN YEARS AGO

Midnight

Harley couldn't stop checking the time. She needed the night to be done, so she could go to sleep in her own bed, wake up and start over, do the right thing. She'd never had reason to question whether or not she was a good person, and now she dreaded that she wasn't.

Harley had begged Grant to talk to her in private, and when he'd finally agreed they'd hurried upstairs, away from the party, and locked the bathroom door behind them.

"I think we should just tell her," Harley had said. "Phoebe loves us both, she'll just have to get over it. Maybe she'll even be happy for us. Maybe it'll snap her out of the mood she's been in lately—"

"No way." Grant ran his hand through his hair. "Phoebe would not get over it. You think you know her, but you don't. We

will never tell her because it would kill her, and I won't do that to her. So this was a big mistake that can never happen again."

Grant refused to look at her and Harley chewed on the inside of her cheek. She'd been growing suspicious that his stress and mood swings weren't just about Phoebe and the pressure he was under, but that he was seeing someone else. He'd avoided too many calls in front of her and was increasingly irritated when she'd question him.

"Where are you going in such a rush?" Harley had asked him a few days earlier. He'd gotten a text and she watched him delete it immediately. She was sitting on the side of her bed, fastening her bra, hot with shame. She was always wracked with guilt after sleeping with him—why couldn't she just say no?

"Nowhere." Grant leaned back against her desk, smiling at her, but he was distracted, already thinking about something else—the text probably. Did she even matter to him? Was she risking her friendship with Phoebe over nothing?

"No, really—where are you going?" Harley tried to sound firm. "Are you seeing someone else? You are, aren't you? Who is she, Grant?"

Grant stopped smiling. "There's no one else, but this has to be the last time. Phoebe will never forgive me and I can't have one more thing for her to be mad about. She's driving me crazy enough as it is."

Harley was hurt. "I promise I won't be jealous, just tell me who she is."

Grant bent over and pulled up his boxers. It was hard to look away from his perfect body, and Harley blushed.

"Jesus, Harley, there's no one else! How would I have the fucking time? But Phoebe's going to find out, you know she is—I can't believe she hasn't already when all she does is worry about me, and this'll kill her and then she'll kill us and I'll never hear the fucking end of it."

Grant had a softness sometimes that Harley wondered if anyone else got to see. A vulnerability that came out when they were lying in bed together, in the few minutes after sex and before he started regretting it and worrying about his sister. He'd play with her hair or kiss her with a smile on his face. But that softness was long gone in this moment. Grant was brushing her off and treating her like a huge mistake and it made Harley furious. At both of them. Why exactly would this kill Phoebe? Because Phoebe wouldn't think Harley was good enough for her precious big brother? They were best friends! Could the girl not be normal for a minute and just relax? Why could the Deans never let anyone else inside their tiny circle?

"Grant," Harley said, trying to sound more relaxed than she felt. "It's been two months and we haven't exactly been safe." God, she hated that she sounded like her mother, but what other explanation was there for how distracted he'd been lately? "Don't I at least deserve to know who else you're fucking, for my health?"

Grant tugged on his shirt. "Jesus, I'm just meeting a friend, okay? For some study notes. It's nothing, calm down. I'll call you later."

Harley watched Grant leave her bedroom in a hurry. She threw some clothes on, waited by the door for a minute and then left her house, heading straight for her parents' car.

She followed Grant for twenty minutes. He looked in his rearview mirror once and she ducked, but he seemed too focused to notice her. He pulled into the vacant lot of the drive-in and she parked off to the side of the highway, loathing herself. Grant clearly wasn't meeting another girl, not in this rundown spot, so she should just leave; this was ridiculous. If Grant saw her following him, it would definitely be over, and she knew it should be, but she didn't want it to be all on his terms. She would not be cast aside like the dozens of other girls he'd slept with and then forgotten about the second he rolled over in bed.

Harley heard a car come up loudly behind her and she lowered down in her seat. Once it had pulled into the empty lot, she peered over the dash and watched a wreck of a red car stop next to Grant's. Both drivers rolled down their windows. Grant passed something through his window that glinted briefly in the sun. They exchanged a few short words and then they both drove away in opposite directions.

Harley never saw the other driver's face, but she breathed a sigh of relief that there wasn't another girl. At least not today. And then her relief turned to shame, and she started to cry on the side of the highway because she didn't recognize herself anymore.

Harley frowned at the memory as she leaned against the wall in Kelsey's blaring living room. Her face had dried after the argument with Grant in the bathroom, but she still wanted to leave.

She watched Phoebe stumble down the stairs and stop at

the window, bang on it several times and then storm to the front door. Phoebe flung it open and stepped out into the storm.

Harley groaned inwardly. Phoebe had been on a tear about Grant ever since she'd picked her up that evening. She knew she should talk to her, help her through whatever it was that had her so bent out of shape, but a part of Harley worried that Phoebe was onto her and Grant, and if she wasn't yet, Harley couldn't risk letting it slip herself—that she was doing the one thing Phoebe would never be able to forgive.

The front door was flung open again, rain streaming in sideways from outside, causing everyone to shriek and clap and open their mouths like it was snowing. Phoebe pulled someone in from outside, dragging him through the thick crowd to the kitchen. Harley craned her neck to see, curious. Who was it, she wondered, who had Phoebe acting so unlike her normally in-control self, and instead so frantic?

Harley checked the time again, as if she hadn't just done that a minute ago. Phoebe could handle herself; she'd just call her first thing in the morning.

BECCA

Becca peered uncomfortably at her face in the door's window. She brushed her hair behind her ears, practiced a smile, checked her teeth—but each movement was reflected strangely back to her in the distorted shadows of the darkened glass. She smiled bigger, but it felt alien. Then Grant walked through the living room to where she stood on the front porch.

When he saw her, he stopped abruptly, confused.

This was not part of their arrangement.

Becca waved as he walked to the door, but she could tell he was in a foul mood. It was the stormy look in his eyes, and that he wasn't trying to hide his limp. Her pulse roared inside her body; she was stressed and she didn't have the energy to be discarded by him again.

Grant opened the door but did not invite her inside. "What are you doing here?" He spoke very quietly, but she knew he was angry.

Becca reached for an answer that might soften his edges, but she was nervous and didn't want to tell him that she came by often—all the time lately—but always stopped herself from coming to the door.

"I was just in the area—"

"Sure." Grant looked quickly over his shoulder. "My mother's home, you shouldn't be here."

Of course Becca knew that Ellen was inside; her car was sitting in the driveway, and Grant was tense and shifty. His mother was a miserable cow as far as Becca was concerned—never letting up on Grant, even after this long, when he was her only remaining child.

"You stood me up, Grant—I wanted to come see why. I worried that maybe you'd fallen down the stairs and hit your head or something." Becca tried to sound light-hearted, but the look fixed on Grant's face was making her sweat.

"Sorry." He stared right through her. "But I had to take my car in. Someone keyed it last night. Right here in my driveway."

"Keyed it?" Becca swallowed. "Who would do that?"

Grant shrugged but his eyes bored into hers. "Kids probably."

"That's awful, but Grant, we had plans—and I told you it was important to me, and then you never showed and I just sat there waiting for you. It was humiliating."

"I said I'm sorry," Grant snapped at her. "Okay? But I have a lot on my mind."

"That's another reason I came by, to see if there's anything I can do to help for tomorrow—"

Grant let out a bark of a laugh. "We're fine, and you need to fucking leave, Becca."

Becca was stung by his rude tone. Had Grant not just stood her up? Humiliated her in public? The list of his cruelties was a mile long at this point. He'd never treated her this badly before; how could they move past it if he was still being so dismissive of her?

Becca stepped closer to the door, to Grant, to the dark living room that always smelled of long-dead things. "I'm on my way back from therapy actually. I needed an emergency session. Like you, I have a lot on my mind."

This was a lie, but it had the desired effect; Grant raked his hand through his hair quickly and smiled at her. It was brief, but a smile nonetheless.

"And how did it go?" Grant asked. "Your emergency session?"

Becca watched his eyes, those beautiful brown eyes, and wished desperately to keep him attentive. "It was a tough one," she said as she cast her gaze downward. "You know how hard all of this is—the memorial, everyone still looking at me like they do, looking at *us*, when none of them can ever really understand—"

"That's it?" Grant interrupted her. "Nothing else?"

"We talked about the accident of course."

Grant nodded, but his jaw was set. "What about it?"

Becca felt a tear slide down her face in frustration; she wanted Grant to hold her, to tell her everything would be fine, that the secrets they'd kept for one another could finally be set free. Then they could start over, try again, unburdened by all the lies.

Didn't they deserve a second chance?

Grant watched her expectantly, and a little apprehensively, as he always seemed to when she mentioned therapy. He was genuinely interested in what Dr. Murphy had to say, which made her feel important, seen.

Becca had asked him once why he cared so much about her sessions, and he'd said that because he couldn't afford to go himself, and his mother certainly wouldn't support it, that hearing what Dr. Murphy said was helping him heal as well. And so she always tried her best to relay what they'd spoken about if it related to him in any way.

But she hadn't been to therapy in years, and Becca started to panic at the look on Grant's face as he waited for her to say something of value. "Just the same stuff," Becca said. "About the accident, not remembering everything."

Grant sighed impatiently. "That's it?"

Becca felt his attention slipping away as he peered over his shoulder, probably listening for sounds of his miserable mother.

"Just how awful it was, waking up in the back seat, and watching you stand there in the rain screaming—"

Grant whipped his head back toward her. "I was devastated. And scared."

"I know."

He opened his mouth; closed it again with an audible click. "That's it, then? The same story?"

"It's not a *story*—" Becca whispered, feeling tears prick her eyes.

"You know what I mean." Grant looked behind him again. "You really have to go before my mother sees you."

"Well, it's just that..." Becca trailed off, arching her eyebrow and watching Grant's eyes narrow immediately.

"Just that what?" Grant nodded, prompting her. "You can tell me you know." He spoke quietly; she had his focus again. "If you remember anything new, whatever it is—we can process it together."

Becca's mind whirred; what could she say that would draw him in and not push him away? The truth?

The truth was she'd woken in the back seat of his truck, dazed and in terrible pain, and seen Grant through the front windshield screaming and throwing his arms in the air and then collapsing to his knees, sobbing.

But the truck had been stopped by the bridge guardrail, and Grant was further down on the opposite side, not near Phoebe at all. It wasn't until Becca had managed to climb out of the truck that she'd seen Phoebe lying broken on the pavement.

Later that night in the hospital, after Grant was so gentle with her as he helped her fill in the gaps of what had happened—that's when Becca had understood the monstrous truth.

Grant had let Phoebe die on purpose; and he'd done that for her.

To save Becca from getting in trouble with the sheriff for causing the crash, for being the reason Grant had lost control. And to protect their secret: that they were in love and Grant was going to leave his sister behind for Becca.

That's why Grant had waited until Phoebe was dead to call the ambulance. To keep Becca safe and protected and out of jail; he'd saved her life by keeping the blame off of her.

They'd never spoken about this out loud; but that fibrous thread bound them together. It was why Grant would ask her sometimes, usually after a few drinks, when he was bold and raw, if her memory had returned, if she remembered anything new. In those vulnerable moments of his, he'd test her, to see if she'd remain loyal and not speak the complicated truth out loud: that he'd done this for her. That he'd killed for her. For wasn't leaving Phoebe to die the same as killing her? It was the ultimate act of love; and a secret that Becca would always keep, even if sometimes she desperately wanted to shout it out: *Grant saved my life! Grant loves me! I am more important than Phoebe Dean!*

Becca thought of that moment often—of Grant's anguish on the bridge that night. Of the torment he'd faced to put her needs first.

"You have to go." Grant was frustrated now. He was shifting his weight to favor his good leg and his eyes were red-rimmed and feral, and she tilted her head because he looked like he had at Flo's the other night—disheveled and distant—when he'd barely spoken a word to her before leaving with that *stranger*. Not to mention that he'd just stood her up today and maybe his car *was* in the shop, but was his mother's car not right there in the driveway and also what looked like a rental right next to it?

How could Grant sacrifice so much for her ten years ago but treat her so poorly now? That stormy night had many facets, but had she not protected him, just as he had her, by keeping some of those truths to herself? He'd been the one driving, had he not? He'd let his sister die, had he not? Becca had lived for ten years with the unbearable burden of guilt of what Grant had done out of love for her, and yet she was still overlooked and ignored in town.

Becca was tired of being invisible in her own story; she was owed more than what Grant was giving.

Becca knew Grant's mood was unlikely to change and so she smiled, but she was spent. "Nothing," she said finally. "I remember nothing new. The doctors told me I probably wouldn't, you know that."

Then Grant slammed the front door shut and Becca stood on the Deans' porch, purple-faced and panting, before spinning on her heel and nearly tripping down the front stairs. As she fell into her car she thought, *Well, this won't do.*

This won't do at all.

JUNE

June grabbed her keys from the counter and the handmade card she'd shoved in a drawer. She walked down the road, away from her house and Wyatt, who was still in the shower after nearly thirty minutes.

AJ was the last person in town she could think of to speak to about her brother. Although she was running out of options, June liked this new feeling—of shutting her front door behind her and setting off with a purpose. And there was something cathartic about walking—one foot in front of the other; the repetitive movement, like a trance, that calmed her—something she needed after the earlier incident with Wyatt and the red car. She'd tried to bring it up again, to be sure Wyatt wasn't just toying with her, but she didn't like the way he'd seemed so alarmed, and so she'd let it go.

She stopped to catch her breath and watched a cricket crawling over the dusty cracks on the road. The way it moved so haphazardly unnerved her, but she watched until it had skittered into the overgrown ditch, trying to find its way home. June kept going, turning at the broken fence that marked their property. It had been Wyatt who had broken the fence, crashing into it years back, and it had never been fixed. An oddity for their father, who had liked things a certain way but who had maybe left the mess there, the mangled destruction, as a constant reminder of Wyatt's wrongdoings.

But Wyatt had changed since he'd been a teenager, and June wondered if she seemed changed to him. More capable, industrious, strong. She was softening her big brother little by little, she could tell. She was glad he was home. They could fix the fence together, she'd mention it when she got back; and she smiled to herself at the list of future plans that kept growing.

June made it past the brown ribbons of dead fields and wide barren lots to the Hills' driveway, still smelling of fresh asphalt. There was a large sign on the lawn about taking down the bridge that the girls had clearly made, a pink bicycle lying next to it, bright living flowers on the windowsills.

The normal family scene didn't sting her today, June noticed. She'd have to ask Wyatt to help her with the front garden. It was barely a patch of dirt, but he might have some ideas. They'd plant some flowers and grow something together. A fresh garden for their fresh start.

June walked up the three front steps, knocked at the door. She noticed a crack in her fingernail and tried to smooth it away with her front teeth. She fixed her hair as she waited, tucked in her shirt. She'd washed her face, was wearing clean clothes that still smelled of laundry detergent.

Linda Hill opened the door. "June," she said, flustered. "Shoot, I'm busy burning something on the stove, why don't you come in before the whole house goes up in flames?"

"Okay, thank you." June stepped into the living room that was cluttered with what she imagined were nine-year-old things: big squishy pillows on the floor, dog-eared novels, a pink plastic manicure set.

She followed Linda into a kitchen that was bursting at the seams with life: dirty dishes in the sink, homework strewn on the kitchen table, a half-eaten apple lying on a chair.

"Have a seat," Linda said, snatching a pot from the stove before it boiled over. "Can I get you something to drink?"

June remained standing, spotting a calendar filled with colorful reminders for soccer games and dentist appointments and mortgage payments. Should she get one of those for her and Wyatt? "No thank you, I can't stay long. I was wondering, are your girls home?"

Linda wiped her hands on her apron. June noticed her nails were pale pink and lovely. June made a mental note of the color and then shook her head; she'd never had her nails done before, not once. But was that something new that she might enjoy?

"Shoot—the girls are at dance. They'll be sad they missed you though."

"I just wanted to thank them for the card."

"Oh, dear," Linda said. "It's the least we could do. Did you get our flowers? I'm so sorry about your mother. I lost mine two years ago. It's hard, isn't it? No matter how old we are, we still need our mothers sometimes, don't we?"

June looked through the big open window, to the swing set in the backyard, to more bikes and scooters and soccer balls. "What about AJ?"

Linda had her head deep inside the fridge. The stove was giving off a burning smell. June thought about turning it off but didn't want to seem rude. "AJ? He's not home either," Linda said, closing the fridge with her hip. "You sure you don't want a tea or coffee?"

"No, I really can't stay, I just wanted to thank you for the card, and flowers." June shuffled her feet, looked down at them for a second. "Say," she said, looking up, trying to smile. "Are you going to the Deans' tomorrow?"

Linda blew her bangs off her forehead. "Only if we can get a sitter. We don't want to bring the girls to something like that."

"But I saw them raising money for it—"

"Right." Linda smiled. "They did that all on their own, made a whole four dollars. I guess the church has been talking about Phoebe Dean, about loss of innocence and all that—bit morbid if you ask me. I'll be glad when the bridge comes down. You'll be voting next week, won't you? We need to move on, the whole town. It was AJ's idea, to bring it to a vote." Linda smiled at her warmly. "Would you like to stay for dinner?"

"Oh, no," June said. "I mean, thank you, but no, I should be getting back, but Linda—the memorial tomorrow—it has me thinking a lot about my brother, Wyatt. Do you remember him?"

"Sure—we had a couple of classes together, and AJ talks about him sometimes, fondly of course."

June blushed at the kindness, not sure if Linda was just trying to be nice. "That party was just down the road from here."

"That's right," Linda said, adding far too much salt to whatever was bubbling away irritably in the pot. "I wasn't there, I was babysitting for my cousins. A blessing in the end."

"I wasn't there either. Was AJ?"

"We weren't together at the time." Linda lifted a noodle from the steam, eyed it, dropped it back in. "But he was, though I think he left before anything really happened."

"Did AJ ever mention seeing my brother there? It was the same night that Wyatt left."

"It was?" Linda looked surprised. "Are you sure?"

The warmth she'd felt from talking to Linda began to fade. "Yes—I'm sure it was the same night."

"Well, shoot," Linda said, brow furrowed. "How did I not know that?"

June blinked. "Well, no one paid much attention to us."

Linda looked stricken. "I never really thought about it like that, so that's shame on me, on everyone I guess. Have you heard from him, then? From Wyatt?"

June wondered, as she stood in the middle of this nice family kitchen, what it would feel like to say: *Yes—he's finally come home.* Would Linda even care? Or would it barely register and Linda would have to pretend to be interested, which would just insult June further. "No, I haven't," June said, realizing she might never gain what she'd hoped to from coming here. Not just information about her brother, but finally being seen, and having her pain acknowledged.

Would anyone ever care about Wyatt? He was a person with feelings and motivations and complexity and loss. But no one had considered him ten years ago, and no one considered him now. Not with the memorial hanging over everyone so they clung to it, wrapped themselves in that old grief, obsessing over it again. Everything felt just like it had a decade ago—except she had lost so much more since then.

"You sure you don't want to stay for dinner? Be warned," Linda laughed, "I'm quite a terrible cook."

"No. Thank you. But I was asking you about AJ at Kelsey's—"

"Right, sorry, look at me all frazzled over a pot of pasta. Never have twins, June, they'll ruin your brain. Um, what about it? Has AJ heard from Wyatt? No, I don't think so."

"No." June shifted her weight, irritated at how difficult it was to make these people see her. "No, did AJ say anything about Wyatt being there, who he went there to see?"

Linda chewed on her lip, thinking. "It was so long ago but here, just one second." Linda reached into her pocket for her phone, squinted at the screen, typed something. "He's good with texts, it'll just be a... There." She smiled at the ping and then held it out for June to read:

Linda: June's here, wants to know if u saw Wyatt at the party at Kelsey's THAT night

AJ: he came late and Phoebe was pissed at him tell June I'm sorry about her Ma and she should vote yes next week if she knows what's best for the town

BECCA

Becca's store manager, Rusty, tugged aggressively on his oily goatee.

"So put the cameras in, see if I care," she said. "This is probably against my civil rights or something, to be accusing me of theft—"

"No one's accusing you officially," Rusty said. "But the cameras are coming next week, Rebecca. Be smart. I owe your dad, but not this much."

Rusty stormed off to the break room and Becca hit the button to open her register, then lifted the cash tray for her cigarettes. She could feel her anxiety grow and twist inside of her; she might need to cut out from her shift early with the way things were going. She should never have dropped by Grant's to try to fix things, because now everything was worse. She closed the register with a hard shove and then shivered as the air conditioning unit above her spluttered to life.

Becca was furious with Grant but he held as many cards as

she did. If he would just allow her to explain to everyone what had happened in the truck, that she would never intentionally hurt Phoebe, that it truly had been an accident that got out of hand, and that they *had* been dating and that he'd spent the last decade protecting her from prison—well, she would no longer be invisible in town, would she? Maybe it would even be worth everyone knowing it had been her fault. Maybe they'd empathize with how hard this must have been for her; maybe they'd be impressed with her devoted loyalty to Grant for all these years.

Becca leaned against her till, praying the last half of her shift would speed up. She needed to be at home where she could think, to weigh the pros and cons of the arrangement they'd had for ten years, to consider if it wasn't worth it anymore.

It was a small miracle that the store was empty so late in the day—except for Mr. Brown, whose cane was clicking unevenly against the floor, setting her even more on edge. He came in once a week for the same seven items; he'd be at her register in less than three minutes. She could time it if she wanted to.

Becca checked her nails and then searched through her purse for her compact mirror, applied some lip gloss with a trembling hand.

Right on cue, Mr. Brown shuffled up to her register and smiled dully with half-missing yellow dentures. She started ringing him up without smiling back.

"Good morning, Debbie."

Becca scowled at him, wishing her hands could work faster. "It's not morning and it's Rebecca. Debbie is my sister. Actually, it's Crazy Becca—didn't you know?"

"Lovely, dear, that cat food on sale?" Mr. Brown asked and Becca flatly ignored him. "No matter then, I'll be taking it anyway—will you be going to that party for the pretty girl—"

"Party?" Becca raised an eyebrow. "It's not a party, it's a memorial. How insensitive, Mr. Brown."

Mr. Brown smiled and handed her a wad of crumpled singles.

"*Pretty girl*," Becca muttered. "You want to know something, Mr. Brown?" She smashed her fist onto the register. "That *pretty girl* wasn't so pretty when she was screaming at me to stay away from her brother. Even though we were together! We had real plans! He gave me this—" Becca rifled at the back of her till and pulled out the necklace she'd been keeping safe back there. "It was his grandmother's and we were going to pawn it for a wedding ring, but Phoebe was so jealous, she just could not let him go. She would never be able to let him go. I thought that after she died it would bring us closer together, but it didn't, so I guess she died for no good reason at all."

Becca shoved the bag of groceries into his chest and Mr. Brown smiled blankly at something above her left shoulder. "Lovely out today, isn't it, Debbie?"

Becca crossed her arms and glared at him, trying to catch her breath as he trundled slowly to the front door.

"Hey, there—Becca?"

"Oh." Becca swung around to the front of her checkout line. "Oh. Harley." Becca smiled quickly, fixed her hair. "I didn't see you there."

Harley's eyes were piercing and Becca wondered how much she'd overheard.

"You doing okay? You rushed out of the shelter yesterday without a word."

"I felt a migraine coming on, but I'm fine now. How's your cat—Sophia?"

"Sabrina. It was nothing in the end. The vet suggested changing her food." Harley eyed Becca suspiciously as she placed her groceries on the belt one at a time: shortening, brown sugar, vanilla. "But you seemed so upset and you didn't even say bye! I hope it wasn't anything I said, I was just trying to be nice to you."

"I said I'm fine. Is this for tomorrow?" Becca rang the items through as fast as she could, glad now for the air conditioning spitting loudly above her, and that it was a light basket. "Cookies?"

Harley continued to stare at her. "Chocolate chip, my grandma Mabel's recipe. Phoebe loved them, we used to bake them together all the time."

"So sweet of you. So that'll be $7.67—"

"I just heard you talking to Mr. Brown about Grant—was that Phoebe's necklace? The one with the locket?"

Becca sighed, drained. "What do you care if it is?"

Harley's eyebrows knit together. "I guess I'm just wondering why you have it in your till at Kramer's?"

Becca handed Harley her change. "Grant gave it to me."

"You should tell Mrs. Dean. She's been looking for it."

"And how would you know that?"

"She said she was looking for it when she called me about the speech. I was telling you about that yesterday? I've decided I can't speak tomorrow."

Becca sighed loudly. "Why not?"

"I feel guilty. It just seems wrong somehow."

"*You* feel guilty? What on earth for?" *I caused the crash*, Becca wanted to shout. *I've been drowning in guilt for a whole decade!*

Phoebe is dead because of me!

Harley smiled sadly and then looked down at her feet.

"What do you have to feel guilty about?" Becca went on. "When you weren't even there."

"No, but you were." Harley looked as though she was realizing this for the first time. "How did she seem, Becca? Was Phoebe angry with me?"

"Angry—with *you*?" Becca could feel her face turning red. Was this really continuing to happen to her? Ten years she'd suffered in silence, and now Harley had waltzed into her store to try to make it all about her? "No." Becca's teeth clenched. "No, she did not seem angry with you."

"Good," Harley exhaled. "Oh my god, that's good. I couldn't live with myself if Phoebe's last thoughts were about me and Grant—" Harley stopped, let out a sad little laugh, shook her head quickly.

"What's that about you and Grant?"

"Oh god, it's nothing." Harley flushed, embarrassed. "It was ten years ago!"

Becca didn't like the look on Harley's face, and when she spoke her voice was high-pitched. "What exactly about you and Grant was ten years ago?"

"Nothing." Harley tried to smile but failed. "This memorial

is really getting under my skin." She picked up her bag of groceries. "Phoebe loved that necklace, so if Grant gave it to you, he must care about you, Becca. It's nice that you've gotten to know each other a bit—a silver lining I guess?" Harley paused as though another thought had just struck her. "So maybe I'll see you there tomorrow?"

Becca couldn't even manage a nod as Harley left the store. She fell back against her till, thoughts whipping through her head, thoughts she could no longer hold onto or control.

JUNE

"This is really fucking weird," Wyatt had said a few hours earlier. "It's just a bird. A dead bird. You kept a dead bird in our bathtub, June."

"This is a nice thing to do," she said. "And it was a cardinal, not just any bird."

"Right, a cardinal." Wyatt rocked on his heels, struggling slightly to stand. "How could I forget—the bird is Mom's ghost come back for a visit. So how you doin' down there, Mom? Comfortable enough for you?"

"Don't be morbid. How does it go, the poem?" June laid the delicate body in the hole they'd dug under the large maple tree, regretting instantly that she'd placed it on its back because now its feet were sticking awkwardly in the air. And its small black eyes were open and she didn't know how to close them. She didn't like that it looked like the bird was still alive and that they were about to bury it. She used the trowel to cover it quickly with dirt before she changed her mind.

"Ashes to ashes, dust to dust—Wy, what's the next line?" June patted the ground hurriedly until it was flat.

"We commit this body to the ground, or something like that, I don't know. Does it matter? I don't think the bird can hear us, Juney."

Wyatt was still wearing the heavy knit sweater that had belonged to their father. How did he have it after so long? The sentimentality of it, of imagining that wherever he'd been—prison was still her best guess, drilling oil in the deep Pacific was another—that he'd hang onto something of their dad's filled her with warmth, and June found that by just looking at him, her breathing started to slow, the disquiet of the dead bird receding.

She was sitting cross-legged under the tree in the shade and held out her hand for Wyatt's cigarette. Wyatt stared at her a minute and then gestured impatiently. June looked down into her lap at her hand, which was already holding one. She blinked, the red cherry about to burn her fingers. She took a last pull and coughed. "Remember Baxter?" she asked.

"Do you?"

"Yes, Wyatt—that's why I'm asking."

"Then yes, me too." Wyatt winked at her, his eyes darkening. "Baxter loved to catch squirrels and bring them inside—it was gross. He'd leave them under your bed."

"Under *your* bed. And that opossum once, which was huge and stunk up the whole house because we didn't find it for days."

Wyatt laughed, the sound getting stuck in his throat like a

choke. "Looked like a giant rat—how did he drag it inside? It was half his size and he was a big dog."

June sat in the back watching the setting sun. The porch was slanted, with protruding rusty nails and rotting wooden slats. Weeds reached all the way up to the windowsills. She could hear the tire swing twist and squeak in the wind, even though she knew it wasn't there. Their father had cut it down in one of his fits of rage because it was something that had mattered to Wyatt.

June flicked her cigarette away because it was making her light-headed and nauseated. She'd never been much of a smoker, and it was her second of the day. The cigarette landed near the small wooden cross she'd made from two twigs and an elastic band, to mark the dead bird's grave.

June looked to the sun that hit the impenetrable tree line at the far edge of their property; the temperature cooling as it continued to dip. The night insects would be out soon, so loud sometimes she couldn't hear herself think.

AJ Hill had confirmed that Wyatt had been at that party. Just like Becca and Mick had thought. June contemplated the letters she'd found at the back of her mother's closet. Wyatt hadn't sent them; he'd sworn to her and she believed him. It just wasn't something that he'd do, which meant someone else had, someone who hadn't wanted them to look for him. June assumed that meant someone knew where Wyatt had gone, and why he'd left. Someone who had kept this information from her for nearly ten years. Kept her naive and enslaved to her worry and anxiety and dread.

June could hear Wyatt in the house, lacing up his sneakers. He always had loved running at night. She was concerned about him; about his deteriorating health and what his involvement was all those years ago.

Just minutes ago, Wyatt had told her that he was ready, that it was time. That he wanted to go to the memorial at the Dean house the next day, to see Grant, to pay his respects. He'd laughed then, delighted with himself, and she'd rushed out of the house to have a cigarette in peace. To think. She hadn't smoked in years, but Wyatt always had a pack and she'd forgotten how much it soothed her.

June leaned against the back door and closed her eyes. She pictured the dead bird reaching up through the soil with a skeletal wing and felt her chin start to tremble. Wyatt wanted her to come with him tomorrow, to talk to Grant with him. She'd agreed but she was scared. Was she ready for this? Had *Grant* written those letters? He'd told her at McCray's that Wyatt didn't want to be found, just like the letters had said. But why? What had Wyatt done? What had her brother been capable of back then, when he was going through something dark, when he was losing himself to something she didn't understand?

June suddenly craved the comfort of her small bedroom, and the gift of escape her headphones and loud music had offered her back when she'd be avoiding thinking of her mother lying on the couch dying, and avoiding thinking of the night that Wyatt left, the night of Wyatt's terrible event.

"*Event*," June said aloud, holding the word in her mouth, tears burning her eyes.

A couple of months after he disappeared, when it had seemed Wyatt wasn't coming home this time, her mother had begun referring to his running away as *the event*. Some days she would make up big sweeping lies about *the event* to anyone who would listen. That Wyatt had met a nice girl and knocked her up and was just doing right by her by living in secret. *He's such a good boy*, her mother would say, *such a romantic*. She'd been completely engaged in the fantasy. But Wyatt was neither a good boy nor a romantic. He'd been completely uninterested in anything but running and trouble.

Or sometimes it was that Wyatt had felt the honorable pull to serve his country and had enlisted in the Army. That he'd been sent overseas because of his superior strength and intellect; that he was currently a highly decorated soldier, but living undercover.

Drilling oil. The circus. The Marines.

Witness relocation.

And the list had only grown.

Depending on how much June had left to give that day, after walking on eggshells around her mother and trying to stay on top of her homework—even though she was failing half of her classes, and with no responsible parent around to even notice—she'd either nod along, or she'd retreat to her room, because her mother lying to herself wasn't something she could bear to watch.

After eight months, and then twelve and then twenty,

everything existed with a faint dusting of loss. Grocery shopping for four, now three, now two; how empty the baskets looked, the curling receipts shorter, the bags painfully light. The thought of decorating the tree without Dad to place the angel meant entire Christmas seasons were skipped. The dishwasher looked so bleakly pathetic with just two mugs and two bowls and two forks.

Well, he better be dead, *her mother would say, on the days she was drinking and brave—referring to June's father, who left for work a year to the day after Wyatt and never came home.*

Her mother spent the first couple of years after Wyatt left sober and raw, and then polished off an entire bottle of whiskey one night, a gift from a neighbor who hadn't been by to check on them in months. A stupid token of his pity, *her mother had disparaged when he left after just a few minutes of unbearable small talk.*

Her mother sat for hours that night on the back porch, cradling the bottle and crying. June stood by the window, horrified and fascinated, as her mother willingly, urgently, lowered herself into a drunken stupor. June helped her to bed when it was nearly morning and the bottle was empty. Her mother smiled at her before she passed out on her pillow—a faraway smile that left behind it a rare peacefulness on her face. June knew, in that moment, that her mother would chase that peace again. She threw the bottle in the trash and sat on the back porch herself until dawn, understanding that something was changing in their house again. That she was going to be left to pick up the pieces. She cried, terrified of being alone; really alone. She stared at the moon and the spray of stars and the dark woods in the distance, teeth chattering but too paralyzed to go inside for a sweater or blanket. The cold comforted her in a way, darted at her, little teeth nipping at her exposed skin; finally, some attention.

When her mother's physical health problems started, the cancer diagnosis felt like another crippling blow. A whole new set of unknowns, and more worry and stress and waiting, waiting, waiting. June had been here before too many times and it felt like a physical injury now; like a broken bone, or a scar split open and bleeding anew. Sometimes she'd hold out her palms, check her face, her legs, her scalp, to see if she was really bleeding; to see if her suffering had finally broken free, manifesting itself as something real.

When the final diagnosis was stage four and her mother flatly refused treatment, the doctor, professionally dismayed, looked to June as if there were something she could do other than shrug apologetically and brace for what was coming. "A few months," the doctor said, resigned. "Here's some morphine, don't tell anyone." But her mother lasted seven months, and in the last couple of weeks, when June knew that her mother lay on the couch dying, and the fear of being alone was so terrifying that she felt hunted by it, that's when she started escaping.

She'd lock the door to her bedroom, put her headphones on, blare music so she couldn't hear her mother writhing or sobbing or, worst of all, completely silent like a corpse, and in that short bit of brief escape, she'd allow herself to pretend.

That her dad was still home. And he'd promised to take her fishing, and he'd kept his word. Atta girl, Juney, *he'd say when she caught something, and she'd beam up at him even though she didn't enjoy fishing, but she loved her dad.*

Or at least she loved that pretend version of her dad.

Sometimes she would simply pretend she was happy. The warm lightness of that—like floating on a cloud. She was happy and her body didn't constantly ring with anxiety and dread. She was happy and her mother was at her old job in the library of the elementary school, and not currently passed out on the couch clutching a bottle to her chest like a precious sleeping infant. She was happy and her brother would waltz through the door from practice, grab the milk and then ruffle her hair as she sat at the kitchen table studying.

Sometimes she let her mind wander unrestrained. Allowed it freedom to go where it wanted, into valleys and creeks and ditches, but holding the reins tight. If it wandered too far she worried she'd get stuck in the pretense—locked in there, unable to find her way back out.

In her escape she was a carefree child, skipping rope on the long dusty driveway, her brother and father playing catch in the backyard under the maple tree. Her mind would keep going, taking her to sleepovers with friends whose faces she could no longer picture, fingers greasy with popcorn butter and salt, laughing uninhibited like only children could. But the sound and feel of laughter in her mouth was like a foreign language; one she might recognize to hear, but not how to sound out herself.

And then her thoughts would unspool further, to people in

her town, to Grant Dean and Rebecca Hoyt, teenagers like herself who had suffered, who could relate to her if she dared talk to them about it. They were branded like she was; she could tell by the way people moved out of their way on the sidewalk, irritated that they'd not had the decency to leave town. Instead they had stayed, and now they dragged their trauma behind them like a ghastly security blanket, tattered and dirty and hardened in the corners with nervous spit.

She wondered after them both sometimes, Grant and Becca—sometimes in sympathy, empathy, relatability—but then her mind would weave on further into a dark storm cloud of rage, because Wyatt had left and no one gave a shit about him, because of Phoebe.

The girl had changed his trajectory.

He'd better be dead, *her mother would say routinely about her father, but never about Wyatt. No one would wish that on him. But clinging to the sliver of hope that he was still out there, obsessing over the infinite ways that he might someday come home, was an excruciating practice of self-flagellation for them. Allowing their wounds to heal slightly, only to split them open over and over again.*

The sun continued its slow descent over the back fields. June's eyes had started to water. If she could gather her courage to drive to the Deans' tomorrow with Wyatt, and if Wyatt followed through with the plan he'd been contemplating for three days, maybe her wounds could finally heal.

She could be born anew.

June wiped her eyes and went inside to wait for Wyatt to come home from his run. To tell him that they could go, that she was ready for Phoebe Dean's memorial.

That she agreed with him; it was time for the Delroys to finally be seen.

GRANT

Grant sped away from his house to a liquor mart two towns over, in the cheap rental car AJ had loaned him. His phone kept ringing—*Unknown Caller* flashing repeatedly on his screen, terrorizing him. The small-town journalist no doubt, hellbent on eking out a story about that night. He turned off his phone, threw it in the back seat.

Grant pulled into the deserted beige strip mall, and stormed into the liquor store. It had three aisles and multipacks of wine in boxes and a discount bin that smelled of stale beer. He grabbed the first brown bottle he saw and threw some bills on the counter. He imagined the salesgirl was Phoebe, and so before she could open her black bloodied mouth to speak, he was out the door.

He drove into dusk, away from West Wilmer, on the two-lane highway. Phoebe sang in the back seat and there was nothing to see but the darkening night sky and flat horizon. He drove until he felt far enough away from it all, and pulled off the road into a field of dead wheat. He turned off his car and opened the door and sat with his legs on the dry, cracking ground.

The day's light was nearly gone, and he reached behind him to turn up the heat. He drank from the brown bottle and squashed a cricket with the toe of his shoe.

He no longer knew what to do about Becca. She was pushing back, standing up to him, showing up to his house, using her quack doctor as bait; testing him, holding things over him—did she remember more than she'd let on?

Grant suspected it was Becca that had left the deer skull on his car, and used her keys to scratch the number twenty-seven into the hood. There was only one other person who knew what had happened that night, but he'd been gone for ten years and would never come back.

Grant touched his wrist—that reflexive habit that had returned recently, that made him sick every time he did it. He considered taking a saw to his arm so he'd stop rubbing the skin where his father's watch had once been.

That fucking watch. That fucking watch. That fucking watch.

"Seven hundred and fifty dollars." The rat-faced man behind the counter said, pretending he was really scrutinizing it and not about to completely rip him off.

"It's a fucking Rolex," Grant snapped, the high wearing off, the shakes settling in. "It's worth like ten times that."

"Not here it ain't," the man sneered. He was missing a tooth. "Five hundred now, jerkoff."

Grant snatched the watch back and stuffed it in his pocket. He owed nearly five thousand; had stolen from the Dairy Bar, had used all of his savings, had tried to make a few deals out of town himself that had just sank him further in the hole. But he'd be damned if he was going to sell the only thing his father had left him for peanuts.

Grant would give Wyatt the watch, explain that it was real gold, a real Rolex; that if he really wanted the cash quick, he'd have to pawn it himself.

Or maybe they could make a deal, some kind of payment plan; surely they could work something out. Wyatt Delroy was smart, calculating—he wasn't about to go off the deep end for five thousand dollars, right? What did he even need the money for anyway?

Grant threw the half-empty bottle into the dark gray fields and shut his car door. He stared, unseeing, through the front window, clenched his jaw, and wished to god he'd never met Wyatt Delroy.

WYATT

His pillow was wet. Wyatt flipped it to hide the mess and used the blanket to wipe dried blood from his nose. He dragged his tongue around his mouth, which was now entirely bruised, tender flesh. His chest burned; his head was blank, his bones brittle.

But Wyatt had dreamed. He'd dreamed about playing baseball. The sun alight in the sky, melting the crown of his head, discoloring the red of his faded cap the longer he stood in the outfield. His parents were beaming and hyper in the stands, happy coils loaded and ready to spring and cheer when he made a big play.

Hundreds of black vultures in the fields surrounding him, standing motionless, eyeing him; waiting.

Wyatt opened his eyes though he hadn't been asleep. The dream was the only one he ever had. Sometimes he'd be the pitcher, sometimes shortstop, outfield and then infield. His position switched because he couldn't remember the one he'd played regularly as a boy; too much time and too much pain had passed for normal memories such as those.

He sat up slowly, his body sore and slack, and leaned against the cool wall. He touched his nose again, but it was clean now, dry; maybe he'd run out of blood to bleed.

"Wy."

Startled, he gasped. His eyes adjusted to June sitting at the foot of his bed. He couldn't make out her expression in the dark room.

"You scared me." His breathing felt strange, irregular. "I didn't hear you come in. What time is it?"

"It's late. You were screaming," June said, facing away from him, rubbing the quilt beside her with an open palm. "I came to check on you."

"I wasn't screaming," Wyatt said. He wished June would stop rubbing the blanket; he could feel the hot friction in his ears. He thought it harder, hoping she'd stop. She didn't.

"You were. You must have been having a nightmare."

Wyatt drew his knees to his chest, could tell one was newly bruised, the skin soft and tender like a peach. "It's okay, June," he said. "You can talk to me."

June stopped moving her hand. The quiet felt nice; Wyatt could feel the silence stuffing his head.

"I had a bad dream." June sniffed softly. "I didn't want to be alone. I hate being alone—it scares me."

"You aren't alone anymore." Wyatt reached for her at the foot of his bed, but she got up to stand at the window. June drew the curtains aside. She didn't speak but the room filled with her sadness. It was harder for her to pretend at night. Wyatt waited patiently to hear what she'd come in to say, because that was what he was supposed to do. That was why he'd come back. To help her. To help her see.

Wyatt watched June's thin body in the frame of the dark window until finally June spoke: "I don't feel right sometimes, Wy. I don't feel right since Mom died. Sometimes I look in the mirror and I don't recognize myself anymore. Sometimes I think that because of everything that's happened to me, I'm not the same person I was before."

"Maybe that's not so bad."

June sat down heavily on the edge of the bed.

"What brought you in here, June? Really."

"I told you, a dream." June lay back, her head touched his feet, he could feel the warmth radiating from her body. "It's the only dream I have lately. You playing baseball. Vultures in the field. Thousands of them. Waiting for you."

BECCA

She should be at home trying to sleep. She should have taken an Ambien, because she couldn't remember the last time she actually had slept. Was it weeks? It was possible. And so was it really that surprising that she was doing the bad thing? Again?

Becca shook the steering wheel because she wanted to scream. She couldn't stop it anymore. It had found its way in; it was burrowing, it was making a home, it was consuming her.

The way they pitied her. Kelsey and June and Harley. This guilty secret Harley had about Grant that Becca couldn't stop thinking about. Her parents suffocating her. Grant's many cruelties. Becca didn't know which of those cut the deepest, but she'd been sliced and sliced and sliced and now she couldn't stop the bleeding.

She parked her car up the road and waited. She wasn't proud of what she was doing, but he'd forced her hand. They all had. And she'd given Grant chances, so many chances. And she wasn't made of steel. She had faults, like everyone else, and she had a set of parents who were making her crazy, and a memorial that was bringing everything back up, and people in town who didn't think she mattered.

And it wasn't stalking if you weren't caught. It wasn't stalking if you were doing it for the right reasons. This was what she'd come to understand after doing some research online. There were forums! She wished they'd been around when she was younger; that whole thing with AJ had been so blown out of proportion. She'd been a kid, and it had been a mistake that she regretted dearly because it had changed things with everyone, her parents included. They never really looked at her the same way again, and it had been hard to keep explaining these things over and over to her therapist. Explaining herself. Defending herself.

"Your mind is finding ways for you to cope, Rebecca, to heal from the trauma of the accident, to add meaning to what happened by creating these fantasies—"

"They aren't fantasies."

"But if they never quite happened like that, if—"

"They are not fantasies!"

Dr. Murphy smiled kindly. "We'll take it up next week."

The forums had plenty of freaks—lots of variations on the *PeepingTom6969* handles—and her opinion of herself went down slightly every time she logged on, but then she'd sit up straight because, after all, she wasn't like them. She was healing from a trauma.

And so she knew things. Like the fact Phoebe's room was completely untouched, frozen in time like a morbid museum. Becca snickered to herself, remembering what that old bat Mrs. Kilsworth had thought—that there was a room in the house dedicated to Phoebe's awards and trophies. *No, you old hag, there certainly is not.* If anything, it was Grant with the accolades! Three whole trophy shelves! But people constantly blew everything out of proportion when they thought of Phoebe. Had she even been that smart? That pretty? That special? Becca remembered the way Phoebe had looked at her that night, like it would be impossible that her brother would be interested in someone like her, like it would be impossible for her to be accepted into their precious fold.

Or was it the accident that had made Phoebe special and unforgettable? The worst irony of Becca's life, really. That the tragedy had made Phoebe more popular than she'd already been, and now Rebecca Jane Hoyt, who had suffered through it, had been pushed to the side. Over and over and over again.

Becca's eyes stung as she stared unblinking at the house. She knew that sometimes when Grant was really drunk he'd wake up in the middle of the night crying, and go to sleep on Phoebe's bed. He'd always get up early and make his way back to his own room, probably so his mother never found out.

Sometimes Grant would have nightmares and scream: *Why why why?* Maybe his mother could hear him shouting. She'd like to warn him about that—so it was one less thing for Ellen to be resentful about—but didn't know how to bring it up to Grant without explaining how she knew he was doing it.

Becca had a collection of doctors she visited quarterly, making sure they didn't keep digital records or take part in a centralized prescription drug program (another great piece of advice from her forum). She visited Dr. Keens for her Adderall, Dr. Bryce for her modafinil, Dr. Ganock for her Ritalin and Dr. Tanaka for her Ambien, which she only took when the nausea became overwhelming and the shakes hurt her teeth because even Ambien, which most people swore knocked them out like the dead, did very little to keep her nightmares at bay. Sorry, her *hypnagogic disorder*, which meant hallucinations so vivid she was terrified to fall asleep at all.

Phoebe sitting on the edge of her bed. Phoebe doing cartwheels on the ceiling of her room. Phoebe straddling her chest and screaming at her to help him. Him, *always* him. *Even in her hallucinations, Phoebe was a good person trying to help her brother.*

Becca dropped her cigarette and stubbed it out. The red embers sparked on the muddy ground. She'd have to rinse the soles of her boots before going inside. There was a hose on the side of the garage she could use if they hadn't turned the outside water off yet. Or maybe she'd track mud all through the house; Grant deserved it for the way he'd been treating her.

Becca brushed the back of her neck, feeling as though someone had just touched her. She looked behind her, saw nothing but the dark and the swell of empty fields behind the house, exhaled. It must have been the wind picking up, because she was definitely alone out here.

Becca shrank into the shadows as Grant's car pulled into the driveway. She could tell by the way that he staggered to the front steps that he was drunk. He drank heavily, which was such a crutch, when she was right there offering to help him! Sometimes she thought he was too proud, even though she loved him unconditionally, but recently—and she felt her chest seize at the bad thoughts that were wearing her down—she'd wondered if there was more to what had happened that night than she'd been able to see. Or willing to see.

The lights turned on on the main floor, the windows lit up like watchful eyes, and she shivered in the dark. When his bedroom light went on, she crept to the side of the house. There was a tree she could climb that stood right outside his room. He'd usually be too drunk to even close the curtains, and he certainly never locked the window, so she could easily slip inside.

She'd stand at the foot of his bed while he slept. She just wanted to know how he was doing, and when he was sleeping was the best way to know. Sometimes he slept soundly. Sometimes he'd whimper and cry out Phoebe's name. Becca liked the nights when he'd be tossing and turning best, the sheets bunched around him like rope, trying to fight off the striped linens. She liked to watch him struggle because it meant that he was still just as tortured and miserable as she was.

At least that's how she used to feel. But tonight, as she stared into Grant's sleeping face, she noticed that his lids twitched erratically, showing the whites of his eyes, and that he had bags and pockmarked stubble on his chin. As drool leaked from his gaping mouth, she felt the resentment thundering within her.

She'd kept their arrangement for ten whole years. Everything had been on his terms, and she'd gone along with it because she loved him, and what if she'd been found guilty of manslaughter—or worse—and been sent to prison? He'd protected her from a ruined life and she owed him everything; something he reminded her of constantly. But as Becca looked furiously around his bedroom, noticing it was quite empty and bland and pathetic, she wasn't sure if he had been worth it.

Grant had lied for her, but she'd lied for him too. She'd told the police he was sober, and he hadn't been. She'd been watching him all night at Kelsey's house and he'd been drinking heavily, fire in his eyes.

She remembered the screaming in the front seat of the car; the Deans had been fighting. Grant said it had been Phoebe screaming at Becca, that it was because of their relationship, that Phoebe was jealous and he was trying to calm her down. But what if it had been Grant screaming at Phoebe? Hadn't Phoebe been looking for him all night? Hadn't she said it was important? Hadn't she said Grant was hiding from her?

Becca rammed her fists into her eyes so she wouldn't see Phoebe's broken face lying in her lap and Phoebe trying to talk, but unable to because of her severed jaw. Becca had leaned down as close as she dared, Phoebe's breathing a sickly rattle, but all that came out was a slow hiss: *whyyyy*, not a word at all but the very last breath of a dying girl.

Becca stood on Grant's bedroom rug, paralyzed. She wished there was someone she could talk to, a friend. Someone who could help her find clarity about what had really happened on that bridge. Had Grant really stood there, hesitating, to protect Becca? Or was it something else, something she didn't know?

She thought of June. June, who had been a friend to her when they were young. Who had stuck by her even when everyone turned on her because of AJ—Crazy Becca they called her. But then she'd dropped everything for Grant, even when June was going through a tough time at home.

June was lost to her, Becca could tell. It had been too long and she'd been too absent because she'd focused the last ten years of her life on Grant. She'd stayed in town, she hadn't gone to college, she still worked at the rundown market just in case she saw him, or in case he needed her.

What did that say about her? What kind of a person did that make her?

She thought then, miserably, of Harley, who seemed to know something she didn't about Grant. Becca had watched Grant lie easily to the sheriff. Had he lied about other things?

Becca felt like sinking to the floor. She couldn't stop herself from crying in the middle of Grant's boring bedroom. She was so lonely and lost. This had all become too much.

Tomorrow she'd remind Grant that she wasn't the only one who'd lied.

She'd remind Grant that she mattered; that she deserved to not just be heard, but seen.

Tomorrow, everything would change.

TEN YEARS AGO

12:58 a.m.

Grant was high and that was bad news. Reggie Nash checked the time; it was nearly 1 a.m. He looked around the packed living room, noticed how slowly everyone was moving, how long lulls in conversation silenced the entire room. More than one person had fallen asleep on the stairs, someone was passed out on the floor, and it made him feel better. Maybe no one would notice that the star of the West Wilmer football team was high as a kite, continuing to slip. Drinking was accepted, applauded even, but drugs—drugs would get him cut from the team. Scholarship coming or not.

Reggie watched AJ across the room staring at Becca Hoyt, who was on the opposite side of the room staring at Grant. The scene made Reg laugh. AJ's parents had made a big show of taking out that restraining order. It had caused an even bigger rift between the families—a feud that had started in high school, his own parents explained—but it would be just like AJ to be jealous if Becca had moved on to Grant. AJ had a real thing against Grant because AJ was a weaker player and couldn't accept it. But wouldn't that also be typical of Grant—to bang Becca Hoyt just because he could, or to take a dig at AJ? Reg was sure that by graduation Grant would have slept with every girl in this town and the next town over; he didn't exactly have high standards. Sometimes he wondered if Grant did it out of boredom, or because it was the easiest option. He loved Grant like a brother, but he was taking the easy way out too much lately.

Grant was perched on the window ledge staring at his feet on the floor; he seemed angry. One of his hands slipped and he shook his head to himself but didn't look up from his feet. Becca smiled at this. Reggie frowned. He should go see what was wrong with Grant, but he was tired, and if he were being honest with himself, he was getting fed up of worrying about Grant.

"You gotta cut that shit out, man," Reg had said yesterday and the day before that and the week before that, and the countless times in the last several months after Grant had finally stopped lying to him about it.

"It's nothing," Grant said, but wouldn't meet his eye. "It's just a little weed, some pills, helps me sleep—you know how important that is."

"Coach'll cut you, Grant. He will. And I know it's not just a little weed. Why risk everything?"

"You don't know shit, Reg, okay? You don't know the pressure I'm under to clinch this scholarship, so drop it. I'm fucking serious."

Reg got up from the couch, kicking a few empty cans as he did. He walked into the kitchen just as someone rushed out, banging into his shoulder. "Hey, man," Reg yelled. "Look where you're fucking going!" But the house was roaring again and the guy was already lost in the crowded living room. He sighed; he just wanted to go home.

"Reginald."

Reg saw her in the corner of the kitchen, sitting at the table alone, hands around a beer.

"Hey, Phoebe, you good?"

Phoebe stood, staggered slightly. "Did you see who I was just talking to? Who came here tonight? He came to find Grant—Grant's in real trouble, Reg."

Reg adjusted his hat, not liking the dark spark in Phoebe's eye, the one that made her look exactly like her brother. "Who came here? What kind of trouble?"

"Well, Reggie"—Phoebe wasn't smiling—"Wyatt Delroy, Grant's drug dealer, just told me a few things."

"Drug dealer?" Reg held the judgmental stare of his best friend's little sister. "C'mon, Phoebe, I'm sure it's not like that—"

"It's been going on for months, but you just don't want to see it," Phoebe said. "I'll stop them both if I have to—it's for Grant's own good and I do not care what happens to Wyatt Delroy."

Fuck, *Reggie wanted to shout,* fuck. *Was Grant really so careless to cheat so badly when he didn't even have to? If Reg was honest, he wasn't sure. But what he was very goddamn sure about was that Phoebe was principled, and that there was probably nothing she wouldn't do—rat out Wyatt Delroy included—if she thought it would save her brother.*

Reg laughed at himself and then smiled at Phoebe. It was late, the party would wind down soon, and he knew he was drunk enough that he wouldn't remember any of this in the morning. Besides, this had nothing to do with him. It was just a drunken sibling spat—lord knows they'd been fighting a lot lately.

"I just saw Grant in the living room, but hey." Reg grabbed Phoebe's slender arm. "He's in a mood, and it's not easy you know, the pressure he's put on himself."

Phoebe frowned. "Even if he's a little lost right now, he'll straighten out, I know it. I know him, Reg."

Reg watched the kitchen door slam shut after her. He cleared his throat uncomfortably. He heard a crash from somewhere inside the house. Or maybe it was more thunder. Whatever it was, something didn't feel right. Something didn't feel right at all.

GRANT

The Day of the Phoebe Dean Memorial

The day he'd been dreading for a month—for ten years—had come. It had stalked him, hunted him down, laid claim to its kill.

Grant heard his mother moving around on the floor below him—rearranging chairs, pushing the couch against the wall, fighting back raw tears at her loss. They came so easily to her, an endless reservoir; had she ever even tried to heal?

It was only morning but already Grant couldn't stand to be in his room. Or in the living room or on the porch. Nowhere in the house felt right, everywhere felt wrong. He was so jittery his temples ached. For the second night in a row he couldn't shake the feeling that someone had been breathing on his face as he slept, but every time he turned on the light there was no one. Just him and his demons.

He looked to the window, the barn, the endless stretch of gray sky beyond. He could run. Find a new town, start over. But it would chase him, find him, drag him down again; he'd be hunted forever, he knew that.

Grant forced his body to move, got dressed. Maybe tonight wouldn't be so bad, maybe it would be nice. He raked his fingers through his hair so hard it hurt his scalp. He stared at a clump of hair in his fist and clenched his teeth; even he didn't believe his own lies anymore.

Grant walked into the kitchen, surprised to see his mother sitting at the table, hanging onto a mug of tea and not busying herself at the stove so she wouldn't have to look at him.

"Morning." He opened an overhead cabinet and saw a pink mug that hadn't been there yesterday. He pulled out the hunk of misshapen clay: *PHOEBE* was scrawled in childish handwriting, punctuated with a tiny handprint. He shoved it to the back of the cupboard and took out a stained white one.

"Grant, I'm glad you're up." His mother's fingers were bone-white, clutching her tea. "Can you please get her journal?"

He leaned hard into the counter. "What?" His voice sounded hoarse.

"The journal, can you get it for me? It's in her bedroom."

The coffee was hot and scorched his throat. He drank it all anyway, welcoming the burn and the split second it overpowered what was happening; his mother had moved the journal again so he would be sure to see it. "Right now?"

"Yes. Now."

"Sure." Grant left the kitchen and this dance of theirs. She was punishing him and he would let her. Phoebe was dead and it was his fault.

He waded through dread back up the stairs to the long hall that creaked underfoot, to the door of Phoebe's bedroom, to the place he would never choose to set foot in; unless he woke up in her bed disoriented and sick and heartbroken, something he was doing a lot lately.

Grant opened the door very reluctantly. The smell hit him first: mint toothpaste and rose water; her.

Their mother would clip roses from the garden, place petals in a bowl of water for Phoebe's dresser, thinking they were her favorite flower, but they weren't. Phoebe had loved wildflowers, the beautiful unruliness of them; how they could bloom in the harshest of conditions.

There was a field of them near the barn. *I think it's what the ocean might look like*, she'd confided in him when they were children and still spent all their time together out there.

Had their mother known Phoebe at all?

Grant held his breath, crossed the threshold. He'd be quick and he wouldn't see Phoebe sitting on her chair or by the foot of her bed, and he wouldn't try to talk to her or try to touch her hair because it had been so soft but he couldn't remember what it felt like anymore. No, he would think of something other than that rain-drenched night and the horrible mistakes he'd made out of reckless desperation, and how shitty his life was now because of them.

Those twenty-seven minutes.

Grant scoured the wooden desk that was covered with Phoebe's things. His mother still insisted that nothing be touched; to remember her daughter, to torture her son—two sides of the same coin.

Phoebe's colored pencils sat in an old football trophy of his; a dusty science textbook was held open with a pink ruler, as if she might run in any minute to finish her homework. Grant's throat ached as he rifled through spiral notebooks and avoided looking at the ceiling, and the stars that he'd helped her put up, the ones that glowed that shade of green that existed only in childhood.

One night before the accident he caught Phoebe on the roof outside her bedroom.

"Phoebe?" He was so shocked to see her out there smoking that he figured he must be drunker than he was. "What are you doing? It's the middle of the night."

Phoebe looked over her shoulder at him and smiled, and dropped the cigarette to the ground. "I'm trying to relax," she said. "The stars are so bright out tonight."

"And is smoking helping you relax?"

"Not really."

"If Mom finds out, you know she'll find a way to blame this on me. Like I forced you or something."

"Maybe not this time," Phoebe said quietly. "Maybe—" But then she shook her head and lit another one.

Grant pushed off from her window ledge but something

stopped him from leaving her room. Phoebe didn't do things like this, not really. He considered climbing out there with her, to talk about the fighting that was erupting between Phoebe and their mother. That he'd been right that morning in the fields—their mother was that cruel. That now that Phoebe was so close to getting what she'd spent her whole life reaching for, their mother had decided she couldn't bear to let her go.

"How could you leave me?" Grant had overheard his mother ask Phoebe. "What's so wrong with the community college nearby? What's so wrong with the home I've made for you? It's been hard, you know, doing everything on my own for this long. I've done everything for you, and this is how you're going to repay me? Abandon me like your father did?"

"But isn't this what you've always wanted?" Phoebe had shouted and Grant had smiled, though it was unnerving to hear them argue. "What was it all for then?"

Grant watched his little sister sitting cross-legged on the roof, her slim back to him, knowing that she must be cold. He should sit with her and watch the stars and bring up the suffocating pressure that filled every inch of their home.

As if reading his mind, Phoebe leaned back on her elbows and tilted her head to the night sky. "Do you think I don't know what you're doing? Do you think you can keep things from me? You can't let me down, Grant."

Grant's mood turned instantly. He was tired of hearing all the ways he was disappointing her. Could she not talk about something else? "And what exactly am I doing, Phoebe? Other than checking on you in the middle of the fucking night?"

"I'm trying my best," Phoebe said. "But if you keep slipping we'll never get out of here—"

"Just flush your cigarettes down the fucking toilet, I can't have her on my back right now," he shouted, and then stormed out of her bedroom.

The journal wasn't on Phoebe's desk so Grant spun around, every corner of her room pulling at him. The light blue bedspread she'd lie on to read; the twinkly lights on the headboard that she'd never unplug; an old hat of his hanging from one of the bedposts. Grant swallowed. She'd often worn his hats, no matter how beaten up or poorly fitting. That she'd loved him so much when he was so unworthy of it, that she'd wasted so much of her precious time on him, made him sick.

He had to get out of there. He turned again, searching, feeling spent and nauseated, and then saw Phoebe sitting on the bed, holding the journal out to him.

"I know you killed me." She tucked her long hair behind her ear. Her nail polish was starting to chip; he knew she'd fix that soon, she didn't like for her polish to chip. "But I don't know why. Didn't you trust me? After everything I did for you?"

Grant tried to grab the worn brown journal, but Phoebe held it over her head. She had two black eyes and a wide gash on her forehead that was pumping blood down her face, dripping onto the collar of her jacket.

"Soon everyone will know what you did, Grant. It's come, it's here. They'll hate you more than they already do—was it worth it?"

He lunged this time, knocking over the heavy cream lamp on her bedside table to grab it. He wiped sweat from his forehead and left the room, slamming the door. He leaned against the wall in the hallway, holding Phoebe's thin journal. It was water-logged, musty; rodents had nibbled half of it away. He flipped through, but just snippets of words were legible: *worried*, *throwing it away*, *lost*. There were some doodles, what looked like dried pools of urine. He kept flipping: *future*, *our plan*, *freedom*, his heart bursting through his chest, and then to the last page, marked with a dried wildflower.

Who's he involved with???

If he won't stop it, I will.

I won't give up on him.

Grant closed the book, careful not to disturb the petrified blue stem that marked her last entry, then took the stairs down to the kitchen two at a time. He dropped the journal in front of his mother, who hadn't moved and was still staring deep into her mug.

"Thank you." She dabbed at her eyes with the edge of a fraying tea towel.

He didn't bother putting his mug away or speaking to her. He grabbed his keys from the counter and hurried out of the house.

WYATT

The water was like ice. When Wyatt flapped his arms away from his body and then brought them back in, the movement made everything even colder. Deep within himself, his bones were numb; his skin was blue under the water. Wyatt held his breath and opened his eyes, that strange sensation of wet on wet, the writhing distortion of everything above him.

He needed air, so he moved himself to sit up, leaned back against the side of the bathtub, felt the water rush from his body, cooling it further.

This was where he felt most at peace. In water. He was light, suspended, otherworldly; a vestige of the womb, perhaps. Of the time when he'd almost existed, but not quite.

The bathtub was too small to float in entirely, but even the slightest buoyancy made him calmer than he'd been in days. Wyatt was losing himself to this house; to June. He could feel it as it happened—this gradual slackening of himself, this dimming.

They were ebbing and flowing together; as Wyatt dulled, June sharpened. This was a good thing; this was the whole point.

The shower curtain was old and yellowing and moldy at the bottom. Wyatt drew the hardening plastic aside, the rusting metal rings screeched along the rod and he cringed—the shrill sound of nails on a chalkboard slipped under his skin.

There was only one towel on the hook and it was June's. There was nothing in the house that still belonged to him. But that was okay. He was no longer a part of this house. Maybe he had never been.

Wyatt stood and shivered as the rest of the water rushed from his body to below him. His feet looked bony and webbed under the inch of remaining bathwater.

He grabbed the towel and wrapped it around his skeletal body. He hadn't eaten anything since he'd returned, and he'd lost more weight—something June had started to notice now that she'd been released from her shock of grief. Wyatt stepped out of the tub, his paper-thin white skin flushed with goosebumps.

The single light above the medicine cabinet flickered in annoyed warning that it was about to give up and finally go out.

He should have fixed that; as he should have fixed everything else around the house. But no, that was not why he'd come back. Lights and heat and broken windows were things that June could handle on her own. He'd come back with something far more valuable to her: Strength. The truth. Knowing. A fresh start. To plant a seed in that patch of dirt she kept talking about; to tend to new sinuous roots. June had always loved being outside, digging in the ground; she'd kept a wriggling pink worm in a jar once as a pet.

Wyatt stood at the sink, dried himself, opened the cabinet with its neat rows of orange bottles. Pain medication, sleeping pills, vitamins, a vast assortment of hard-pressed powders that had tried their best to keep their mother alive; and when that scale tipped, as comfortable as possible as she died.

What a joke, Wyatt thought bitterly. Death was too final to be comfortable.

The orange bottles were all empty, so Wyatt shut the cabinet door. He bared his remaining teeth in the mirror, gnashed them violently at his reflection. Tried to count how many he'd lost since he'd come home. At least five, maybe six, but all in the back. None yet so visible that June could know that he was peeling away from himself. He had wanted to tell her the truth so many times, but had stopped, told himself to wait. If it was too soon she'd force him to leave, and he knew she still needed him.

Wyatt saw his mother lying on the flimsy cot in the ambulance—the frailty of her spent body and the yellow of her skin, and the profound sadness that color represented. June might not yet, but Wyatt understood their mother's need to lie to herself about him, her wayward son. The lies she spun had kept him alive and them tethered. He forgave their mother for getting lost in the pretenses of her never-ending fantasies—that he'd joined the circus or the Marines or was deep in the Pacific, drilling oil—because he knew they weren't weakness, but slivers of hope. A way to keep afloat in the bottomless unknown. A way to survive. And who were the remaining Delroys, if not survivors?

Wyatt leaned closer to the mirror, the light still flickering on and off in the small cold bathroom. His left eye had the purple outline of a bruise forming, and his nails, despite constantly trying to clean them, were still tar black and most were ripped and split or missing altogether.

There was a soft knock on the door. Wyatt turned to the shy sound. "Just a minute."

"Wyatt?"

"I just need a minute, I'm almost done."

June opened the door a crack. "Wyatt?"

"What is it?"

She hid her face behind the door. "Are you sorry?"

Wyatt drew the towel tighter around his waist.

The light flickered with an audible buzz he could physically feel, and then the bathroom sank into complete darkness. "Am I sorry for what?" he asked into the black.

June breathed shallowly beyond the door; her nails squeezed the side but she wouldn't show herself to him. "Are you sorry that you left that night? Because then Dad left, and then Mom gave up. Are you sorry that you did that, that you left me alone? It was so hard, being in this house without you."

Wyatt fiddled with the light switch, wondered if that would help. He dried his hands on the towel and then tightened the bulb gently. The light flared briefly, enough for him to see his face in the mirror, and then went out again, pitching him into thick, oppressive black; there were no windows in their bathroom.

"Yes, Juney." Wyatt spoke to her thin white fingers gripping the door. "I'm sorry."

"Do you mean that?" June whispered. "You're not just saying that, are you?"

“I’m not just saying that. I am sorry. Are you sure about tonight? You’re ready for this? I can go alone if you want. There’ll be no turning back—things will change. Do you understand?”

June pushed the door open an inch, stood on her tiptoes to peer over his shoulder at his reflection in the mirror. Muddy light seeped in from the hallway. He watched her eyes widen and then adjust until she could see him. June was startled and then confused and then fearful. “Sorry,” she said, quickly shutting the door.

“Are you sure you’re ready, June?”

Wyatt was grateful for the silence that answered him. He didn’t have the strength for another fraught conversation about the shapes of June’s grief, about whether there were birds in her room or their mother at the foot of her bed. These were round and tiresome arguments, even though he was pleased she still had fight left, even if it was just with him for now.

“Just another minute,” Wyatt said loudly, but he knew that June had left the hallway to sit on the couch, legs tucked under her, picking at the skin of her fingernails, waiting nervously for him.

Wyatt tried again with the string and the switch and the bulb, burned himself this time, but there was one last shot of light. A quick burst, enough to make out his hand with the broken talons, clutching the frayed string, his thin twig-like red arm with the short white hairs sticking straight up, his orange crooked beak, his tar black feathers, his red baseball cap.

No, no, this was all wrong. He leaned forward to rap the mirror with his hooked avian beak, until the image of the vulture disappeared and he was there again in the reflection. Wyatt. As he had been: young, troubled, lost; the catalyst.

As he had been.

Wyatt smiled in the dark, for tonight he was not only the catalyst, but the reaction; the reckoning.

GRANT

He sped from his house, fleeing his sad, spiteful mother in their kitchen, his sister he missed so much it ached, this life that was closing in on him. Driving at one time had relaxed him, but not anymore. Now he sat in a tiny box, suffocating. How had it come to this? How had he ruined so many lives?

Grant drove aimlessly for what felt like hours. He fidgeted with the internal temperature of the car, cranked open the window and fiddled with the dials on the stereo. There was nothing but country music on the local stations so he turned it off and drove in silence until the silence was deafening, and he turned it back on and found the first thing that wasn't country: a preacher with a gravelly voice reading from the Bible. Fine—anything was better than silence screaming at him.

Grant clenched his jaw, clutched the wheel and refocused on the road. On the fragmented brown fields. On the sky that bisected the flat horizon, and the occasional speck of bird. On the new bright signs stuck into dead lawns that were multiplying like rabbits. He'd have to show up next week to the church basement or the school gym to plead his case—that the bridge had to stay up; that Phoebe wouldn't have wanted it any other way.

Do it for Phoebe, he'd plead, feigning earnestness, and the image made him retch.

Grant picked up speed, was flying dangerously now, trying to outrun what he'd done.

He turned the wheel hard, chewing up loose gravel. He could see the old water tower in the distance—*W ST W LM R*—the letters half washed-out, the boarded-up drive-in next to it. He passed three abandoned barns on his left, blackened and craggy, sinking slowly into the dry ground until they'd eventually become a part of it.

He recognized with a start where he was, and hesitated before pulling into the parking lot nervously. He slid his sunglasses on, forced his hands to release from the wheel, felt blood flood his numb fingers.

He watched through the frosted glass door as the sheriff left his office to stand at reception, toothpick in his mouth, grinning down at the pretty receptionist.

Grant sat in the parking lot for ten minutes, pretending that he was about to put an end to it all, pretending that he was a better man than he was. That he could walk right through that door and file a report of what had happened that night. The whole sequence of events.

Well, son, the sheriff would say sternly but appraisingly, *good for you for finally telling the truth.*

But it wouldn't happen that way. The sheriff would cuff him in disgust and then lose sleep himself over how unjust it had been that Grant Dean had spent the last decade a free man. That if the sheriff had only just pried a little, or investigated the crash site at all, it could have given the town closure. Saved it. Saved them all.

The sheriff would polish off the bottle of whiskey he kept hidden in his desk drawer for really tough days, appalled that Grant Dean had spent the last decade waking up in his warm bed and earning a paycheck and having sex whenever he wanted to and throwing the football for Reg and Heather's boys and occasionally having fun and even sometimes, though not often and not for long, forgetting.

"You're right, big brother." Phoebe poked her head up from the back seat. "You're a monster. It is amazing though that no one has figured it out. Maybe you always were the lucky one."

"Lucky?" he said, rubbing his eyes. "*Christ.*"

"You can still tell the truth." Phoebe caught his eye and then looked out the window of the car, not able to stomach him. He stopped himself from reaching for her because he preferred her this way—angry. It was better than when she was young and alive and unaware of what would come bearing down on her at his hand. "You can still be who I thought you were."

Phoebe flung open the car door, but sat there a minute with her feet barely skimming the ground. "You promised me that you'd do the right thing. You could keep at least that one." And then she hopped down, whistling, as she rounded the corner of the sheriff's office.

Grant wiped the sweat from his neck and shoved his forehead onto the steering wheel, pushing on it until he saw stars. He exhaled loudly at the floor of the car; he was tired. He was so tired. What would happen when he finally cracked? It felt inevitable.

He threw the car into reverse and drove the other way, the twenty minutes to the bridge.

The autopsy report had concluded that Phoebe died about forty minutes after the initial impact of the truck into the guardrail. Forty minutes of lying on the bridge in the rain, dying. He tried not to wonder what her last thoughts might have been, if she'd had any. He prayed she'd been knocked unconscious and never woken up, though in his gut he knew that was unlikely, partly because he'd thought he saw her moving as she lay there with Becca, and partly because he just knew.

He touched his wrist, still bare. Of course. That fucking watch. He clenched his jaw until his temples burned.

He suspected the report was in his house somewhere, maybe in the back of his mother's closet or in the bottom drawer of her jewelry box. He knew his mother would have kept it; it being the last remaining shred of Phoebe's life. Not just the official cause of how she'd died, the hard proof that she was really gone, but the last new thing relating to Phoebe. There would be nothing new about his little sister anymore.

Phoebe would never blow out another candle, or marvel at the vastness of the stars in the sky, or laugh, delighted, at the lights of the town fair, not caring who heard her earnest joy; she would never get married, have children, leave town.

"The New York Public Library has forty miles of books under a park. The same park had a cemetery once." Phoebe hadn't

looked up from the book she was reading but told him, excitedly, the second he walked into the kitchen.

Tired from practice and still slightly hungover, Grant leaned over the sink, running the faucet until the water was cold. "Okay, Phoebe, I'll bite—and?"

*Phoebe looked over at him and laughed; later, he would remember the way the sunlight hit the table where she sat, but not the sound of her laughter. "Well, Grant—*and*—at first I thought books and people buried underground together was really creepy, but now I think it's poetic. Come on, don't look at me like that." She laughed again. "Just think about it—two completely different things going on and on forever. What could be more beautiful?"*

Grant had come to the bridge to look over the railing. He spent twenty-seven minutes staring down into the swirling water. He was bleary-eyed and dizzy by the time he looked away. His fists pulsed and his eyes stung.

Twenty-seven minutes. It was the exact length of time he'd spent saving himself. He'd been soaked with rain and blood and panicked desperation and had spent nearly half an hour frantically serving his own needs, bargaining with Phoebe's life, rather than saving her.

He watched the river another minute. The calm that some found being near water was the opposite for him. To him the river was a battleground; the water fighting itself, churning and spitting and frothing; angry and vengeful and filled with dark secrets.

Grant walked slowly back to his car. He'd spent the better part of the day driving around town, staying away from the house, but sensed that as he drove away from the bridge, cutting it close to the start of the memorial at his house, it had come for him.

It was a similar feeling to that night ten years ago. Something was fracturing; something was coming undone.

Phoebe yelled at him, but it felt different. Her voice was loud enough for some people to look, despite the frenzied chaos of a high-school party, but he wondered if she was just going through the motions. If she was angry with him as a reflex.

Grant had dragged her into Kelsey's empty kitchen. He couldn't tear his eyes from hers. His little sister. Just us, *they used to say.* We'll be okay. *Phoebe squeezed a red plastic cup, but there was something new in her eyes, something he couldn't place.*

Was Phoebe finally tired of being disappointed? Was she about to give up on him? She had suspected too much for too long; what would she do if she thought he was a lost cause, that he had broken his promise, that he had let her down?

The thought of Phoebe jumping from their island terrified him.

Grant snatched the cup from her hands and threw it against the wall and then grabbed onto both of her thin arms. He dragged her through the kitchen to the back door.

"You need to work out more." Phoebe fought to escape. Grant squeezed harder. "But you have drugs for that, right?

You might need more of them because they don't seem to be working."

"You don't know what you're talking about—"

"Wyatt came here to find you! How stupid do you think I am, bringing him right in my face? You owe him a lot of money! You spent all of our money on drugs for football?"

"That's not true." Grant dug his fingers into her skin, nearly drawing blood. "I didn't bring him here, so whatever you think, you're wrong, and you're definitely not going to open your fucking mouth to anyone—"

"You tried to pay him off with Dad's watch?" Phoebe was quite drunk. "Do you respect nothing? What's happened to you? You're scaring me—I don't know you anymore."

Grant touched his naked wrist and felt himself rage at all of the things that were slipping away from him. "Phoebe—fuck! Let's just talk about this, okay? It's important that you know—"

"Wyatt told me everything—the steroids, that he's going to tell your coach if you don't pay up, that the watch wasn't enough. He has no loyalty to you, Grant—he's dangerous. Did you see him tonight? He has nothing to lose! He could really hurt you." Phoebe wrenched her arm from his grip, dark purple marks forming where his hands had been.

Grant yanked her arm back down again, saw on her face that he was really hurting her; gripped as hard as he could. "Phoebe." Grant could feel her pulse pumping under his hands; they were outside now and it was pouring rain, but they were halfway across the lawn, nearly at the truck. "I have it under control, I know all about Wyatt*—I could finish him—"*

"This was for both of us!" Phoebe screamed, but she was hard to hear over the rain and the anger pounding in his head. "Why do you think I've tried so hard? I've tried for you—for you*! So you can get away from this and have something better!"*

Phoebe managed to pull away from him, but with nowhere else to go, she climbed quickly up into the truck. She looked behind her to the back seat, startled. "Becca?"

"I need to talk to Grant." Becca was half-asleep and slurring. "We have plans."

Phoebe looked at her brother with eyes that seared.

Grant needed to think but he didn't have time. He knew Phoebe wouldn't be able to keep this to herself. It wasn't even the drugs, it was the cheating. The principle. That he'd wandered so far from her, that he'd kept lying and broken her trust. Even if Phoebe tried to keep it to herself to protect him, and he knew she would try, it would eat away at her.

No one knew his sister better than he did.

"Phoebe, please..." Grant was terrified; had she really confronted Wyatt? Wyatt, who insisted on secrecy. Wyatt, who wouldn't know if he could trust her. What did any of this mean? What if she told his coach? Would she do that to him? Fuck, what if she already had? "Phoebe, this is my life, we need to talk about this alone." Then he screamed into the rearview mirror: "Becca, get out of my fucking car!"

"Wait—Becca." Phoebe turned quickly. "The big house on Maple, right? My brother is scaring me a little and I need some time to think, so we'll drop you off on the way. We'll just have to take the bridge."

JUNE

You look nice," Wyatt mumbled. "Really pretty, Juney."

June watched him fumble with the seatbelt with hands that were stubborn and slow. She was driving to the memorial because he didn't have a driver's license or wallet. Small particulars that made it seem as though he were floating above the surface of the earth without leaving an imprint or disturbing anything.

Mrs. Lloyd was increasingly begrudging about loaning them her car. *Again, June? But you just used it!* June had asked her anyway. She was feeling better, stronger, the colors outside a bit brighter; her mother continuing to slowly recede.

Wyatt finally managed the belt; click. "Quite the event tonight I guess."

June pulled out of their long, overgrown driveway and gave him a funny look. "What was that?"

"What was what?" Wyatt stared out the window as dusk

settled around them, purples and pinks and oranges aglow. June noticed his hair was matted and sticky at the nape of his neck, despite all the time he'd spent in the shower.

"Nothing, just that it's a memorial, not an event. Just that you used that word right now—*event*."

Wyatt shrugged slowly and blew on the window, forming a rounded heart on the glass. "Memorial, *event*, what's the difference?"

"Nothing, no difference."

Event. June held it in her mouth and then said it under her breath. She was pleased it wasn't causing her any discomfort at all, that it had thawed into just a word. She found herself smiling at her brother beside her, at their bond, at his company over the last few days—as strange and volatile as it had been.

"What did you want to be when you grew up?" June asked, the thought striking her suddenly. "I never asked you when we were kids. Maybe you can do that, be that. You're young, there's still time."

"Dinosaurs," Wyatt gurgled as he wedged himself against the side of the car. "Paleontologist?"

"Oh?" June felt uneasy. "Funny, Mrs. McCray said something like that when I was in the hardware store yesterday."

Wyatt exhaled shakily onto the window again, his breath bleeding onto the glass. "Drop me off before the house."

"Before the house?" June's heart sank. "Are you not coming inside?"

Wyatt drew his hand to his mouth and spat, the wet sound lingering in the car. He held his palm out so June could see his tooth in a glob of red blood. His canine. He'd already lost his molars; June had found them and considered keeping them safe for him somewhere, but in the end she'd buried them with the bird. Wyatt wiped his mouth with the back of his hand. June tried to look away from the blood but found that she couldn't. She felt the familiar prick of tears. "Wyatt, I made you a doctor's appointment for tomorrow. I'll take you and stay with you the whole time. We'll figure this out together; it's going to be okay."

Wyatt angled his head awkwardly. His eyes couldn't focus on her. He looked so tired, so thin. "I know you're a good person, Wy. I know things would have been different if Dad hadn't pushed you away, if Mom had stood up for you. And I know you're not feeling well, that you're very sick. Thank you for coming back home. I love you, Wy, you're a good brother."

Wyatt knit his eyebrows together, trying hard to focus, and then snapped out of it and smiled, a kind smile, crimson blood smeared on his remaining teeth like he'd lifted his head from a kill. "Of course I came home for you. You're my little sister, Juney." Wyatt used the hem of his sweater to wipe his face clean. "You've done good, with your questions and your prying. I knew you'd be able to do it. So you go inside first—find Grant and tell him that I'm back and I want to talk; he'll know what it's about."

June was trying hard not to cry. "Why can't you just come in with me? You don't have to hide anymore; they probably only care about Phoebe still anyway, especially tonight."

Wyatt pinched the bridge of his nose, turned back to the darkening window. "Phoebe was a good girl. She never got in trouble—I did."

"That doesn't make it okay."

Wyatt swung his head back. This slow pendulum act was frightening her. He looked so unwell. June was afraid he was dying, that he had the same cancer their mother had and that he'd come back to clear his conscience before he died. The cancer had taken their mother in seven months; how much time did Wyatt have left?

He smiled grimly, patted her gently on the knee. "No, it doesn't make it okay, it makes it rather tragic. But you'll be fine. You're stronger than you think, June, I know you are. You can go in there and talk to people. You can tell Grant that I'm back and I want to see him. We can all three of us have a nice little chat. See? It wouldn't work if I told you, June. It has to be Grant. It has to come from him."

BECCA

Becca turned off her phone, silencing the calls from her parents and Debbie. She'd deal with her parents later, and Debbie would get over what she'd done. Right now her whole frequency was off. Everything was confusing her; she had too many voices in her head arguing about what she actually remembered about the accident, and what she'd been told and whether any of it was true.

Becca steeled herself, took the time to smooth out her new black dress, set her shoulders back, attempted eye contact with anyone who looked her way. But after ten or so minutes, she realized that no one cared that she was there. That although she'd been a big part of that night ten years ago—had been *very badly injured* even—that when in Mrs. Dean's orbit, she'd been relegated to nothing more than a passing thought. A mere slip of a thought. A wisp.

Becca couldn't catch her breath. She needed to calm down if

she was going to talk to Grant. Confront him. Becca scanned the living room but he was still nowhere to be found. There were a dozen people milling about but no one she cared to talk to. No one interesting. No one who would really see her.

Becca nodded curtly at a customer or a neighbor or a friend of her parents, but remained secure in her corner, waiting for Grant, smearing soft cheese onto crackers and shoving them one by one into her mouth.

The cheese was pungent so she tried a mini quiche, but that was too crumbly, so she gave up on the appetizers and, feeling extremely on edge and fidgety now, strode hurriedly around the living room calming herself by looking at porcelain knickknacks and stacks of old-fashioned books and trying her best to avoid being roped into small talk because she didn't think she could manage it.

Across the room, Becca was surprised to see that June had come and was nodding politely at something Reg Nash was saying. Heather looked in her direction and waved her over, but Becca couldn't bear it—not another conversation where people looked at her as if she didn't matter, when wasn't this entire thing her fault? Would they even be here tonight if it weren't for her? No, those days of being ignored were over; she just needed to do something quickly before finding Grant. Becca spun on her heels and found the stairs to the second floor.

Phoebe's room was such a pleasant change from Grant's empty one. The bed was light blue, their favorite color, and had a canopy over it with twinkly lights that still worked. Mrs. Dean must change the battery pack whenever they went out, because she seemed to care a lot more about her dead daughter than her living son.

The blankets smelled of dust and mildly of urine. Grant, Becca figured, passed out and sleeping in Phoebe's bed. Becca plugged her nose and lay back on the bed for a minute, staring at the cobwebs under the canopy until she felt the wave of nausea pass. She turned to the bedside table, sat with the bowl of jewelry in her lap. She removed Phoebe's pearl earrings; Phoebe's gold necklace with the locket; Phoebe's thin bangles. Becca put them all back in the bowl. She had to be careful; she was owed these treasures but she couldn't keep anything for too long. She couldn't have anyone notice they were missing.

Becca opened the closet, picked up some of the folded sweatshirts from the shelves, smelled them. Moved to the hangers, ran her hand along the tops, touched the plastic bag that hung at the very back. Becca hesitated, her spine tingling, before she unzipped the bag and brought the hardened leather jacket to her cheek. She could still smell blood and sweat from that night on it.

Becca pictured Phoebe lying in the rain, the pink of the jacket slowly blooming to red. She zipped the plastic bag back up, left the closet; it was a horrible image.

There was a very small bathroom attached to the bedroom. Because nothing had been touched, there was a thick blanket of dust on everything, and rust sprouting on surfaces, and mouse droppings in corners and dead insects everywhere, but still, Becca loved the bathroom because it was as if she were stepping back in time to when they might be having a sleepover, or had convinced their parents to let them study together, when in reality they'd be trying on makeup and gossiping about boys, and mostly talking about how she'd marry Grant one day.

Just like she'd always wanted.

Under the sink were bottles of nail polish, but they'd all dried up and could no longer be opened, the polish hard as cement. She'd tried once to break one by smashing it against the tub, but it had made such a loud thunk that she didn't dare try again.

The rest of the drawers were filled with Phoebe's makeup. Becca opened every lip gloss and tried them all on. Most of them were solid and had long finished rotting and were now putrid and cracked, so she just smelled those before returning them to their special spots.

In Phoebe's makeup bag she found one blush that wasn't too spoiled, but she had to use her fingers because she couldn't find any brushes. She'd remember to bring one of hers next time.

Becca looked at herself in the mirror. She had used too much electric pink blush, but it had been Phoebe's and so she left it there; a piece of Phoebe on her skin. With her hair so long and dark now, she looked a bit like her, like Phoebe. Becca smiled, pleased. Grant loved his sister so much. She hoped he'd notice. Maybe it would make their conversation easier.

Becca left the bathroom and made her way to the bedroom door to leave, but then stopped, eyeing the corner of something sticking out from under the ruffled bed skirt. She bent down, and pulled out what looked like the remains of a very old journal, then sat back down on the bed. Becca opened it and flipped through tattered pages that were quite unreadable, but realized quickly that she was reading Phoebe's diary.

Becca's heart stopped. She'd been in this room dozens of times—how had she never seen this before? She looked quickly to the closed door, thought she heard footsteps outside. Becca held her breath and flipped to the last few pages, read quickly, felt tears prick her eyes. *Yes*, she nodded, her heart swelling. *Yes*.

The bedroom door swung open and Becca sprang up. "Oh," she gasped. "I didn't hear you, I was just—"

Grant stood in the doorway, eyes narrowed in confusion, and then reared his head back and laughed. "Is that my sister's goddamn makeup on your face? That's rotten and ten years old? You look like a clown."

"Grant." Becca reached for him but he backed away from her. "Grant, we need to talk. You can't keep treating me like this—"

"Wait—are you reading her journal?" Grant's face had gone so red it was purple; Becca watched sweat stream from his temples. "Please tell me—*Becca*—that you are not in my sister's bedroom reading her private journal. You're not, you could not be doing that—I refuse to believe this is happening."

"No, just wait, please." Becca stood on trembling legs. "It says right here that she knew you were involved with someone. Phoebe already *knew* about us, so maybe others did too, and we don't have to keep it a secret anymore—"

Grant snatched the journal from her hands and shoved her hard in the chest. Becca fell back on the bed, winded and afraid. "Harley!" Grant screamed down in her face. "It was Harley!"

Grant raised his arm as if he might hit her, but then threw his head back and laughed until the veins in his neck bulged blue. Becca watched in horror as spit flew from his mouth; her heart shattered inside her chest. Harley? Harley's secret and guilt. Harley, this whole time. "How could you?" Becca had painful tears in her eyes. "How could you do that to me, seeing us both at the same time—"

Grant stopped laughing abruptly. He looked down at her slowly. Breathed heavily. The room fell silent. He stared at her without blinking; his eyes seared. Then Grant balled his hands into fists and shoved them into his pockets, where Becca could see through the fabric of his jeans that he continued to open and close them; flexing, throbbing.

Becca stood up from the bed, backed away nervously; she'd never seen him like this before.

"I need you to listen to me," Grant said carefully. His jaw was so tight, bone showed through his stretched skin. "I'm done with this—with you. It's over, whatever this is. God, this has been hard, and you've made it so much harder, do you know that? Do you care? It doesn't matter now, but honestly, you've always scared me." Grant smiled a crazed smile and Becca stepped closer to the door, away from whatever was happening to him, her heart stuck in her throat. "No, wait, don't go yet, because I've always wanted to ask you this: do you make up these lies because you love the attention, or are you actually completely fucking insane?" Grant pointed to the door and opened his mouth to scream: "*Get the fuck out of my sister's room!*"

GRANT

Grant had to use the wall in the far corner of the living room to prop himself up. It was very hot and he was drenched in sweat.

There were about thirty people now, the couches were full, the chairs that had been set up around them also full. People had broken into small groups, whispering; the occasional nose was blown.

A few judgmental eyes found their way over to where he stood alone, but would just as quickly flit back as they resumed their conversation. If anyone had heard him screaming at Becca upstairs, no one seemed to care.

He was drunk but didn't know what else to do to get through the night, so he just poured himself another. The ice bucket was getting low; he should fill it before his mother had to seek him out, annoyed to have to engage with him. Grant grabbed the bin just as someone tapped him lightly on the shoulder.

"Grant?"

"Oh." Grant nearly dropped the bucket. "June?"

June fiddled with the strap of her purse; he noticed she had bitten her nails to the quick. "I'm sorry about Phoebe."

Grant clutched the bucket to his chest. "Thank you."

"You're right, it never really goes away."

The condensation from the bucket seeped through his sweater, soaking his chest. "No, it doesn't."

"What happened to your hand?"

Grant held it up, surprised. The sloppy bandage job he'd done had loosened, and his knuckles peeked out, cut and bloody. He'd forgotten already that he'd punched a hole in Phoebe's wall after he forced Becca out. Better than punching Becca, although he might still do that—the night wasn't over yet. Could he kill her? The thought felt strangely comforting. "Accident," he mumbled.

June looked around the room, still fidgeting with the thin leather strap of her shoulder bag. "I see Becca is here, and she looks upset." June tilted her head to look up at him. "You doing okay, Grant? You're pale, have you eaten? It's important to eat at these things."

Grant set the bucket down and found he could not tear his eyes from June's face, that it was actually quite pretty. "Can I get you a drink?" He looked around stupidly, as if a bar might have sprouted in his living room, and not like he was the bartender and would have to complete this task himself.

"Okay," June said. "I'll have whatever you're having."

"Just about to fill the ice." He waved toward his kitchen, felt that movement might steady his nerves. "Will just be a minute—"

"I think I'll come with you. There's something I want to talk to you about."

Grant spun on his heels and nearly lost his balance. He walked to the kitchen door and pushed it open, noticed his mother speaking quietly to a young woman he didn't recognize.

"This is Lisa Stewart." His mother gave him a strange look. "She's a journalist writing about the bridge and your sister—"

But June was right behind him and he could not consider his mother's resentment or the mousy small-town reporter he'd been avoiding. The woman was like a dog with a bone, to be here in his goddamn house during a private memorial for his sister, but right now he had to force his brain to churn through the whiskeys, to somehow make it through the next hour and then the hour after that. As much as he'd been dreading it, the night was so much worse than he'd expected it to be.

"June." His mother motioned for Lisa to follow her. "I'm sorry for your loss. I'll drop off a casserole next week—"

"No, thank you, ma'am. I don't need your charity," June said and then leaned against the kitchen counter that had every square inch covered with dirty dishes and half-full glasses and balled-up paper napkins with a fall floral motif.

Lisa raised an eyebrow and jotted something in a small notebook. His mother frowned deeply at June before she walked back to the living room and her guests.

Grant fumbled with the handle of the cupboard, reached for a full bottle of whiskey, unscrewed the cap after several tries, poured one tumbler, and then another, pulled out the ice drawer, sucked on the cold air, tried to think, *think*, shoved his injured hand into the razor-sharp ice, might have cut himself more but couldn't really tell, filled the bucket and turned very reluctantly to June to hand her the drink.

June took a small sip. "Are you sure you're okay, Grant? You seem different."

He shut the freezer door, set his glass down beside him, spilling liquid everywhere. "I'm fine, thank you for coming."

June turned to the large window and the dark night outside. "I find these tough, these anniversaries—they bring everything back so clearly, don't they?"

Grant blinked sweat from his eyes. "Yes."

"We're trying to figure out what Becca was doing there. Did you pick her up on the side of the road or something? Was she hitchhiking?"

"She was waiting for us—me—in the back seat."

"Oh, dear—that's just so unlucky. And you're what?" June looked sad. "Toying with her? For a whole decade? That's cruel, isn't it? Are you a cruel man, Grant? I think you might be, and to be honest, you scare me so it definitely wasn't my idea to come tonight. I'd rather be at home."

Grant looked desperately at the closed kitchen door, praying for someone to walk through—anyone—to save him. "My mother really appreciates that you came."

"It was my brother's idea—Wyatt thought I should come."

Grant swallowed too fast and then had the terrifying sensation that he was choking. Had he heard June properly? Was he that drunk? Was he that affected by today's date? By seeing Crazy Becca in his sister's bedroom touching her things? By the deer skull on his car hood? By people talking about the bridge again, that horrid monument to all he'd done wrong? He focused on the whiskey sliding down his throat, the whiskey that was not actually blocking his airway, just slipping into his body, lighting it on fire, scorching it.

He tried his best to smile at June but imagined he looked ridiculous. "Thank you for coming tonight—"

"Finally, some good news for once, right? I don't get much of that." June looked out the window again and Grant stepped away from her. "I know you remember my brother, Grant. I know I saw you together on my driveway and I know he was at that party, but when I asked you about him, you lied to me. When you could have done the right thing and told me the truth. Do you know how long I've wanted the truth, Grant?"

Grant stared at June's black dress and slight back, wondering if he might be sick right there on the kitchen floor.

"I'm fine. Don't look for me. I'm sorry." June said, turning, smiling weakly at him. "Did you send those letters to my mother? I think you did. You told me at the hardware store that Wyatt didn't want to be found, but you couldn't have known that unless you know where he went. And why." June sighed. "My mother kept the letters from me, didn't think I could handle it maybe, I'm not sure. They're cruel letters, aren't they? Making it seem that Wyatt wanted us to forget about him—but no matter now, because Wyatt's back. It's a miracle in a way."

"But your brother ran away," Grant choked out.

"He did, but he's back now, and he really wants to speak with you. He says you'll know why."

BECCA

She sat on the back stoop of the Deans' house. Her heart was broken and her mind was racing and her phone wouldn't stop ringing and she was on her fourth cigarette, but nothing was helping to calm her down.

Becca answered finally: "I'm busy."

She heard Debbie try to soothe the baby on her hip. "Mom's hysterical, Becca, where are you right now?"

"I'm at the memorial because I was there that night. What—are you jealous that something interesting happened to me—"

"It's not interesting, it's sad. Because you don't even know them. And have you considered that they probably don't want you there, constantly reminding them of that terrible accident—"

"Of course he wants me here—"

"*Rebecca!*" Debbie yelled, and Becca clamped her mouth shut, stunned. "You're a complete stranger to them! No—worse—you're a vulture circling for attention or meaning or something, so *if* Grant is keeping you around, there's a reason for it. And you should find out what that reason is! Go ask him right now, and don't stop until you get an answer and then move on. You don't owe that asshole—"

"The accident was my fault, you know. Me and Phoebe got in a fight in the truck and Grant lost control because of it and then he lied to the sheriff to protect me—" Becca stopped mid-sentence. The last couple of days weighed so heavily on her that the words she'd cocooned herself with sounded different. They sounded wrong. And so she tried different ones: "We were dancing at the party together, me and Phoebe." But those ones sounded wrong too. "We were all having fun."

No, Phoebe was dancing, and you were watching from the corner, by yourself.

"Phoebe told me to stay away from Grant because she didn't want us to be together. She threatened me that night."

No, Phoebe was looking for Grant because she was angry with him, it had nothing to do with you.

"Oh," Becca whispered quietly into the phone. "Oh, no."

Becca felt faint as the world tilted, and the last ten years of avoided calls and texts and Grant doing the bare minimum flashed before her eyes. Everything on Grant's terms. Everything she'd given up. She went back to Grant's expression as he'd sat beside her hospital bed. She'd thought at the time that it was one of sympathy and love, but now Becca realized what it had really been: cold calculation. Grant had understood that because she remembered very little, it gave him a way out. And then he'd manipulated her. Blamed her. Someone who wouldn't question anything he said; someone who would do anything to protect him, as long as he showed her some attention every now and then.

Becca lifted her wet face to the sky; she watched the moon and listened to the soft cooing sounds of her sister's baby on the other end of the line. Becca thought of the life she'd put on hold for Grant and then said to Debbie: "Grant said he couldn't be with me anymore because it was too hard, that I reminded him too much of the accident and his sister."

"Rebecca, I love you, but you have to wake up—you didn't have a secret relationship and you weren't going to run away and get married. Didn't Dr. Murphy talk to you about these fantasies being ways for you to cope with Phoebe dying right in front of you? That you were in the wrong place at the wrong time; just really unlucky, Becca. But it's been ten years now. Grant doesn't care about you, he's using you. And you should find out why so you can move on. Get help—please." There was a slight pause before Debbie went on: "And don't think I don't know what you tried to do with Mom and Dad either, implying that because my husband is working late—because he made *partner*, something I was waiting to share with them myself—that he's having an affair. Jesus, Becca, we'll deal with that later. I have to go now."

Debbie hung up and Becca lit another cigarette even though she was shaking. Her heart was battering inside her body, trying to run away from her. She touched her chest, could feel the hot, furious pulse. Becca looked up to the dark sky again; blew out a thin stream of smoke. She closed her eyes, tried to gather the strength to remember everything that had happened once she woke up in the back seat of the truck.

it had been raining so hard that water poured through the broken windshield soaking her clothes and filling her mouth and mixing with blood where she'd bitten her tongue and everything tasted salty and warm and she started to choke

but she managed to unhook her seatbelt and the sudden release winded her

she fell to the pavement and saw Phoebe's foot was missing her shoe and her toes were painted light blue and she crawled to Phoebe over broken glass that cut her palms and smeared blood along the ground

she was dazed and looked around on all fours and could see that they'd broken through the railing of the bridge

where was Grant

she heard screaming

but it wasn't her because she was having trouble breathing and it wasn't Phoebe because Phoebe wouldn't wake up

wake up Phoebe please wake up

Grant where are you

her eyes were open but she couldn't see anything and her head was cracking like an egg

Grant help us Phoebe won't wake up Grant help us why aren't you coming please we need help

I'm so scared

and then she was cradling Phoebe's head in her lap and

Phoebe was making sounds but Grant wasn't coming to help them he was standing at the side of the bridge

standing at the side of the bridge screaming

Grant she isn't moving there's so much blood and half of Phoebe's face is missing her jaw her white teeth her tendons her veins pumping blood onto Becca's legs

Grant your sister is dying

but Grant is screaming down into the river as if looking for something he's lost, screaming something she can almost make out, screaming, screaming, he's screaming: why.

he's screaming why

JUNE

June rarely touched alcohol, but took a sip of her drink to stop her hands from trembling. She was nervous being in the kitchen alone with Grant because he was so obviously uncomfortable. He'd finally managed to relax his face, but she could tell by the way that his lips curled that it was hard for him to do. He also couldn't stop rubbing his wrist; it looked almost raw.

"Am I making you nervous, Grant?" June surprised herself with the words and her ability to say them, but in the last half-hour since she'd arrived at the house, she'd grasped onto something she hadn't in a while: confidence. Probably because Wyatt had decided to come inside in the end, and he'd sat right in the middle of the living room in a high-backed chair, wearing their father's old suit. It was short in the legs and terribly outdated, but that didn't matter because no one noticed him sitting there. Which meant Wyatt had been right, that the town was still so fixated on Phoebe Dean that he'd been able to slip in unnoticed.

They could be invisible until they were ready; until all of the pieces were in place.

Vultures, all of them, June. Never forget what they did to your brother and us, promise me.

Grant's face was ashen and June faltered slightly in her resolve. She wanted her brother to reclaim what he'd come back for—his reputation, his space in town, a life out in the open—but there were still some things she didn't understand.

What did Grant hold over Wyatt to have kept him away and quiet all of these years? Had Wyatt seen something? What really happened to Phoebe Dean? Had Wyatt done something to Phoebe himself, and then waited until both of their parents were gone to come back to confess? This thought was June's darkest, and she quickly flicked it away with her wrist because she knew her brother wasn't capable of that.

He couldn't be.

June gathered her strength by grabbing at the air, something she used to do as a kid. She was ready to hear it; all of it.

Grant's eyes kept darting around the kitchen, and she could tell by his sloppy movements that he was drunk. She'd seen this pure intention a thousand times with her mother: the insatiable thirst for everything to dull and blur and go away.

June placed her glass on the counter, rallying herself to be brave. "Grant, I'm sorry about your sister. And Becca. Whatever's going on there, I'm sure it hasn't been easy for her."

Grant avoided looking at her.

"Do you need to sit down?"

Grant stared at the bottle on the counter; his neck was slick with sweat.

"Do you need some water? Can you hear me—Grant?"

"I'm fine," Grant said far too loudly for how close they were standing. He grabbed the bottle and held it tightly, his knuckles blanching. "Thank you for coming—"

"You'll never guess," June said, the cadence of a regular conversation electrifying to her. "But Wyatt has come tonight—he really wants to see you."

"What?" Grant swung to her so fast he lost his balance, slamming his hand down on the counter to try to steady himself. "What did you just say?"

"Can you believe it?" June tried to smile through her frayed nerves. "That after all of this time, he's here now?"

Grant stared at her. He didn't blink. She watched the blood drain from his face more than it already had. Grant was white as a sheet. He put his glass slowly to his lips and drank every last drop. He wiped his mouth with the back of his hand. "I don't think I heard you—"

"Wyatt is here, in your living room. He wants to speak with you."

"Wyatt?"

"Yes—Wyatt."

Grant made a soft choking sound and then cleared his throat. He narrowed his eyes and then opened them wide. A look of resignation slid across his face, warming it, the white turning slightly pink again, fresh blood pooling under the surface of his skin. His face broke into a grin that made him look demented.

So much could change in an instant; June knew this better than anyone.

"Wyatt Delroy." Grant tilted his head back and laughed at the ceiling. "Well, shit." He relaxed his shoulders and shook his head, still laughing. He poured himself another drink, opened his mouth to speak, closed it, opened it again but was interrupted by the kitchen door slamming into the wall. Grant dropped his tumbler, shattering and spraying glass all over the floor.

"Shit." Grant opened the cupboard under the sink to grab a dustpan and brush. "Becca—Jesus *Christ*."

Becca stood in the doorway, surveying the damage.

"Hi, Becca," June said with a little wave.

"What are you still doing here?" Becca asked her. "I mean, it's great to see you I guess, June, but I'm surprised you're still here. You said you weren't going to come, and you didn't really know Phoebe."

"Well neither did you."

Becca blushed and turned her attention to Grant, who was on his hands and knees scraping glass very clumsily into the dustpan. "June, I need to speak with Grant alone."

Grant dropped his chin to his chest and yelled to the floor: "You cannot be fucking serious—"

"Oh, yes, I'm very serious," Becca shouted back.

June watched all of this closely, trying to understand what was passing between them.

"Grant!" Becca screamed so loudly that he flinched. "Grant,

we're going to talk right now—I know you've been using me because of my feelings for you." Becca chewed on her lip but June could still hear the tremor in her voice. "You've made a fool of me for ten years, even after everything I did for you! I deserve more than this, so—*yes*—we're going to talk right now or I'll tell the sheriff the truth. That you were drunk, that there was no deer, that you and Phoebe were fighting in the truck—that I don't know why you waited so long to call for help, but I do know that none of it was my fault."

Grant swung his head from Becca to June, his eyes darting around frantically. He nodded several times to himself and then visibly deflated. Grant stood slowly and said, "Okay." He let out a long hiss of breath. "I can't do this anymore either. It's been hard, the lies. So many lies. But let's go somewhere private."

Grant stumbled to the sink and dropped the dustpan in it. He snatched the whiskey bottle from the counter and then nodded at Becca—and then, to June's surprise, he nodded at her too, face solemn and resigned. "Follow me." Grant headed for the back door. "Both of you."

"Wait," June said quickly. "What about Wyatt?"

Grant held the open door in his hand, the wind blowing in from outside smelling like cold leaves, like fall. He hesitated, tense. "Right," Grant said. "Wyatt. Just tell him to meet us out in the barn I guess."

GRANT

Despite it being too dark to see, Grant was desperate for forward momentum and picked up his pace. It was dark but he wished it were darker. He wished it was the kind that felt thick, so he could get lost and cease to exist. He knew that it had finally come for him. The truth. But he wasn't ready for it. There was no way for him to prepare. He had lived for so many years under the weight of it all, but he was terrified to come out from under it.

To shed this skin despite it being one he loathed.

Grant saw something ahead. His heart pounded in his ears, breaking up the panic slightly. He squinted to make sure he didn't lose sight of it. There were no stars tonight; just a few curls of gray cloud in the empty sky.

He reached it, the old barn. Their old barn. He scrambled blindly around the exterior, scratching his body and clothes on bent nails and slats of jagged wood and funnels of moss until he found the door.

Grant grabbed the knob, now rusting and sharp. He pushed too hard and sliced the palm of his hand on the warped metal, but the sting didn't register. He used all of his weight, and the door screeched against the uneven hay-strewn floor, splintering further into nothingness.

Grant stood in the doorway, trying to focus. There was a lantern, he remembered, to the right of the door, and waterproof matches below it.

He was taller now and banged his elbow into the glass, but managed to catch the lantern before it fell. The matches were harder to find. Grant used the toe of his boot but had no luck, so he reluctantly dropped to his hands and knees. He pulled his shirt up to cover his nose from the stench of age and rot and rodent shit.

Grant was blind and in the dark dared to move only an inch at a time, afraid of what he might touch, afraid of what might be in the barn with him.

After crawling half a foot he touched the long rectangular box with the rough striker on the side. He watched the blue flame lick across the wood of the match. He held his breath as he turned around, the lantern lighting the shadowy space in rings of dirty yellow.

Grant saw a pile of textbooks and childish graffiti on the far wall. He walked closer, raised the light: *G & P 4 EVR* glowed back at him. He traced Phoebe's scrawled letters with his finger, wishing to feel her.

Under the boarded-up window was a small makeshift kitchen. Both cupboard doors were open and something inside darted, catching his eye. He stumbled away, trying to recover from the frayed feeling it gave his spine with a quick shake of his head. It didn't help; he was too exposed, it was still too dark. He turned around again.

"Hello?" Grant said, his voice immediately sucked away. "Phoebe?"

He shivered, feeling foolish. His hand trembled but he lifted the lantern as high as he could to illuminate each of the dark corners.

There was an empty bird's nest in one; the leaves and gathered debris arranged like a bowl. Grant let out a tight hiss of breath. Phoebe would have liked that, he thought; she had always loved birds. He clutched at his chest, pinching his skin, his heart breaking a bit more, a crack and a deep ache he was familiar with but had never gotten used to.

Grant moved his arm to light another corner. There was a crumpled mass, a dead animal. He staggered instinctively away from it, to avoid the smell—another instinct, that there'd be a smell. But this had been there so long it was odorless and mostly bones and mostly gone; now just a whisper, an imagining.

"I'm sorry," Grant said aloud. "Phoebe, I'm sorry I didn't choose you."

Grant knew he couldn't keep living like this; that the end had come whether he was ready or not. The secrets and the guilt would soon take over until he would no longer recognize himself. Was there maybe still some good left in him? He wasn't sure.

He heard a rustling in the corner, wondered if Phoebe was in here with him tonight. He hadn't dared hope for anything in a long while, but there was the smallest sliver of it—that by confessing, which he knew he had to do, he'd finally make his sister proud.

BECCA

"I left that skull on your car." Becca couldn't catch her breath. "I thought it would make you want to see me."

Grant was unrecognizable in the dim light of the lantern. Becca could hear his words but they weren't resonating. She tried scrabbling to the surface to escape this nightmare; to escape what he was telling her.

"The twenty-seven too," Becca confessed, dazed and embarrassed. "I don't even know what happened in that time, and I was there. You made me think it was all my fault."

Everything that Becca had thought and felt and known for the last decade was nothing but a lie. A manipulation. Was she that pathetic? She'd wasted ten years trying to protect Grant; but what he was telling her made him nothing but a monster.

Becca had lied to get him out of trouble. She'd been at his beck and call because she thought she loved him. Because of the guilt she'd lived with day in and day out for being the reason he'd swerved and Phoebe had died. Grant had ruined her life, but she'd allowed it.

In the strange abandoned barn, Becca's thoughts turned to her sister. Her sister and her nieces and nephews who lived six hours away. Becca wanted suddenly, desperately, to hold her sister's newborn baby and cry on her sister's couch and have her say: *You can stay as long as you want. You've made mistakes, but they were rooted in loyalty and love. It's not too late to start over.*

"How could you do this to me?" Becca shouted at Grant. "You blamed me when Phoebe was angry with *you*! I was just there. Like everyone thinks, like everyone knows. You've made such a fool of me."

Grant's face was grotesque in the flickering light.

"You're sorry?" Becca felt hysterical, like the walls were caving in. "I'm the only person who cared about you and look what you did. You manipulated me for a decade to protect yourself, just in case I ever remembered what really happened."

The rage swelled in Becca's body and she started to scream and pound on Grant's chest; he stood and took it all.

"You look so ugly when you sleep," Becca started to sob.

They both turned suddenly, peering through the thick dark, to the barn door screeching open again.

JUNE

It took a while for June's eyes to adjust to the empty horse stalls and ancient bales of hay, and the faint light in the far back corner.

"Hello?" she called out, her voice shaky.

"Over here."

June followed the hush of voices deeper into the vast hollow space. The door swung shut behind her and she jumped and nearly screamed. She was sweating from the walk, and now the untouched heat of the barn clung to her skin. June was afraid. Of the thick dark, of the smells and deep corners and strange shadows and the knowledge that everything inside had long been abandoned. "Hello? Becca?"

"Over here."

June took small steps across the rough floor, arms in front of her so she didn't knock into something or someone. When was the last time anyone had been in here? Was there another door she could use if she wanted to leave? And where was Wyatt?

June was close enough now that she heard whimpering. Becca. She turned in that direction until she could make out weak light on the ground. June kept her hands in front of her, taking one slow step at a time. She hit something with her foot that caused her heart to stop, as whatever it was skittered across the floor. June sweated into her eyes and wiped them; another step, one more, and then the outline of a body sitting on the ground in front of her with his head in his hands, breathing loudly. Grant.

June drew back and tried to make out the door that she'd just come in through. She didn't want to be in here anymore, with their dark secrets and hidden pain. This was a mistake. She wasn't ready for this.

"June, is that you? Grant just told me, he told me everything, but I didn't know, I swear I didn't, I don't know what to say." Becca's voice was already hoarse from crying. "I'm so sorry, I swear I didn't know, he kept it all from me—he lied to me. He blamed me. He *used* me. He made me think this was my fault. You have to believe me, please. I'm so sorry—I swear I didn't see." Becca was crying again, the sound echoing around them loud as gunfire. "Grant told the sheriff we hit a deer—but I didn't see him, I swear." Becca fell to her knees, sobbing.

June kept backing toward the door. She wanted to leave now. Right now. Grant's head shot up from his hands; in the lantern's light his eyes were wild, primal. "June—it was an accident—"

"Stop, please stop." June was so afraid; *where is Wyatt.* "Wyatt should be here—"

The door to the barn swung open behind her. A gust of wind blew through, disturbing the loose hay. The moon shone down between cracks in the roof, lighting up dancing dust motes like flakes of prehistoric snow. It was beautiful. June felt Wyatt come up beside her, and she relaxed. He could take over. June smiled weakly at him, but he didn't look at her. Wyatt stared straight ahead, locked on Grant.

"June?" Grant said.

June didn't like the way Grant was looking at her, so she turned her attention to Becca who was rocking on the barn floor, clasping her head tightly in her hands. Becca's wailing had settled into hacking sobs and a repeat of: "Oh my god. Oh my god. Ohmygod. *Ohmygod.*"

"You're breathing really fast, June."

June found her way back to Grant's voice. She realized he had stood up from the floor and was in front of her now, holding the lantern. June couldn't make out Grant's face, just a big round light. Had she lost time again? Why did that keep happening to her? How long had she been in the barn?

June didn't like what was happening; there was something wrong with the barn. It must be haunted. There were ghosts in here. June took a step backward. And then another. She gripped her hands together and felt that two of her nails were broken. Fear seized her as the scene in front of her didn't change: Becca continued to cry on the floor, head in her hands, elbows on her knees, and Grant was still standing, wavering drunkenly, but looking at her like he was going to speak to her again.

But why was no one asking Wyatt where he'd been?

Why was no one surprised to see Wyatt?

June turned to Wyatt, her big brother who had come back for her, who had chosen her.

Dread swept in from outside, just as Wyatt had. Cold air clinging to her ankles, sliding up her calves, to her waist, traveling the length of her spine, into her hair. June moved her eyes from Becca on the floor to Grant, who had stepped closer to her still. Grant lowered the lantern, laser-focused on her now, and opened his mouth to speak.

June shook her head. No, she didn't want to hear what Grant had to say. No. She didn't want this anymore. She wasn't ready. She shouldn't have come; this was a mistake. June grabbed Wyatt's hand so they could leave. His felt like ice. June squeezed, Wyatt squeezed back. She tugged his arm so he'd look down at her, so she could break the trance he was in, staring daggers at Grant, who she realized was talking to her.

"What?" June was so confused, sounds moved in and out around her but June couldn't hear anything over her racing heartbeat and the bright living pulse in Wyatt's cold hand.

"Breathe," Grant was mouthing to her, shiny with sweat. "You're hyperventilating. I need you to know it was an accident, but you're going to pass out if you don't calm down."

June turned again to Wyatt, who wasn't wearing the gray suit anymore but their dad's old sweater; it wasn't cream-colored, but covered in blood. She tugged his arm hard and Wyatt moved slowly to look down at her. His face was ghastly and June started to cry. He had two black eyes and his mouth and lips were cracked and dried with blood.

"Wyatt?" June reached for him, to touch him, to touch his

face. "What happened to your face? Wyatt, what's happening to you?"

Grant was shouting at her but he was moving in slow motion and she still couldn't hear him. June shook her head, trying hard to focus, but she had started crying like that night she sat at the kitchen table and felt like she was splitting apart and would never survive this. Would never survive being alone. But then Wyatt had come home. Wyatt had come back for her.

"What?" June asked, and sounds crashed into her all at once, a tidal wave of noise, and Becca was standing next to Grant, shouting at her too, sobbing that she was sorry, that she didn't see, she didn't see, she didn't see him.

She didn't see him.

June was terrified but dug in for the energy to ask: "Didn't see who?"

Becca put her hands on June's shoulders, but June was splintering, splintering, splintering, like she had that night at the kitchen table, before Wyatt came back. Before her brother, who deep down was a good person, came back for her. He had.

"Didn't see what?" June tried to stay focused on Becca, who had transformed into a shell of guilt. Moonlight shone down onto Becca's tears, making them bright somehow—*pretty*, June thought, *that's pretty*. June turned to Wyatt, who was smiling at her, his eyes black holes sunken into his white skull, his mouth an empty yawning hole because he was missing all of his teeth.

I didn't see him. I didn't see it happen. He shouldn't have been on the bridge, it was too dark, the rain—I didn't see him, June, I'm sorry, I'm so sorry.

Sounds swarmed June's ears, wind or bees or some other insect, wasps maybe; they'd come in on the breeze for this purpose, and she couldn't discern who was speaking anymore or if they were words, or sounds, or air, or thoughts.

June wrung her hands together to feel something real; the nail on her thumb was starting to heal. "Wyatt?" June said. Her body was weak, she needed to sit down. "He loved to run on the bridge. My brother? But he's right here."

It was too dark.

It was raining too hard.

It was an accident.

"But Wyatt is right here."

Becca was lost now, wailing and thrashing against Grant's chest, ripping his sweater, tearing at his face, spit and tears flying from her mouth, landing on the floor. Grant pulled her into him, muffling her screams with his body, and he opened his mouth to let out his own tortured sound and June looked behind her to see if the keening was wolves or coyotes; they had those here.

"Hit him?" June found the words to say. "You hit him?" It made no sense. Had she ever said those words before, *hit* or *him*? Hit. Him. June didn't think so, they were new words, *new*.

June readjusted her hearing in the dark, *crank*, and her eyes, *work*, to the barn, to the barn, to here, *I'm right here*, to Becca sobbing into Grant's chest and the reality that Grant was screaming at her: "June, goddammit, calm down!"

June looked beside her and her heart sank and her legs buckled. "Where did he go?"

"June, you have to breathe—"

June was frantic, looking around her, spinning like a top, but it was so dark and her pulse was so loud in her head. June spun until she was dizzy but the barn was still empty except for Becca and Grant. "Where is he? He was just here."

"June, Jesus Christ, you need to breathe." Grant grabbed her shoulders and shook her hard.

"Wyatt," June said, terrified of the looks they were giving her, the looks of pity and remorse and guilt. "Wyatt was just beside me."

"I should have called 911 earlier, I should have told the truth, I didn't mean for it to happen, you have to believe me—but, June, there is no one else in here."

"Wyatt," June spoke softly. She loved the feel of his name, of her big brother's name.

"I'm so sorry." Grant spoke loudly, and finally June heard him. "But Wyatt is dead."

TEN YEARS AGO

1:28 a.m.–2:01 a.m.

Grant felt himself snap somewhere between dragging Phoebe from the party before she made a scene and finding AJ's crazy stalker in the back seat of his truck, waiting for him.

"We'll leave together." Becca was close to passing out. "Get married—"

"Shut up!" Grant screamed, and the sheer power of his voice made him swerve dangerously on the slick road. "Everyone just shut the fuck up and let me think!"

"I'll tell your coach if Wyatt doesn't, or I'll tell the sheriff about you and Wyatt." Phoebe spoke so quietly he knew she meant it. "I'm doing this for you, don't you know that?"

Grant couldn't see out the front windshield; it was too dark and the rain was too heavy. "You wouldn't do that to me."

"It's cheating and it's probably killing you, and you'll get

caught and you'll regret it because you are better than this. Even if you don't believe that anymore, I still do. Maybe you can come out from under it if you do the right thing, but you have to do it now."

"The right *thing? You'd ruin everything for me? My one chance to get out? Isn't that what you've always wanted? To fucking leave?" Grant shook the steering wheel, but pulled back hard before he fully drove on the wrong side of the road. "You'd jeopardize my future, our plans, because of your principles? You're just a fucking child, Phoebe! You don't get it, you're impossible—"*

Phoebe threw her hands out in front of her and screamed: "Grant—look out!"

Grant opened his eyes minutes later, dazed. He was soaked, and blinked a few times at the massive hole in the front windshield of his truck. He fumbled with his seatbelt, smelled gasoline and blood, and fell out onto the road. His eyesight adjusted slowly, his head and heart and leg throbbed in tandem.

Grant stumbled back a foot from the wreckage and realized he'd hit something, lost control and driven straight through the guardrail of the bridge.

He could see in the back seat that Becca's head was at an awkward angle and deep cuts covered her face and chest, but she moved slowly, mumbling to herself. Phoebe in the front, though—Phoebe was in bad shape.

"Phoebe, oh god." Grant moved toward her but fell to his

knees, splashing dirty rainwater into his eyes. "Phoebe, hang on." He held his breath to focus through the sickening pain, and reached across the seat to his sister, whose body was slumped forward against the dash, her face unrecognizable. "Phoebe." Grant unbuckled her belt. "Hang on, you'll be fine, just please hang on."

He pulled her from the truck and lay her on the ground. She looked so small and broken lying there. It reminded him of the time he'd carried her home from that party in his arms. "Phoebe, just hang on, you're going to be okay."

Grant dragged himself to the front of the truck. Through the one headlight that cut through the rain, he could see that what he'd hit was lying by the side of the bridge, twitching.

No. No. No.

Grant bent over and vomited. He tried to catch his breath but he couldn't find enough air to breathe. He stood on trembling legs and wiped his mouth with the back of his hand. He clamped both hands around his left thigh to drag it; he knew it was broken, but he couldn't think about that right now. The agony began to lessen as his body went into shock. He made it to the side of the bridge and collapsed to his knees.

"Wyatt," he choked out. "Oh my god."

Wyatt lay on his back; his eyes blinked wildly in confused fear. There was blood everywhere. Wyatt's chest was caved in where the truck had hit him. Grant could see Wyatt's ribs through his sweater that was no longer white but dark, dark red.

Wyatt tried to hold up his head but couldn't. "Grant," he rasped, a sickly shuddering sound. "Help me—"

"Hang in there," Grant said, still blinded by the look in Phoebe's eyes when she said she'd tell his coach and the sheriff. The lengths he knew she would go to save him. From himself? From their mother? Maybe they were one and the same.

Grant looked from Wyatt's mangled body to the river. Phoebe didn't have any proof; just what Wyatt had told her. Phoebe had been drinking. And Wyatt wasn't exactly trustworthy. Grant could make his sister see that it had all been a misunderstanding, a mistake. That he could be better. That he could get back on track. Find his way back to their path. Phoebe loved him. He could fix this.

"Hang on." Grant lifted Wyatt's arm to check for his father's watch. He saw it on Wyatt's wrist and breathed. Grant stood, looked around through the thick sheet of pouring water and dim car light. He had rope in his trunk, and he dragged his broken leg through glass and blood and broken car parts to retrieve it. Grant saw Phoebe moving her mouth on the sidewalk. "Phoebe, hang on, I'll be right there," he hissed through clenched teeth. "Just please hang on."

Grant knelt back by Wyatt, looped the rope around his ankles, and then looked around frantically. He saw a large broken piece of cement, tied the other end of the rope to it, and with all of his strength, pushed Wyatt over the side of the bridge.

"No—" Grant reached for him, remembering he hadn't taken the watch. Grant screamed down into the water, looking on in horrified disbelief as Wyatt's body sank, was gone.

What had he done? This was not who is—what had he done?

"Wy!" Grant screamed until he was emptied of air, and then

turned in a daze to see Becca had climbed out of the truck and was sitting with Phoebe, who was still lying on the ground.

Grant hobbled over to them, clutching his leg. "Phoebe, I'm getting help, hang in there, please, hang in there—it's going to be okay."

He avoided her disfigured face, her open unseeing eyes, and squeezed her hand gently, remembering the time she'd taken his while they watched the sunrise. Grant choked on a sob as he shuffled to the end of the bridge, where he knew there was a payphone.

He placed the call and collapsed to the ground. As he waited for the ambulance, he thought only of Phoebe. He'd spend the rest of his life making this up to her. They'd leave town together. He'd do whatever it took. He'd prove to her that she was right, that he could be better; that he was worthy.

When Phoebe woke up in the hospital, he'd be by her side. A good, decent person; a changed man. He'd keep his promise.

Just us, we'll be okay.

EPILOGUE

June hesitates before stepping onto the narrow bridge. She almost didn't come. She ran out of the barn, away from Grant and Becca, disoriented and terrified. Now she sees Wyatt far ahead, leaning against the railing over the water. He turns as she approaches and smiles and waves; she cannot manage a smile, but does wave back.

She reaches where he is and stands next to him, her big brother. Wyatt glows in the moonlight; ethereal. They turn in unison to watch the dark river below.

Although he is much taller, she can hear his teeth chatter. June draws her arms around herself and feels that she too is shivering. It's cool tonight, nearly fall.

The water under their feet is moving fast, but is so black she can see the reflection of the trees along the banks and the perfect slice of bright crescent moon. It's so beautiful, serene. She can see why Wyatt loved running here. She's not sure why she never came before; she'll do that more often now, before they take it down.

Or maybe she'll fight for them to keep it up; to have a place to come to remember, to mourn. The town will listen to her now; they'll have to.

In the river's glass reflection, she is a tall matchstick but her face is missing; an empty space. June holds up one hand and her mirrored reflection waves back. She turns to Wyatt to do the same but he's staring straight ahead at nothing.

June turns back to the water, to wave with the other hand, and realizes she can't see Wyatt's reflection on the black surface; it is hers alone.

She turns more slowly this time. He's there, standing beside her, stoic and unmoving. She turns back to the water; it is just her thin body and the trees and the moon.

Wyatt speaks, and it is as though the voice is hers: "I have to go back now, June."

"But I don't want to be alone." June touches him and feels the unyielding chill beneath the thick sweater.

Are you really here? she wants to ask him. *Did you really come back for me? Am I going to be okay?*

"You'll be okay. You don't need me anymore, Juney."

June watches him climb up and over the side of the railing. Wyatt moves quickly, deftly, and she reaches out for him to be careful, *come back where it's safer, Wy*, she wants to say, but she drops her arms, letting him go.

"Would you have come back to us that night? To me?"

Wyatt looks down from where he stands with those big dark eyes. He smiles at her, shakes his head, amused. He leans far out over the river; the wind grabs hold of his sweater and tugs at him; they are so very high up.

"Would things have turned out differently if you'd come back? Would we have been okay, Wyatt? Would Dad have stayed? Would our family have been okay?"

"You know I can't answer any of that for you, Juney."

"But I need you, Wy." June's voice trembles with pleading but she speaks softly, or perhaps not at all.

He smiles at her again, his face so young under the light of the moon. Without another word he lets his hands drop to his sides, and Wyatt falls down into the churning water without a sound or a splash. June watches long after he's gone, the water hiding his body once more with hurried strokes; the river resuming its natural rhythm; the pounding of the tide, the hiding of secrets.

The rush below her hypnotizes her as she waits for her tears to dry and her breath to settle and her pulse to calm. She is patient and kind with herself. She finds that when she touches the tender space below her eyes, they are still sore but the tears feel different; they're warmer somehow, comforting.

June feels an unfurling and opens her palms to the moonlight. Her skin is smooth and unbroken. She touches her face; it is damp but also intact. She feels the thin skin of her chest and the thrum of her heart and a beating of something else, something new, something just beginning: a seed of relief born from knowing.

She has lost so much, but she is here.

She is still here.

June watches the river another minute. The moon brightens and she can see her face in its reflection now. It has returned to her. She wipes away a tear, and then another, and nods softly at the black mirrored water, at the shape of her grief that has returned to its resting place, at Wyatt, who gave her what she needed.

She pushes off from the side of the bridge to find a payphone. The same payphone that was used too late all those years ago. She calls the sheriff and leaves an anonymous tip about the body of Wyatt Delroy at the bottom of the West Wilmer River, under the bridge where Phoebe Dean died. A hit-and-run. Divers will be needed. Grant Dean should be questioned. He knows it's coming.

When June hears sirens in the distance, she slips away into the thick dark night and starts her long walk home alone.

READING GROUP GUIDE

1. How would you describe Grant's relationships early on in the book? What prevents him from allowing people close to him?

2. Where does Becca get her patience for Grant? Do you think her forgiveness is a strength or weakness?

3. How does Becca think about her role in the accident? Why does she weaponize her experiences against her family and neighbors?

4. How does Wyatt interact with June? Why is the power dynamic between them so skewed?

5. Describe Phoebe and Grant's relationship. How did their ambitions for each other become destructive?

6. How did Becca keep the secret about her relationship with Grant for ten years? Why does she start telling people about it when she does?

7. June and Wyatt both feel at times like their family was invisible compared to the Deans. How do they each respond to that feeling? How can we make sure that everyone in our communities feels seen and valued?

8. If Grant had told the truth on the night of the accident, how do you think things would have unfolded differently for Becca and June?

9. What do you think is next for Becca and June? How will the truth change their trajectories?

10. What does Wyatt represent in this book? Do you think he was really there or a figment of June's imagination? If so, why? Or why not?

A CONVERSATION WITH THE AUTHOR

What was your inspiration for *Twenty-Seven Minutes*? What are the first decisions you make when you start writing?

My mother died very quickly after a pancreatic cancer diagnosis in 2018, and I felt like the rug was completely pulled out from under me. I wanted to write about that feeling, of the fear that comes with everything in your life changing in an instant, and how dark and transforming grief can be.

I start writing with a feeling or a concept that I want to explore—this time it was regret, loss, and grief—and then I'll figure out how I want the story to end, either in terms of plot or in terms of how I want the reader to feel when the story is over.

The small-town rumor mill is almost its own character throughout the book. Did you grow up in a small town?

That was really intentional, so thank you for this question. No, I didn't! I grew up in downtown Toronto. But my mother, who was so much of the inspiration behind this story, did. She grew up on a farm in a very small rural town, and I spent time there, especially as a young child. Those visits really shaped me, maybe because the farm was such a starkly different place from where I grew up. I'm so grateful for those memories and experiences from my childhood with her.

Both Phoebe and Wyatt were heavily shaped by their reputations during their high school years. How do our expectations dictate student outcomes?

This is such a great question and one I think about a lot as a mother of two kids who'll be starting high school in a few years. I think external expectations can put a tremendous amount of pressure on students, too much sometimes when we should really be listening to them, to their goals and abilities and really try to support and empower them in finding their own path.

June and Becca both have significant lapses in reality. As you were writing, how did you keep track of what they believed versus what was truly happening?

This was really difficult! But when you spend so much time living in a story it becomes easier to remember what's real and what's in their minds. But even still, I would lose sight of things sometimes, especially with Becca. Process-wise, I would keep a list going of the main plot points and then Post-its of misdirection and reality lapses for both Becca and June, and I would read and read and read again to make sure everything lined up properly.

What does your writing routine look like?

I'm what they call a "pantser" or a discovery writer so if I use an outline, it's a very vague one. When I'm plotting, I need to listen to music, and I work best with large chunks of uninterrupted time to get into a groove and let the writing flow; I have to let it out or I'll lose sight of it. I'll write seven to eight hours a day until I have a rough draft done. After that I'll start to revise, which takes much, much longer than the drafting process but can be done in shorter bursts.

What are you reading these days?

I'm so glad you asked! I've finished some great books recently: two debuts, *Home* by Cailean Steed, which is a thriller about a cult, and *A Good House for Children* by Kate Collins, which is a gorgeous Gothic horror. And I was lucky enough to read an advanced copy of *The Whispers* by Ashley Audrain, which is just as brilliant and unflinching as her debut *The Push*.

ACKNOWLEDGMENTS

This story was born from the crushing grief of losing my mother, very suddenly, to pancreatic cancer in 2018. To the heartbroken grievers out there: I see you, I am you, and I'm so sorry.

To my superstar agent, Hayley Steed, thank you for your keen editorial hand and for never giving up on me. To the rest of the wonderful team at the Madeleine Milburn Literary Agency, thank you for everything you do, and do so damn well.

To my incredible editors, Lucy Dauman, Anna Michels, and especially Bhavna Chauhan, I have never stopped pinching myself! Thank you for your unwavering enthusiasm for this story and these characters, for your brilliant editorial insight, and for your endless guidance and kindness; working with you has been an absolute dream come true.

To everyone at Doubleday Canada, Headline UK, Sourcebooks, and beyond, who have had a part in shaping this novel, from cover design (infinite gratitude to Jennifer Griffiths, Emma Rogers, and Jonathan Bush for their incredible designs) to marketing and everything in between—I am indebted to you, even if we've never met.

To my guardian angel, Ashley Audrain—without you I would have thrown in the towel long ago. You are the best writing partner, encourager, and friend, all wrapped up in one shining package.

Thank you to my most loyal and trusted first readers—oh, the vulnerability of sharing those early drafts!—with special thanks to Gillian and Val. I am forever grateful for the many (many!) years of friendship and your tireless encouragement and support.

Writing can be a very lonely and isolating endeavor; to my family and friends, both new and old, especially Sara, Rosemary, Kat, and my mother-in-law, Tina, who have never stopped believing in me—thank you with my whole heart.

Lastly, to my wonderful husband and incredible children—it has been one long and bumpy road. I am overwhelmed with gratitude for you three—for being my number one fans and champions, for your support in all the little ways and big, but mostly for never giving up on me, especially when I wanted to give up on myself.

ABOUT THE AUTHOR

Ashley Tate worked for over a decade as an editorial writer and editor for various publications as well as Canada's first online magazine. She lives with her husband, two children, and their dog, in Toronto, Canada. *Twenty-Seven Minutes* is her first novel.